The
Secret Wife

OTHER TITLES BY STEVE ROBINSON

The Penmaker's Wife

The Jefferson Tayte Series

In the Blood

To the Grave

The Last Queen of England

The Lost Empress

Kindred

Dying Games

Letters from the Dead

The
Secret Wife

Steve
ROBINSON

Copyright © 2020 by Steve Robinson.

Published by Alchera, London.

ISBN-13: 979-8649012676

Cover design by Emma Rogers.

For my wife, Karen

PROLOGUE

Crows-an-Wra, Cornwall
1844

In my dream my body is enveloped in flame, and yet I feel no pain. I see myself burning, as if looking through the eyes of another, impassively observing my own death. I feel nothing, but I can smell it. The acrid air excites my senses and I awake, my heart beating close to panic. The smell is still present, as real as the sweat on my brow. It is the tang of smoke and a house full of charred objects now blackened and unrecognisable.

Sophia!

My first thought is for my daughter. I throw back the heavy bedcovers, and in the darkness I rush to the door. When I open it, I am no longer in darkness. To my right, the corridor is ablaze and I instantly catch my breath. Sophia's room is that way, beyond the flames that lick the walls and cling like fiery demons to the ceiling.

I do not hesitate for a moment.

'Sophia!' I call as I run to her, unafraid.

Hot smoke fills my lungs and I begin to cough. My

eyes sting and stream until I can barely see out of them. Flames now crackle and hiss around me as the heat becomes stifling.

'Sophia!' I call again, her name spluttering from my lips.

I reach her door and try to turn the handle, but it burns my palm. I see the paint, blistering and peeling from her door. I try again, and this time I wrap my hand in the folds of my nightgown. A quick turn and the door opens. Then, as the flames reach out for me, I am pulled back.

'Rosen!' a voice calls. 'It's too late.'

I shake my head. 'No! It can't be.'

'She's gone!' the voice insists. 'Sophia's dead.'

I begin to weep, knowing from the intensity of the flames inside her room that it must be true. The thought overpowers me, and my body fails me at last. I go limp. I feel myself falling, but someone catches me. It is my husband, Richard. He begins to drag me, wheezing and barely conscious, from the flames.

'Our daughter,' I utter, too weak to be heard over the fury of the fire.

I struggle as best I can, struggle to be free so that I can go back and save her, but it does me no good. My husband's grip grows firmer, my heels scrape faster along the coarse weave of the runner that lines the corridor until the air begins to clear, the heat of the flames to give way to the cool night.

When we stop, Richard looks down at me. I do not see sorrow in his eyes. I see pity. 'I'm sorry,' he says, but his cold apology is not for our mutual loss. He is sorry for me, and for what he is about to do.

I see a narrow length of cloth and a hessian sack. He

takes the cloth and forces a section of the material into my mouth. I try to scream, but the material stifles my cry. I struggle weakly as he wraps the cloth uncomfortably tight around me and ties it off at the back of my head, rendering me mute. Then, with wide eyes, I watch him bring the hessian sack closer to my face. I shake my head and begin to kick my legs, but other hands soon catch my ankles and restrain them.

Someone else is there.

Confusion engulfs me. What is happening to me? Why? Before I am able to see the figure at my ankles and know who it is, I see another piece of cloth, held in the palm of Richard's hand. He presses it firmly to my mouth and nose and I am forced to breathe its sweet-smelling vapour. I feel dizzy. The world around me begins to distort and fade.

Then I am in darkness again.

CHAPTER ONE

Rosen

Only a fool takes freedom for granted, but are we ever truly free? I had always thought I was, but just as a child is controlled by parental constraint, so is a married woman governed by her husband's will. To be truly free, one must live without rule or boundary, and yet I now found myself encumbered by both. I had not once in the twenty-five years of my life considered such things before now, but until now I had never been forced to.

Where was I?

I had awoken more drowsily than seemed natural, to the scratching sounds of what I imagined could only be mice or rats scurrying beneath the floorboards. I cannot say it was morning, because to own the truth I had no idea what time of day it was. The numerous bedcovers felt like sheets of roofing lead on my chest, pinning me down. As soon as I opened my eyes, my eyelids begged me to close them again, to make the dizziness stop. When I tried to move, the pounding in my head warned me to do so very slowly. I blinked against the bright glow from a single skylight in the roof above me, my only source of light in the room, and began to take in my surroundings.

The single ironwork bed and I were in one corner of a small, sparsely furnished room that offered no clue as to my whereabouts. I did not recognise anything about it. There was a washstand and bowl in the corner at the foot of the bed, and on the opposite side of the room, beneath closed window shutters, was an old wingback chair. Its faded green cloth was close to threadbare in places, and there was a small pile of books beside it. As soon as I sat up and heaved the bedcovers aside, the small fireplace to my right had me wishing for firewood and a match with which to light it, but it appeared that I, Rosen Trevelyan, the lady of Crows-an-Wra Manor, was no longer to be afforded such luxuries.

Yes, I remembered who I was, but little else with any certainty. I had been in and out of sleep for what felt like several days, although it might just as easily have been several hours for all I knew. The dream came and went, over and over, but still I could make no sense of it. My head continued to ache with such a persistent throbbing that it distracted my thoughts, causing me to question how much of it was real. And yet here I was. That much was certain. I had been rendered unconscious by my own husband's hand and brought without awareness to this unfamiliar room. But what of the rest?

What of Sophia?

Tears began to well in my eyes. Was the fire real, or in my delirious slumber had I only imagined it? The cold air in the room pulled me from my confusion and I swung my legs out of bed with a shiver, aware now of my breath swirling before me. I took up a blanket, wrapped it around my shoulders, and gravitated towards the pool of sunlight in the centre of the room, where I sat in my nightgown and my blanket, staring at the door. Was this room to be my prison? Had my husband locked me away here like a common criminal? There was no question in my mind that the door would be locked, the shutters at the window, too. I would test them in time, of course, but I was not yet ready to confirm my fears.

I do not know how long I sat there. It was long enough for the pale winter sunlight to warm me a little and make me feel myself again, although the shadows the sun cast on the bare floorboards had moved no more than a few inches, so it cannot have been long. Judging by the angle of the sun, I thought it must be late morning or early afternoon, and I already knew how much I would miss its light come nightfall, were I still here.

My thoughts continually drifted back and forth through my dream, or my stark reality if that was what it truly was. I remembered that someone other than my husband had held my ankles while he subdued me. Who was it? Who else was there? A few candidates wandered through my mind, but one remained. It was Richard's mother, Mariah. Was she to be my jailer? I knew Richard had no stomach for such duties, just as I knew Mariah would likely relish them.

I stared at the door again, wondering who would come. Surely someone had to, sooner or later? I noticed then that there were two hatches in the door: one in the middle of the upper half, the other abutting the floor. Their purpose was clear. The upper hatch would allow someone on the outside to look in without having to open the door and risk my escape, while the lower hatch would be used to pass food and water in to me, and to collect my toilet. Why was this happening to me, I wondered again, and wherever was I? It was clear that I was not at Crows-an-Wra Manor. I knew my own home too well. But where, then? I could not imagine the answer to either question.

At length I stood up, my legs weak and numb from having moved them so little. I went to the chair and stooped to pick up one of the books from the pile. It was The Old Curiosity Shop by Charles Dickens, and beneath it was Rob Roy by Walter Scott. I recognised them at once as my own copies. One even had my name written inside, as if I needed any proof – a gift from Richard. I loved to read, everything from Faust to Frankenstein. As I went through the pile, I knew I had read every one of them at least twice, some perhaps half a dozen times.

I put the books back and straightened the pile. Then I went to the window shutters and tried to open them. As I had suspected, they were firmly locked. I rattled them several times in my frustration, but they held fast, so I turned away again, contemplating standing by the door and calling out until someone came. As I turned away from the window, however, I drew in a familiar smell. It was the same smell that had awoken me in my dream. Something was burning, or had recently burned. Its acrid tang still hung in the air. I put my nose to one of the small gaps in the shutters and drew a deep breath. This time the pungent smell made me cough and pull away. I had not imagined it.

It had to be Crows-an-Wra Manor.

If it was, it could only mean that I was much closer to home than I had at first thought, but I was sure I had never once set foot inside this room. I shook my head.

'Not Crows-an-Wra Manor,' I said, already talking to myself, 'yet close by.'

It struck me then, not least because there could be no other explanation. I was inside the gatekeeper's cottage where Jenken, the groundskeeper, lived.

'Jenken!' I called, going to the door at last.

I made a fist and began to bang on the upper hatch. Had it been Jenken, then, who had held my ankles while my husband held that cloth to my face and rendered me unconscious? The impertinence of the man!

'Jenken!' I called again, certain now that it had to have been him, not Mariah as I had first thought.

I banged and I banged, wondering as I did so how Jenken, who had always been kind to me, could be involved in such a thing. Then I stopped banging on the door, my fist shaking in mid-air. Yes, Jenken had been kind to me, and he was especially fond of Sophia.

'Sophia...' I uttered, my voice faltering.

The fire was real. It was all real. The heady smell of the smoke fumes and the charred remains of the life I once knew suddenly filled my senses, and in my mind I was back outside Sophia's room as it burned.

I began to scream, and I wept so hard that it drained every ounce of my strength. I crashed to the floor, shaking and telling myself over and over that it was not true. Then I heard footsteps creaking on what I imagined was a staircase beyond the door.

Someone was coming.

CHAPTER TWO

I could not run back to my bed fast enough. There were so many answers I wished to demand from whoever was coming up those stairs that I should have had the courage to stand there and face my jailer when the hatch opened, but the sound of his or her approach on the stairs outside my room had me quaking like a frightened little girl, afraid of her own shadow. I quickly wiped my eyes, leaped back into bed and pulled the covers up around me, cradling them to my face as I listened and waited for the hatch to open.

The echo of footfalls against the floorboards drew closer and closer. I quickly determined that they were not heavy footfalls. It could not be Jenken. When the sound was immediately outside the door, it stopped, and in the ensuing silence I drew a long, sharp breath and held it. The silence seemed to last a lifetime. When at last the hatch opened, I let my breath go in a quiver and shrank back into my pillows. The thin, unadorned face that appeared so suddenly, like a portrait in the hatch's frame, was, as I had earlier suspected, that of my mother-in-law, Mariah.

'I see you're awake then,' she said, her voice sounding unusually gravelly for a woman's, which I ascribed to her having spent too many of her long years barking orders at people.

I did not answer her, but gradually, as I became accustomed to seeing her familiar face at the hatch, I lowered my bedcovers and sat up again. I expect it was my imagination, influenced by the situation I had suddenly found myself in, but I thought Mariah's sharp features looked quite sinister. Her steel-grey hair was scraped back from her face, being only partially visible beneath her linen cap. The tightness of her bun lifted her thin eyebrows higher, causing her dark brown eyes to stare into the room as if examining me with the intensity of a falcon hovering over its quarry. At her neck she had a white lace collar, which curled high beneath her chin, causing it to jut forward with authority. She pursed her lips and they instantly took on a spiteful appearance.

'Look at the state of your hair,' she said as she continued to study me in return. 'I suppose I shall have to bring you a brush, but don't expect me to brush it for you.'

I drew my hair around in front of me. It was matted with knots, which, given the circumstances, should not have surprised me – hair as long as mine tangled easily. As conceited as it undoubtedly was at this terrible juncture in my life, I could not bear to see it looking so dishevelled. Ordinarily, my maid, Charlotte, would brush it every morning and every night before I went to bed, sometimes taking as long as an hour if I had been out riding. She would brush and brush until it was as smooth and shiny as the cook's copper skillets. But these were clearly no longer ordinary times.

'Are you hungry?' Mariah asked, her tone short. 'Thirsty?'

I had not thought about it before now, but I was. I swallowed and my throat felt parched. I nodded.

'Lost your tongue now, have you?'

After a pause, I raised my head, mustering what little assertiveness I could find, and indignantly answered, 'No, I have not,' meeting her curt tone with my own.

'Pity!' Mariah snapped back. 'It would have saved me the bother of finding ways to keep you quiet. If I hear you screaming again, you'll have no food for a week!'

I didn't care. I just wanted answers. 'Why are you doing this to me?' I asked, my eyes imploring her to explain.

Mariah did not answer at first. She laughed to herself. 'Why am I doing this?' she repeated. 'My dear, if it were up to me, you would by now be dead. Do you think I will enjoy having to watch over you day and night, bringing you food and water and taking out your filthy, stinking toilet?'

'Dead?' I said, hanging on to the word in disbelief. 'But why?' I asked. 'Will you not tell me?'

'You'll know why soon enough,' Mariah said. 'Perhaps in the meantime you should ask yourself why you have not been a better wife to my son.'

The remark both surprised and confused me. 'I have been every bit the good wife to Richard these past seven years.'

Mariah's top lip twisted into a hateful expression. 'You were never good enough for my son.'

I stared back at her, wondering how long she had waited to say that. I had not for a moment in all those years believed that she particularly liked me, however much I had wanted her to. 'It's just a matter of time,' I kept telling myself. But try as I had to gain her approval, she had never accepted me. Now I understood the full extent of her hatred, or perhaps her jealousy. Did she not like to share her son with another woman? Could any woman have been good enough for him, in her eyes? At least we both now knew where we stood on the matter.

'Is that really why I'm here?' I asked. 'Because Richard no longer finds me a good wife, or is it that you do not regard me a worthy enough daughter-in-law?'

Mariah shook her head, as if pitying me. She clearly had no intention of elaborating.

'If you will not tell me why this is happening to me,' I said, 'will you at least let me see my daughter?'

Mariah's pitying expression deepened. 'Your daughter?' she said. 'My dear, you know very well that is impossible.'

Despite the smell of the fire, still lingering in the air beyond my confines, I could not believe that my dream was real and that Crows-an-Wra Manor had, at least in part, been reduced to ashes.

'Where is she?' I asked. 'Where is Sophia?'

'Surely you remember the fire, don't you?' Mariah said, her brow creasing. 'It was two nights ago now. After Richard dragged you away from Sophia's room, you were so overwrought that we had to keep you sedated. It was for your own good.'

I shook my head. 'Please!' I begged. 'Do not torment me like this. Lock me away if you must, but let me see my daughter.'

Mariah's lips began to twist as her features hardened. She pushed her face further in through the hatch, as if to make what she was about to say perfectly clear to me, although she could not have spoken more plainly. 'Your daughter is dead!' she said, almost shouting at me. 'Sophia was asleep in her room. It burned, her with it, along with half the east wing.'

'No,' I said, with surprising calm. I shook my head at her. I did not believe it – would not believe it. But I had seen it with my own eyes, hadn't I? 'You won't get away with this,' I told her. 'You know what my family will do when they find out. It will not be long before they wonder where I am and come asking after me.'

Mariah startled me then. Her coarse laughter was so unexpected. 'No one will wonder where you are, Rosen,' she said, 'least of all your family.'

The notion seemed preposterous to me. 'Of course they will,' I insisted. 'Why would they not?'

Mariah gave me a cold stare. 'Because they believe you are dead,' she said. 'Your funeral is tomorrow at St Buryan's, when Sophia's remains will also be laid to rest, the two of you side by side, sharing a single grave in the family plot. It was hurriedly arranged, but given the circumstances—'

'What circumstances?' I cut in. 'How can a funeral be held for me when I am clearly still very much alive?'

'You know it, and I know it,' Mariah said, 'but as far as your family is concerned, you died along with your daughter in the fire.'

'In the fire?' I repeated, wondering how this could be. 'But where is the evidence? My father would demand to see my body.'

'And see it he did,' Mariah said, a smug expression washing over her face. 'At least, he saw what was left of you – your charred bones and your smoke-blackened rings. Such a tragedy.'

I thought Mariah could not have sounded less sincere. 'Whose bones were they?' I asked, somewhat tentatively, because Charlotte was suddenly in my mind again. My maid and I shared such similar proportions that I shuddered to think it could have been her in my place. 'Don't fret your pretty little head, dear,' Mariah said. 'It was no one you knew.'

'Did Richard kill someone?' I asked. 'Did you?' I added, reflecting on Mariah's earlier words about killing me if it were down to her.

The notion set Mariah laughing again. 'There was no need for such measures,' she said. 'All we needed was a body, and a dead body would serve well enough as long as it could be passed off as yours. There are still people prepared to dig them up for the right price, you know?'

'Bodysnatchers?'

'Who else? It may no longer be a viable business these days, but there are plenty of people around who will happily turn their trade to just about anything with enough encouragement.'

'It's grotesque,' I said, scarcely able to believe that my husband and his mother could contrive such an unthinkable scheme, let alone follow through with it. But to what end? I was still really none the wiser.

'So, you see, Rosen,' Mariah continued, 'no one will ever come looking for you.' She began to close the hatch, but she paused. Her face suddenly filled the frame again. 'You would do well to keep that in mind,' she added. 'Your death would not be mourned a second time should you become too much of a burden to me.'

CHAPTER THREE

As soon as the hatch closed and I heard Mariah's footsteps recede towards the stairs, I leaped out of bed and ran to the door. I felt the sudden urge to beat my fists on it again, to smash it down and run screaming from the cottage in search of my daughter. But what was the use? I would not be able to break the door down, and my banging and screaming would only bring Mariah back to scold me and threaten me again. I needed sustenance. I had to stay strong and survive, if only to discover for myself the truth of what had happened on the night of the fire, and whether or not Sophia really was dead. I would not believe it without proof.

I took my blanket to the chair by the shuttered window, where I pulled my legs up beneath me and sat huddled with my thoughts. I did not cry for Sophia. I could not mourn her death until I knew it to be true. To mourn is to believe, and knowing now what Mariah was capable of, I would no longer give credence to a word she told me. As I looked up at the skylight, wishing the glass were cleaner so that I could better see the blue of the sky and the passing white clouds, I began to wonder whether Sophia was the reason I had been locked away. If Sophia really were dead, had I, as her mother, become of no further use to my husband? Or was it that, for some reason, neither of us was now welcome at Crows-an-Wra Manor? Had the fire been started on purpose to rid Richard of us both?

I shook my head. It made no sense. If that were the case, why keep me alive? A shiver ran through me as I considered that Sophia might very well be in the same situation. Had a child's bones also been found among the ashes, courtesy of the bodysnatchers my husband had hired? Had she, too, been locked away somewhere, cold and alone as I was, believing her mother to be dead? I could not bear to dwell on the thought. In truth, I had no idea what was going on or why, but somehow I had to find out.

'But how?' I asked myself.

Mariah would only tell me what she wanted me to hear, and Richard... What would Richard tell me? That is, if I ever had the chance to speak with him again? I shook my head, knowing that neither of these people who had once been so close to me could ever be trusted again. I had to escape, plain and simple, but as I looked around the sparsely furnished room again, I thought the task seemed impossible. Even if I could lift the chair on top of the bed and climb up, I still could not reach the skylight. The window was surely my best hope. I stood up and tested the shutters again, more forcefully this time. As before, the slats rattled in their frames, but they were otherwise as strong as the oak tree they had been made from – and made quite recently, judging by their unblemished appearance. Whatever was going on had clearly been planned well in advance.

I sighed to myself and sat down again with a shiver as I pulled my blanket more tightly around me. What had I done to upset my husband so? My thoughts turned back to my earlier conversation with Mariah. Had I really not been a good enough wife to Richard? The very suggestion offended me. Surely I had been dutiful in all areas of our marriage, and Richard had never once voiced his displeasure to me. It was a cruel torture to be treated like this without knowing of what I had been accused. What could I possibly have done to offend Richard so much that my punishment demanded such cruel treatment?

There had to be more to it.

Richard had loved me, hadn't he, just as I had loved him? Not to begin with, of course – our marriage was arranged between our fathers long before we met, great regimental friends that they were – but surely Richard's affections for me had grown as strong as mine had for him over time? Or perhaps I had naively chosen to believe what I wished to believe. My current circumstances certainly attested to that. I stood up and began to pace the room, wondering over and over what I could possibly have done wrong. I had to make sense of the matter or it would drive me mad, but I could find no answer beyond the simple, evident truth that my husband no longer cared for me.

A noise in the chimney distracted me and I knelt before it, eager for the comfort of any sound the outside world had to offer. It intensified as I listened, and I knew the din well enough. It usually preceded stormy weather, not that such things were any longer of concern to me. It was the sound of a hundred or more gulls squawking, come inland for shelter, and I welcomed their presence, as I would equally welcome the sound of the wind and the driving rain on my roof when it came. I had never before thought of gulls as songful birds, but I had never before appreciated their shrill music as I did now. I sat listening to them with my back against the fireplace, until the skylight turned grey and my room was all in shadow.

With nothing to do with my waking hours, I might have fallen asleep there had I not been stirred from my somnolence by a creaking floorboard beyond my door, heralding Mariah's return. I stood up and went to the door, meaning to confront her again, face to face this time, with the same question I had asked her previously: what had I done to deserve this? When I reached the door, however, it was not the upper hatch that opened, but the lower. It distracted me entirely from what I meant to say. I looked down and watched as an old pewter tray was slid into the room. My stomach groaned at the sight of the bread and cheese that was laid out on it, but I was far more overcome by thirst at the sight of the water, glistening from the top of an old brown leather cup. I knelt down and drank it back so fast, so wastefully, that it streaked down my chin and my neck, wetting my nightgown.

'Thank you,' I called as the hatch slammed shut. My words, born of sincere gratitude, sounded meeker to my ears than I might otherwise have intended.

I had expected the upper hatch to open then, for Mariah to reply and enter into further discourse with me, but she did not. Instead, I heard her light footsteps on the stairs. I wanted to call out to her, to bring her back to me, if only for her cold company, but I did not. In a moment she was gone, and I was left alone again with my thoughts.

CHAPTER FOUR

The storm foretold by the gulls lasted a number of days. Much of the time I would lie on my bed, looking up at the rain on the skylight, listening to its pitter-patter until the hypnotic rhythm lulled me to sleep. In truth, I could not say with any accuracy how long had passed since Mariah had brought my first meal to me. Perhaps I should have followed the example of Edmond Dantès, one of my favourite fictional characters, and made a habit of marking the passage of time by scratching lines into the walls with my fingernails, but I refused to. I saw no purpose in torturing myself further by counting the number of days I would be made to endure my confinement.

I had awoken with another violent headache. It reminded me of the first time I awoke in that unfamiliar bed. With it came the same sense of unsettled sleep, and of recurring dreams that were so vivid as to be real. I sat up and turned down my bedcovers. My nightgown had changed. I recognised it as my own, but it was not the same one I had been wearing when I last fell asleep. The embroidery, sewn by my own hand, was entirely different. Now there were yellow sunflowers where there had previously been violets. I noticed then that the backs of my hands, which were usually so pale, were particularly pink and bright, and they felt just a little sore. They had been scrubbed – I had been scrubbed. I had not dreamed it. Without my consent I had been stripped in the night, and then washed and dressed in a clean nightgown.

I thought back to my meal the evening before: a thin stew of potatoes and mutton. As I ate it, I had tasted nothing out of the ordinary – but then, with only two meals a day, I was kept hungry enough to have eaten just about anything without complaint or care for its ingredients. Apparently, however, some extraneous and powerful solution had been added, rendering me unconscious, and causing my head to throb with pain on waking. There was no other explanation for it, and it made perfect sense. Why should Mariah risk coming into the room while I was fully awake?

Mariah...

I heard the toe of her shoe kick at the door again – it was the sound that had awoken me. 'Tray!' she called, kicking the door once more with a thud so loud it shook my nerves.

I saw that the lower hatch was already open. I supposed my body's reluctance to stir from sleep was testing her patience and I almost fell out of bed in my haste to push my meal tray out to her, my limbs not feeling quite my own. That was how mealtime worked. I quickly learned the routine. Mariah would only slide fresh food and water in to me if I first slid out the tray from my previous meal. Again, she would not risk coming into the room to collect it for fear of me trying to escape, and the hatch meant she had no need to. My confinement had been very well planned indeed.

'I'm coming,' I called, looking for my tray through eyes that were still blurry from sleep and the after-effects of whatever drug I had been given. It was at the foot of the bed.

'Hurry about it!' Mariah snapped back. 'I haven't got all day.'

I slid the tray out to her, and the sound it made as it grated over the rough, gritty floorboards caused me to wince and clutch at the side of my head. In the name of heaven, would I have to suffer this pain every time I was in need of a wash and clean clothing? At that moment I would rather have remained dirty.

My tray was snatched away from me before I had pushed it halfway out. There was a rattle and a clatter on the other side of the door, and then a fresh tray was slid through. There was only fruit, bread and water this time, and little of it – no meat or cheese.

'Chamber pot?' Mariah said with displeasure.

I looked over at it, sitting beside the washstand where I kept it. 'I – I have not yet used it,' I stammered.

The upper hatch shot open and Mariah peered in at me. 'Quickly then,' she said. 'Haven't I been standing out here long enough already?'

'You mean now?' I asked, my voice sounding small compared to hers. 'While you wait?'

'Yes, now,' Mariah snapped. 'Or do you want the stink of it in your room all day?'

I did not, but neither did I wish to use my chamber pot while my mother-in-law stood watching over me. But what choice did I have? I went to the pot and began to lift my nightgown. I could feel her eyes on me, and the feeling was already making me uncomfortable. I paused and looked back at the door, certain that I would not be able to use the pot while Mariah looked on. In spite of everything, I would retain some dignity.

'Would you please close the hatch?' I asked, trying to be as polite as I could.

Mariah shook her head and sighed. The hatch slammed shut.

'Thank you,' I called, maintaining my manners even if hers had abandoned her. I would be the model prisoner Mariah would have me be. I would do everything she asked of me without complaint. If I were to understand why this was happening to me, and prove for myself what had become of my Sophia, it would not serve me to upset Mariah more than she already was. As I slid my used chamber pot out through the hatch, however, in truth I would rather have tipped the contents over her head.

'About time, too,' Mariah said as she snatched it from me.

She was about to close the hatch, but as much as I disliked her company, I did not want her to go. I still could not stop asking myself what I had done to offend Richard, and Mariah was the only person who could help me to understand why she felt I had not been a good wife to him. I had already decided that there was no merit in the direct approach. She would not tell me plainly or she would have done so by now. I had to get her talking again, though, and hope that something might come of it.

'Did Richard ever love me as I loved him?' I asked, watching the lower hatch.

It did not fully close, but remained half open as Mariah said, 'I strongly doubt you would still be alive if he did not.'

That at least was something, I supposed. 'How is Richard?' I asked, pretending to care after what he had done to me. 'I expect it must be close to the anniversary of our wedding by now.'

'He's well enough,' Mariah said. 'What of it?'

'I was thinking about our wedding day, that's all. It means it will soon be spring. It's very cold at the moment.'

'You've enough blankets to keep you warm,' Mariah said. She scoffed. 'Come summer, you'll be telling me you're too hot.'

The thought of still being in this room when summer arrived almost overwhelmed me. I steadied myself and continued to steer the conversation in the direction I had previously determined. 'Richard looked very handsome on our wedding day,' I said, recalling his youthful, angular features. He was twenty then. I had just turned eighteen.

The lower hatch closed, and I thought I had lost my opportunity for the time being, but then the upper hatch opened again. I backed away. I have no idea what I was afraid of. The door was locked, after all, and even if it were not, Mariah was an old woman of no greater physical threat to me than I was to her. Even so, I could no longer relax in her company, and the closer I was to her hateful stare, the less at ease I felt.

'Richard was handsome, all right,' Mariah said, nodding her head in agreement. 'But you soon changed him, didn't you – you and your family? How quickly you drained the joy from his eyes.'

'Yes, I suppose I must have,' I said, pretending that I had come to realise what a bad wife I had been to Richard. 'His father wanted our marriage, though,' I added, recalling both our fathers' ruddy-cheeked smiles as they stood proudly beside us in the parish church at St Buryan. 'As did mine.'

'And look where that got you,' Mariah said, her eyes wandering around my dismal little room as she spoke. 'Richard should have heeded your brothers' threats and left you standing at the altar. It would have been far better for both of you.'

'Richard told you what my brothers said?'

'Of course he did. With his father, God rest his soul, always away with his regiment, who else did he have to confide in? Harm you or make you unhappy in the slightest, they said, and he would have all four of them to answer to.'

'But they were none of them serious,' I said, smiling to make light of it. Mariah, however, did not see any humour in the matter.

'They were serious, all right,' she said. 'It aged Richard overnight. He was afraid to put a foot wrong. A good wife would not have stood for it.'

'But surely that is not why I now find myself here in this room, is it?'

Mariah slowly shook her head. 'Do you really not yet understand? You have not been a good wife because you have failed in the most important of all your duties.'

With that, Mariah stepped back and slammed the hatch shut, leaving me standing cold and alone once more, wondering what she meant.

Failed in the most important of all my duties...

The answer came to me as suddenly as a sneeze. Mariah had given me the answer I was looking for, even though she would not say it directly. My duty as a wife was, according to my wedding vows, to love, honour and obey my husband, but there was another unwritten duty that was so deeply ingrained in the doctrine of marriage as to be taken for granted.

I had failed to give Richard a son and heir.

A shiver sent me hurrying back to my bed in search of what little warmth still remained. There was no sun at the skylight today; rather, the picture above me was of a plain grey canvas. The storm may have passed, but its echo would undoubtedly linger for several days more. I pulled the bedcovers up around me, too lost in my thoughts to care, or to pay any notice to my thirst or my grumbling appetite. After our marriage, I had not fallen pregnant easily. Two years passed before Sophia was born, and despite all our endeavours since then to have another child – to provide a son and heir for Richard – it was not to be. There had been complications during Sophia's birth, complications that were no doubt to blame for my inability to fulfil the most important of my duties in the eyes of Richard and his mother.

So that was it. Richard had no further use for me because I could not provide him with a son, and as he could not divorce me – divorce being granted only in the rarest of circumstances – he had locked me away. I had become his secret wife, believed dead by all who knew me, because he could not bring himself to have me killed. But what kind of love would see me live out my pitiful existence in this manner? I considered then that he might only be keeping me alive because I was the mother of his daughter, or perhaps it was because Richard still believed my brothers' threats. I had no doubt that they would make him suffer greatly before his own death should they ever discover what he had done to me.

I had to get word to them.

CHAPTER FIVE

I puzzled my mind for days, trying to think of how I might communicate my predicament to my brothers, but it served no greater purpose than to occupy my thoughts for a time with something other than my Sophia. I had no pen and no paper with which to write a letter, and no one to take it to them if I had. There was no apparent way to get word out unless I could first free myself. So, as the days passed, I put the idea aside, having resigned myself to wait and hope that some means to achieve these objectives would eventually present itself. In the meantime, I bundled myself up with blankets most days, and sat in my chair and reread my books to distract myself.

A week or more must have passed. My meals came and went with obstinate regularity. I swear if I had an initial reference to go by, then I could easily have known the time of day by the opening and closing of the lower door hatch. 'Cuckoo!' I would sometimes call to Mariah when I was in no mood for conversation. Heaven knows, Mariah rarely was, and for that I was frequently grateful because she never had anything pleasant to say. Today, however, there was a kindness I wished to ask of her – two things, in fact. I had not found the courage to do so earlier in the day, but I was resolved to ask her at my next opportunity, which by my reckoning would be very soon. There had been occasional sun at the skylight today, but despite being on the cusp of a new season, the cold of what must have been a harsh winter refused to yield to spring's inexorable return. It was by now dark outside. I was partway through Jane Austen's Persuasion, having sought the companionship of Anne Elliot for the afternoon, reading by the silver light of the moon while my eyes were able to. I had just finished another page, having to pause every now and then as the clouds shrouded the moon and made it too dark for me to discern the words, when my second meal of the day arrived. I could smell it before I saw it. It was pilchards again, a fish widely caught in the seas off Cornwall, and landed in their thousands at Newlyn.

The old tray from my earlier meal was already waiting beside the hatch. I hurried to it, steeling my nerves as I went. The hatch opened, and without speaking I slid my tray out to Mariah. She in turn slid the pilchards through, along with a bruised apple this time and my usual cup of water. The hatch closed and I stood up, willing my mouth to open and speak the words I wanted to say. I heard Mariah pick up my old tray. She was about to leave.

'Mariah?' I called to her. 'May I speak with you?'

The tray was set down again, and a moment later the upper hatch opened. This time Mariah's sharp features were accentuated by the shadows her lamplight cast as she held the flame up to the opening so that she could better see me.

'Yes, what is it?'

'I – I...'

I faltered. I had not once stammered before my incarceration, but Mariah now filled me with such a sense of dread and foreboding that I often found myself tongue-tied in her presence.

She sighed through her nose. 'Speak, girl!' she snapped, 'and be quick about it.'

'I'm bored,' I told her, skipping all the pleasant preamble I had intended to say in getting to the point of the matter. 'I have read all these books so many times that I'm sure I could recite many passages from them word for word.'

'Would you like me to bring more books?' Mariah said. 'Is that it?'

I thought more books would always be welcome, but if they were from the house then it was likely I had already read them many times, too.

'No,' I said. 'Before I was brought here, I was in the midst of embroidering one of Sophia's gowns. It was to be for her birthday. It can't be far off now, and I should very much like to finish it in time.'

A smile cracked at the corners of Mariah's lips. 'But my dear Rosen,' she said, her tone condescending, 'where is the sense in embroidering a child's gown when the child is dead?'

I hated to hear Mariah speak like that. She was wrong. She had to be. 'All the same,' I said, not daring to contradict her, for she would certainly not yield to my request if I did, 'I should like to finish it.' I tried to appeal to her good nature, if any remained in that cold heart of hers. 'You can understand that, can't you?' I added, looking at her as earnestly as I could, trying to find a little sympathy, but it seemed she had none to give.

'It burned,' she said, her eyes widening, as if taking pleasure from the pain she knew she was causing me. 'It all burned.'

As much as I wanted to run and bury my face in the shadows so I no longer had to look at Mariah's hateful stare, I stood my ground. 'My silks then?' I said. 'Perhaps some new lengths if they have also perished. I don't mind which colours. I just want something to do. I can embellish the embroidery on my nightgown, and when there is no room left, I'll embroider the bed sheets.' I swallowed the lump that had risen in my throat. 'Please,' I added. 'Or I fear you may soon have a mad woman in your care.'

Mariah seemed to take me seriously at last. 'Very well, I'll see what I can do,' she said with reluctance. 'But I'll make no promises. You behave yourself and keep quiet, and we'll see.'

She began to close the hatch. 'Wait,' I said, moving closer to the door. 'There was something else I wanted to ask you.'

'Haven't you asked enough of me for one night?'

'Yes, I'm sure I have, but...' I trailed off and brought my long hair around into the lamplight. 'My hair has become so knotted,' I added, showing her the matted strands that I could barely now draw my fingers through. 'I should like that brush you mentioned, if you would be so kind.'

Mariah scoffed. 'Perhaps you'd like some soap or a solution of ammonia so you can wash your hair, too,' she said. Her sarcasm was palpable. 'Anything else?'

'No,' I said. 'That's all.'

'Eat your pilchards,' Mariah said, and then she closed the hatch and walked away.

I could feel my heavy limbs shaking as I took my tray of pilchards to the armchair and sat with it in my lap, and this time I was not shaking from the cold. I gave a long sigh to help relax myself again, happy to have found the courage to ask Mariah for these things, yet uncertain as to whether she would bring me either. I picked up my book again, but the strong lamplight had ruined my eyes for reading by the pale light of the moon, and it was growing paler now by the minute.

CHAPTER SIX

Another week passed without interest. Every day seemed so much like the last that I would not have known a full seven days had come and gone were it not for the repetitive pattern of my meals – although with pilchards in such ready abundance in the area, I was brought them twice a week, so whenever I was disposed to calculate the passing of time, I had to be mindful of that. One whole week, and I had received neither of the things I had asked Mariah for.

'We'll see,' she kept telling me when each morning I would remind her about my silks and my hairbrush. Well, today I awoke with a familiar headache, entirely without need of the latter. My nightgown and bed sheets had been changed, my skin scrubbed clean, and my hair savagely cut from my head. I thanked the Lord that I had no mirror in which to see my reflection because I would surely no longer recognise the gaunt-faced woman staring back at me.

Needless to say, I did not put my tray out that morning. When Mariah came with my first meal, I lay beneath the blankets on my bed, quietly crying to myself, senseless to the toe of her boot banging repeatedly on the door, and to her hateful voice calling to me. I would rather go hungry to spite her. Why she never took my old tray out when she came in to clean me and change my bedding, I do not know. Perhaps it was to ensure that I had to put the tray out each morning myself, so she would know that I had not died in my sleep. Tray or no tray this morning, she would know from my sobbing that I had not.

I imagine it was early afternoon when at last I rose from my bed, the smell of the previous night's drug-laced pilchards still hanging in the air. And there was something else. It was birdsong, more tuneful and sweeter than I had heard in a long while. I went to the fireplace and sat beside it to listen more closely, and very slowly a smile crept up on me. It was surely spring now because, aside from the mounting excitement I could hear in the birdsong, the afternoon air felt so much warmer. Had the weather turned at last? I hoped so. Spring was my favourite season, and how I longed to see its promised miracle of life burst forth around me.

I closed my eyes and rested my head back against the brickwork of the fireplace surround, and in my mind I began to picture the vast estate around Crows-an-Wra Manor as it gradually shook off winter's cold embrace. Visitors had often commented on how everything seemed to come into bloom earlier here than in other parts of the country. I could already see the ever-cheerful daffodils that lined the carriage drive, and the bluebells that brought life and colour to the woodlands. I imagined myself flying above them all, as free as the songbirds, to the vast camellias and magnolias that had always been among my favourites, and out over the myriad wildflowers to the ever-restless sea.

If only I could have remained lost in my imagination for ever, but it did not last. I caught myself heaving a pitiful sigh as I opened my eyes again and was instantly thrust back to my grim reality. I was beginning to miss the simple pleasures that merely being outside can bring to the senses: the scent of the flowers and the smell of rain after a dry spell. I wished with all my heart that I would see the flowers again, and walk among them with my Sophia.

I might have indulged my self-pity with a tear at that moment were it not for the sound of a dove cooing at the top of the chimney. It was so loud, and it came so suddenly, that it startled me. Instead of crying, I laughed to myself at my own fragile disposition.

'Coo-coooo-coo,' I called back, trying to mimic the bird. Was it a collared dove? I thought it was. The wood pigeon's low, throaty tones were never quite as delicate.

The dove answered me, or so I liked to think. 'Hello,' I said in reply, glad of its company for as long as it might last. 'It's a lovely day, isn't it?' I added, peering up through the skylight at a patchwork of fluffy white clouds against the blue.

I heard another call then, similar to the first, but more distant, as if another dove was somewhere on the roof above me. I willed it to introduce itself to me at the skylight, but it did not. A moment later I could hear both doves together at the top of the chimney, gently cooing to one another. My smile broadened. Were they nesting in one of the chimney pots? How lovely that would be. I began to whistle to them – one of Vincenzo Bellini's tunes that I had previously enjoyed playing in the parlour on the fortepiano. They continued to coo as I whistled, then over our music I heard another sound and I immediately fell silent to better hear it. People were talking – two voices that were quite distinct.

I was surprised at how acute my senses were becoming. I could read by the light of even the slightest crescent moon, and now it seemed as if I could have heard the spring flowers opening if I listened to them intently enough. Perhaps it was an effect of the chimney acting like an ear trumpet to the outside world, or merely a consequence of my confinement denying me in other ways. Whatever the reason, I was glad to hear words other than Mariah's and my own, although I soon realised that it was Mariah talking. But to whom?

'Drinking?' Mariah said. 'At this time of day?'

'That's right, madam,' the other voice said. 'Got himself into a right stupor he has, too.'

I knew the other softly spoken voice at once. It was Jenken, the groundskeeper. Although he was related to Mariah, he knew his place and was mindful of proper servant etiquette. I wondered if I called out to him whether he would hear me as well as I could hear him. What did I have to lose other than my meagre rations of food and water?

'Jenken!' I called up the chimney. It made the doves flap and fuss above me, but the conversation between Mariah and Jenken continued.

'Where is he?' I heard Mariah ask.

'Sitting among the ruins with a bottle,' Jenken said. 'I couldn't talk it off him.'

Their chatter fell silent then. There was only the cooing of the doves.

'Jenken, it's me!' I yelled, as loudly as I could manage. 'It's Rosen!'

My voice drove the doves off the chimney this time. Their flapping must have drowned out my words, or else the chimney was having the opposite effect for them, because no one seemed to hear me.

'Very well,' Mariah said. 'I'll handle it. Take me to him.'

With that, their conversation quickly diminished. They had moved away, and within seconds I could no longer hear them at all.

I stood up and ran to the window. I began to beat my fists repeatedly on the shutters, hoping Jenken might at least hear the sound and wonder what had caused it. He had surely been evicted from the cottage prior to my incarceration, made to live in the servants' quarters at the manor, I expect. With no one else living here now but Mariah, he would be forced to wonder what had made the sound. I banged harder and harder, and then I stopped. A slat in one of the shutters had cracked. I stared at it, foolishly thinking of the trouble I would be in if Mariah found out. But what did it matter now? What did anything matter? I took hold of it and frantically began to pull it this way and that. It continued to work loose, until very soon I found myself holding a foot-long piece of wood in my hands. There was suddenly daylight at the window. I put my eyes to it, and through the grime on the windowpane I saw Crows-an-Wra Manor for the first time since the fire.

The gatekeeper's cottage was set at an angle to the main gates and the carriage drive. With my little attic-room window facing into the grounds, it meant that I was able to see the manor house almost in its entirety. It had not been so long since I last looked upon its sturdy granite facade, but somehow it was not the same home that I remembered. My memories were of happy days, first as a wife, and then as a mother, watching Sophia grow with a heady mixture of trepidation and joyous wonder in equal measure. Now, as I looked out through the thin layer of mildew on my window, I could only see it for the grim, grey structure it was, standing half in ruins, as I now was. My eyes wandered and I saw Mariah and Jenken, his lumbering frame dwarfing hers. They were pacing along the carriage drive towards the house. No one had heard me. I gazed at the daffodils that lined the drive, but they were not yet in bloom as I had imagined. If it was spring, then I could not see it.

I turned away with my shoulders slumped. I should have tried to smash every one of those shutters to pieces, then opened the window and tried to jump down, but I did not have the strength for it. Even if I had, how far would I get? That is, if I could even make it down from the window without breaking my legs or my neck. The cottage had three floors and my little room was at the top. The gates would also likely be locked, and I expected that Mariah would be quick to return, for she did not dare to leave me unattended any longer than was absolutely necessary. What if she came back to find me breaking the shutters? What would they do with me then?

No, that would not do.

I took another last look outside, not at the house, but at the budding trees and the deer grazing in the distant fields, and I set the piece of shutter back into place as if it had never been disturbed. I thought it better for now to have a window to the outside world, through which I could see people coming and going to and from the house, than to have no view at all should my little secret be discovered.

CHAPTER SEVEN

Last night I dreamed I saw Richard again, but it was not a pleasant dream.

Far from it.

Several more days had passed since I had broken the slat from the shutters at my window, and every day I had stood with my eyes pressed to the gap, observing the outside world from my limited, if welcome, perspective. I had looked for my Sophia until my feet were sore from standing so long in one place, but my eyes had not once found her. In truth, they had seen very little to excite my senses. Mariah came and went, but was never gone long. Surprisingly few of the servants were to be seen, and there were no carriages or visitors calling at Crows-an-Wra Manor at all. I did see Jenken again, tending to the grounds from time to time, but he was always so distant. I thought he was sure to help me if he knew I was here. His heart was too kind not to. His mind, having matured incommensurately with his years, had rendered him too innocent and untainted by the things that might poison the minds of other men upon reaching adulthood. If only he would come closer, so that I might make him aware of me and let him know that I was still alive.

I took great pleasure in watching the rabbits at dusk, and my pair of collared doves, although I could not see them, had returned to their nest-making among the chimney pots, so I was no longer entirely without company. I do not count Mariah in this. I had not uttered one word to her since she had cut off my once beautiful hair. However, my doves and I, and now the rabbits, were fast becoming the best of friends. I told them how cruel Mariah was to me, and I told them about my dreams, but not yet about my dream of Richard. I had not liked to think about that, let alone talk about it. I had tried burying my head in one book after another all day to take my mind off the matter, but it filled the space between the words and would not go away.

I sat up in my armchair and closed my book, surprised to find that the light was already beginning to fade on yet another empty day.

'Perhaps it would be good to talk about it,' I told myself.

I set the book down on the pile with the rest and went to the fireplace. I listened, trying to determine whether my friends were there.

'Coooo,' I called. 'Are you there, my collared doves?'

My question was met with a low, warbling reply. Was Mrs Dove already sitting on her eggs? Was she as anxious as I had been when I first fell pregnant with Sophia?

'I have another dream to share with you, if you will listen,' I said. 'The upper hatch in my door was opened late last night, much later than when Mariah sometimes looks in on me before she goes to bed. I couldn't see who it was at first, but then I heard the key in the door and it opened, spilling lamplight into my room. It was my husband, Richard. You remember him, don't you – the man who dragged me from the flames on the night of the fire and locked me in this room? Well, as confusing as my dream was, the shape of things never quite settling, I could see Richard clearly enough.'

I paused and pictured my husband's face as I recounted my dream to the doves, comparing his image with that of the man in my dream. It was most certainly Richard. His dark brown hair was a little longer and more unkempt than usual, his full sideburns even more pronounced, but his pale grey eyes, shining bright in the lamplight, could not be mistaken by one who knows him so well. They burned with such intensity as he came into the room and closed the door behind him.

'He'd been drinking again,' I told the doves. 'He came to my bedside and leaned over me, as if to kiss me, and his breath reeked of brandy. He did not kiss me. Instead, he pulled back my bedcovers and stared at me for several seconds before he was compelled to look away. I'm sure he hardly knew me, half-starved and as thin as I am, my hair so much shorter now and more untidy than his own. I found myself asking him why he had done this to me, and where Sophia was. I implored him to tell me that she was not dead, as Mariah had said. I asked him over and over again, but my words were mute.'

I thought ahead to what came next in my dream and my hands began to shake. 'You've probably heard enough,' I told the doves, not wishing to go on. 'Shall I tell you about Sophia again instead?'

Silence.

'Very well,' I said, and then I found myself lying to them – lying because I could not bring myself to recount another word of my dream. 'We embraced,' I added, smiling to myself as if it were true. 'Richard told me he was sorry and that he was going to let me out very soon, and that Sophia was waiting for me. Isn't that wonderful news?'

I forced myself up from the cramped position I had settled into and went back to my chair. I threw myself on to it. In my dream, Richard had not spoken a word to me. Unable to look at me a moment longer, he threw me onto my belly and pulled me up onto my knees. I felt his hands clenching my buttocks, and then he sodomised me. I screamed and I screamed, but I made no sound. Richard had never done that before, and I found myself supposing that, as unlikely as it was given my failure to provide him with another child, he could not take the risk that I would fall pregnant now that he had forsaken me.

I kept telling myself it was only a dream, but it did not help, any more than it would have helped if I had told it to the doves. I knew this because, as much as it felt like a dream at the time, there was no question that it was not. My bruises were evidence enough, and I had awoken with another of those familiar, sickly headaches again.

CHAPTER EIGHT

As the weeks passed, Richard visited me in the night on most washdays to take advantage of whatever drug Mariah was stirring into my meals. Time and time again he came to me to satisfy his carnal urges, knowing I would not be able to fully awaken and resist him. Perhaps he believed I did not know he was there, and that I could not feel his presence, but I did. I felt everything, yet I could do nothing.

At times I would hear him behind me, quietly sobbing to himself, and he would utter words beneath his breath that I could not fully comprehend. Was he saddened by what he had done to me – what he had reduced me to? Was he making his apologies to me? I liked to think he was, because he had every reason to be sorry. I had already vowed to myself that should I ever be free to do so, I would make him sorrier still. Edmond Dantès' revenge against those who had wronged him would appear kind by comparison to the things I would have my brothers do in the name of my revenge.

It was late morning and I was at my window, looking absently out through the gap I had made in the shutters, wondering whether Mariah knew about Richard's visits and their purpose. I suspected she did and that, being the doting mother she was, she readily indulged him. I was also wondering why Richard had suddenly stopped coming to me. I knew he had stopped, for now at least, because my body had been scrubbed clean twice since his last visit and he had not come to me once in all that time. It was not that I minded his sudden abstinence – far from it – but I was curious as to the cause.

Where was he, and where was everyone else, for that matter? I had seen no one but Mariah, and occasionally Jenken, in days. Surely there were too many servants in service at Crows-an-Wra Manor for me not to see them all at one time or another, and before my incarceration never had a week passed at the manor without a carriage or two coming or going. Yet I had not heard a carriage in what must be weeks now. Had that been Richard's carriage? Was that the reason he no longer visited me in the night, because he had left me here with Mariah? If so, I wondered for how long.

It was a sunny day, which made it all the more unusual that I had not seen anyone in the grounds or at the front of the manor; such fine weather usually brought people outside. I undid a few of the buttons at the neck of my nightdress, wishing I had something lighter to wear, or just something different for the sake of change. I imagined it was mid-April by now, perhaps almost May. Mariah would never tell me, saying that such things were no longer of concern to me, so I had to trust in nature to assist my guesswork. It had certainly become much warmer recently, and more colourful outside. Most of the trees were now in leaf to some extent, and the spring flowers were beginning to fade. The nights were still chilly, but by the afternoon I usually found myself wishing for an open window and a cool breeze. I was sure that in another month or two I would be complaining that it was too hot, just as Mariah had said.

For no great reason or purpose, which aptly describes most of my waking hours, I was watching the manor house, or as much as I could see of it through my broken slat. There was something about the house that deeply saddened me today. It had once been so full of life and laughter, with parties to look forward to and plentiful parlour games. To earn their Christmas box, we used to make the servants dress up and put on plays for us from time to time, and the greater their performances, the greater their reward. It was such fun, although I could not imagine the likes of it ever happening here again. Now, as my eyes drifted from one dark, empty window to the next, all I could imagine was that I was in a graveyard, looking upon countless headstones. There was no life left inside Crows-an-Wra Manor. Of that I was certain.

But wait…

Movement caught my eye and I pressed closer to the slats to better see what it was. There was someone there at last. At first I thought it must be Jenken, because the figure's heavy build was not dissimilar. On closer scrutiny, however, I saw that the figure was not nearly as tall. A moment later I determined that the person was wearing a white bonnet. It was a woman. More importantly, she was heading my way. I took her for another of the servants at first, but I could not place her, and the further she came along the carriage drive, the more convinced I was that I had not seen her before. She had a trug over her arm, as though out to collect flowers. She was striding with enough authority to have anyone who saw her believe she owned the estate, but her simple black attire, and her unadorned servant's bonnet, told me otherwise. I thought she had to be a new servant, but who was she, and why had she been employed at all when there were already so many servants? I did not linger on the matter. Instead, I found myself thinking that, whoever she was, she had been employed without my approval. It was an affront to my former position as lady of the house, but what say did I now have in such matters?

I watched her stoop to cut a tulip stem. She placed the flower in her trug, and then I heard a sound that froze me to my core. I caught my breath. I heard footsteps on the stairs. Mariah was coming. I could not have spun around any faster. I picked up the broken slat and tried to force it back into place so that Mariah would not notice it, but I was suddenly all thumbs. I dropped it with a clatter, and as I bent to pick it up again I heard her at the door. I shot to my feet again, leaving the broken piece of slat where it was, just as the upper hatch opened.

'Mariah,' I said, noting more alarm in my voice than was intended. I breathed more calmly. 'Whatever brings you here? Do you have an extra meal for me today?'

'No,' Mariah said, studying me with greater curiosity than usual. 'Although by the look of you, an extra meal might be in order. I wouldn't want Richard to think I'd starved you to death.'

I looked down at myself and thought my nightgown now hung more loosely on my frame than I remembered. I supposed it showed in my face all the more, too. 'I am becoming rather thin, aren't I?' I said, moving back towards the window to be sure that Mariah could not see the broken shutter.

'Pale, too,' she said. 'Are you well?'

'Yes, I think so,' I replied, although I'm sure neither of us would be surprised if I were not.

'Come closer.'

Those two words filled me with dread. I did not want to move an inch.

'Did you not hear me, girl? Come here so I can have a better look at you.'

I stepped towards her, thinking it would be all right as long as I kept myself between her and the broken slat at the window, but the arm of the chair was in my way.

'I'm really quite well,' I said, taking another small step.

'I'll be the judge of that. Now come along!' Mariah insisted.

I took two quick steps, moving awkwardly around the chair. Then I practically sprinted to the hatch, pressing my face close to it so as to block out most of the room.

'Whatever's the matter with you today?' Mariah said, taking a half step back. 'Here, let me feel your forehead.'

Mariah's hand felt like a cold facecloth against my skin. I may have looked pale, but inside I was flushed from the warmth of the day and the fear of discovery.

'A little warm,' Mariah said, 'but nothing to concern ourselves with.'

'My room is rather warm today,' I said. 'That's all it is.'

'There! Didn't I say you'd be complaining about the heat soon enough? There's nothing I can do about it, so you'll just have to put up with it.'

I would have put up with anything at that moment just to make her go away. I took a step back towards the hatch in the direction of the window, hoping I was still blocking her view of the broken slat. 'If not to bring me food or water, then why are you here?' I asked, meaning to get to the point of her visit as quickly as possible.

My sudden directness seemed to take Mariah aback. Her thin eyebrows rose high on her forehead. 'I am here,' she said, 'because we are soon to have a guest at Crows-an-Wra Manor, and I need your assurance that you will do nothing to draw attention to yourself.'

'A guest?' I repeated, at the same time thinking her request entirely unreasonable given my circumstances. After all, why should I not draw attention to myself if there was some possibility that it might lead to my freedom?

'Yes, but you need not trouble yourself with who it is or why they are here.'

Those questions did trouble me, but I knew I would get no answers from Mariah if she did not wish to give them. I wanted to ask her who the woman I had seen gathering tulips was, too, but I caught myself in time to prevent the blunder. If Mariah knew I had seen the woman she would question how, and then my little secret would be up.

'Have I not already proven myself to be the model prisoner?' I said, with a touch of sarcasm. In truth, I had thus far been far too good, but all the while I received food and water and had breath in my body, I would wait for the right opportunity to be free of that room when the time came.

'Just the same,' Mariah said, 'if you keep quiet and make no fuss once our guest has arrived, you shall have a reward.'

'What reward?'

'I shall bring you more books to read – books you have not read before.'

I should have liked the opportunity to once again read books that were new to me, but it was not what I had in mind. 'I want my silks,' I said. 'And my embroidery needles.'

Mariah pursed her lips and drew a deep breath through her nose. 'Perhaps,' she said. 'Once you have shown me just how quiet, how invisible, you can be. Books first, then your silks. Would you like that?'

'Yes, I would. I'd like that very much.'

'Very well, then. I'll not hear a peep out of you from this moment forth. Do we have an agreement?'

I nodded, wondering whether she really meant to let me have my silks, or if she was just teasing me again. I thought she would give them to me this time. She knew I could raise such a holler if I chose to that their guest could not fail to hear it at some point and question its origin. Perhaps I would do so anyway, if their guest ever came within earshot of the cottage. Yes, I would play along and bide my time. An opportunity was sure to present itself before long.

CHAPTER NINE

Who was coming to Crows-an-Wra Manor?

The question vexed me for days, and I sensed the importance of the matter, to Mariah at least. Thus far, since we had struck our bargain, she had been true to her word and had brought me a new book each day with my first meal. From whence she obtained them, I do not know, but I had read none of them before, and it was a delight to be able to lose myself for a time in their unfamiliar pages. My hope remained strong then that I might soon have my silks with which to embroider to my heart's content, although I would not do so merely to pass the time. I had another, far more serious purpose for them. With my silks I could embroider a hidden cry for help, stitched into a fold in my bed sheet so that the laundry maid might discover it on washday.

I told the doves everything Mariah had said, of course, but they were less interested in the matter than I. They now had other, more important things to attend to. Their chicks had hatched, and what a joy it was to sit by the fireplace and listen to their pitiful little cries every time one or other of their parents returned to the nest with food for their ever-hungry gapes. I was sitting below them now for company, talking to them every now and then about the stories I had read in my new books, and about our visitor. I couldn't help but keep coming back to that, whether they cared to listen or not.

'I wonder if that's why Richard hasn't been to see me lately,' I said. 'Do you think his absence concerns our new guest?'

I thought it did. I fully expected Richard to return at the same time with whoever it was, and I imagined it had to be someone important. I tried to think of the people close to Richard.

'He doesn't have many friends of any great import-ance,' I told the chicks. They were silent now, listening intently to my words, or so I liked to think. I suppose they were really just waiting for their next meal, as I ever seemed to be. 'Most of the family's important friends were friends of Richard's father,' I added. 'Do you suppose one of them is coming to encourage Richard to follow in his father's footsteps and join the Hussars? It wouldn't be the first time that has happened, but they would be wast-ing their breath.'

One of the doves must have returned with food be-cause the chicks began to squeal again.

'I know,' I said, as if in answer to them. 'Richard vowed he would never go off to die in some foreign land as his father eventually did.' I paused. 'If not a friend of Rich-ard's father,' I added, 'I wonder who else it could be?'

I continued to think on the matter, listening intently for their answer. What I heard next, however, was some-thing altogether unexpected. I heard voices, soft at first, and then one rose as if in anger. It was Mariah.

'You're to leave this instant!' she said, her sharp tone

echoing in the chimney. 'It's just like you to call when you know Richard's away.'

'Come now, Mariah,' the other voice said. 'I've only just arrived, and besides, it's you I want to talk to first.'

It was a man, but clearly not one of the servants. I sensed I knew him, or had once known him, but as yet I could not place his haughty tones.

'You're not welcome here!' Mariah continued. 'Now be off with you, or I'll have Jenken see you off.'

The man laughed at the idea. 'You wouldn't dare,' he said. 'Besides, I really don't think it would be in your best interest – not until you've heard what I've come here to say. If you care for your son half as much as I know you do, you'll hear me out.'

The voice came to me at last. It belonged to Giles Trevelyan, Richard's older half-brother. I had not seen him in a number of years, and neither to my knowledge had Richard. If Richard knew he was here at Crows-an-Wra Manor now, especially in his absence, he would be furious. I had only ever known them to quarrel and fight, and never more so than since their father had died and Richard, whom their father deemed less apt to squander everything, had inherited almost the entire estate. But what was Giles doing here now? I couldn't imagine, but I was not surprised to hear that Mariah wished him to leave. His last words, however, had seemingly given her cause to reconsider.

'What do you mean by that?' Mariah asked, her tone mellowing.

'I mean, my dear Mariah, that I know.'

It fell quiet for several seconds, and I pictured Mariah studying Giles, her questioning eyes boring into his. Then at last she said, 'What do you know?'

'More than enough,' Giles said, a cool edge having crept into his tone. 'You see, I was in London not so long ago. It was just before Christmas – lots of parties in London around that time, of course. Well, I had been invited to one party in particular, and bless my soul if Richard wasn't there. I imagine someone must have obtained our name in connection with our father and invited us both. You know how the social circuit works. Anyway, I was about to extend a peace offering to my dear brother, it being Christmastime and all, when I saw the daintiest delight of a girl on his arm.' He paused. 'You can see where I'm going with this, can't you?'

'I'll hear it just the same,' Mariah said, her voice now sounding a little less confident to my ear than usual.

'Very well,' Giles continued. 'I stopped in my tracks, of course, wondering what to make of the situation. Where was Richard's wife, I mused? Why was Rosen not on his arm? I could see no sign of her, and there was Richard with this young woman clinging to him like a limpet. I thought at first that he'd simply been adopted for a dance – he always was a handsome fellow – so I decided to make myself scarce and observe them. Needless to say, they did not dance together – not in the usual sense, that is. I followed them out on to the balcony, keeping my distance, and it was then that I knew in no uncertain terms that a romantic bond existed between them. I did some digging around after that, bent on discovering who this girl was, and blow me down if it didn't turn out to be the very same girl Richard has just recently married.'

At hearing that, I gasped so loudly it upset the chicks in their nest. Were my ears deceiving me? Did Richard really have a new wife, and so soon after my apparent death? Was she to be the guest Mariah had told me about?

As hard as I tried, I could find no reason to question what I had just heard Giles say, and in many ways it all made perfect sense to me now. During the months before the fire, Richard had been to London several times on estate affairs – at least, that is what he had told me. Then, I had had no cause to doubt him. Now, however, it was clear to me that he had all the while been courting his new wife.

And Mariah... Both she and Richard had left Crows-an-Wra Manor together recently, and for some considerable time. Mariah had said she wished to visit her ailing older brother in Bristol, whom she hardly ever saw, fearing that his ill health meant there would be little opportunity to do so in the future. Richard had said he was needed in London on extended business and had kindly offered to take Mariah to Bristol on his way there, offering to collect her again upon his return. I doubted now whether any of that was true. The idea of Richard having a new wife now cast a different light on so many things. It brought his entire evil plan tumbling into place before my eyes, as if I could now see every part of it in vivid detail.

So too, it seemed, could Giles.

'A startling coincidence,' Giles said. 'Wouldn't you agree? There was my brother, courting this young woman in London, and elsewhere I'm sure, while his wife was still very much alive. Then his wife dies tragically in a fire, and just a few months later, Richard has a new bride to replace her – a bride, one might say, who had already been primed for the position well before Rosen was dead. You can see why I find this all a little suspicious, can't you?'

Mariah laughed at him, but there was a nervousness to it that told me how agitated she was becoming. 'Do you know what you're suggesting?' she said. 'Do you suppose Richard started that fire on purpose?'

'Yes, I do.'

'And you believe he did so in order to kill Rosen, freeing him to marry again? It's preposterous!'

'That was my assumption,' Giles said. 'At least, it was merely an assumption at first. Then I arrived here to find that most of the servants have been given their marching orders, and that you, dear Mariah, are holed up in the gatekeeper's cottage. It all strikes me as very odd. Very odd indeed.'

'I merely wanted to give the newlyweds their space and privacy,' Mariah said. 'As for the staff, we had far too many in the first place. I've kept the cook, of course. We have Jenken to tend to the grounds and any other handiwork that may be required, and I've hired another, very able-bodied woman, worth at least three regular servants, to look after the household with me.'

'Ah, yes,' Giles said. 'I believe I've met her. Ada Cobb, she said her name was. Not much to look at, and I certainly wouldn't want to get into a brawl with her. I'm sure she's very able-bodied indeed. You clearly haven't warned her about me yet, have you? She was quick enough to let me in when I told her who I was. Anyway, I don't accept it.'

'What, exactly, don't you accept?'

'Any of it. You expect me to believe you would give up the luxury of the manor house to live in this peasant's hole, and that you intend to muck in with the household duties? No – you're hiding something, aren't you?'

'I'm going to fetch Jenken,' Mariah said. 'You're to leave here at once.'

'Oh, I'll leave, all right,' Giles said, 'but not before I've satisfied my curiosity. She's here, isn't she? You've got Rosen locked away with you in the cottage. That's why you've moved out of the manor, to keep a close eye on her here. That's why you've let most of the staff go, because with so many people running about you can't trust that one of them won't some day stumble across your wicked little secret.'

I had to put a hand to my mouth to stop myself from crying out with joy. Giles had worked it out. He knew I was here.

'Stop!' Mariah shouted. 'You're not to go in there. Jenken! Jenken! Where the devil are you?'

Of all people, Giles was coming to my rescue. From what I had heard, it seemed that he had pushed his way past Mariah and was now coming into the cottage to see for himself whether his deductions were correct. A moment later I heard the sound of a door banging somewhere below.

'Get out! Mariah yelled, her voice now much louder and closer, not echoing in the chimney as before, but hollow through the floorboards beneath me.

It was as if no time had passed at all when I heard heavy footfalls on the stairs outside my room. I shot to my feet, staring at the door's upper hatch in anticipation. My heart was beating so fast I thought it would burst from my chest at any minute.

When the hatch shot open, I saw a face so like Richard's that I was startled by it at first. I thought it was Richard, and that he and Mariah were playing some cruel joke on me for their leisure. But no, although they shared the same full brown sideburns and striking, pale grey eyes, this man's jawline was less pronounced, his hairline a little more receding. It was Richard's brother, Giles, and I was never more pleased to see him.

'Giles!' I said, almost out of breath just standing there.

'Well, well,' Giles said as his eyes took me in. 'If it isn't all true.'

Mariah was behind him then. 'Come away from there, or—'

Giles spun around to face her. 'Or what?' he cut in. 'I really don't think you're in any position to threaten me, are you? Not after what you've been party to. No, if there's any threatening to be done, I'll do it, and why shouldn't I? You've never liked me – never cared for me as a stepmother should – and I can't say that Richard doesn't have it coming to him.'

Mariah fell instantly silent. Giles's face was once again framed in the hatch. He smiled at me. 'Come closer,' he said. 'Let me have a good look at you. I've never seen a ghost before.'

I stepped closer until I was standing in a pool of sunshine beneath the skylight.

'My word, you are a ghost,' Giles said. 'Look at you, so pale and thin, and whatever have they done to your hair? You look more like a boy – a young street urchin, I'd say. I can hardly recognise you.'

I wanted to rush to him and cup his face in my hands, embrace him as my saviour as soon as I was able to, but a sudden change in his expression warned me to be cautious. His formerly warm and pitying smile had begun to twist on his face into a self-satisfied smirk.

'I've seen enough,' he said, and then he closed the hatch with such a thud that it jarred my entire body.

I ran to the door, uncertain of what Giles meant. Surely he had seen enough to know I was alive and in great need of his help, but why did I sense that his actions were being driven by an ulterior motive? I stood still for a moment, willing the door to open and prove my suspicions wrong, but it did not. Instead, Giles confirmed them. He did not care about me, only for himself. His next words revealed his true purpose in coming to Crows-an-Wra Manor.

'This is priceless, Mariah, I must say,' he said, laughing to himself at his own good fortune, as he must have seen it. 'But don't worry,' he added. 'I can keep a secret, although it's going to cost my brother dearly.'

I could hear Mariah and Giles walking away from the door, leaving me to rot in my disagreeable little room for all either of them cared. I was speechless. How could Giles be so mercenary? Where was his humanity? If he ever had any to begin with then it had clearly abandoned him, as it had Richard and his mother. Beyond my door, I was aware that Giles was still talking, but I had become insensible to his words. He no longer had anything to say that I wished to hear. A rage unlike any I had ever felt before began to rise within me. I felt it surge through me, giving me strength. I thought, to hell with Mariah's request for my best behaviour when Richard returned with his new bride. I no longer cared for her rewards. I would not be the good prisoner she wanted me to be. I began to beat my fists so hard on the upper hatch that it started to crack under the weight of my blows. It should have hurt, but I did not feel a thing.

'Let me out of here!' I yelled. It was a repressed cry that came from deep within me.

I strode back into the room, to the chair and my pile of books, and with all my might I began to hurl them at the door, snapping their spines and ripping out their pages. At that moment, I did not care for anything, and I did not let up when I heard a key rattling frantically in the door lock. When the door began to open – the first time I had ever seen it open – I threw my books harder.

'Stop this!' Mariah called, but I would not listen to her.

I saw her face at the opening and I threw a book right at it, causing her to back away with a jerk as it landed. Giles quickly replaced her, and I threw a book at him, too, but he did not flinch from it. Instead, he continued into the room, his hands held ahead of him to block my assault.

'You're only making this worse for yourself, Rosen,' he said. 'Now calm down, won't you?'

I would not calm down. I took up a pile of books and backed away towards the shuttered window as he came further in after me. I flung them at him ceaselessly until one caught the side of his head. He winced from the blow, touched a hand momentarily to where the book had struck, and then he ran at me so fast that I could not evade him. He slapped the remaining books from my hand, and as I tried to run past him he grabbed me and pinned me to the back of the armchair.

'Hurry, Mariah! I have her, but she's a feisty little thing.'

I twisted and squirmed beneath him, but he was too heavy a man – grown fat, no doubt, at the expense of others. I wondered why he was calling out to Mariah to hurry, but as soon as I saw her enter the room, I realised. She was holding a small brown bottle in one hand and a piece of cloth in the other, and I was immediately reminded of the night of the fire. Mariah rushed to the side of the armchair, dousing the cloth with the contents of the bottle as she came. Then, just as Richard had done that night, she forced the ether-soaked material over my face while Giles continued to hold me down. I began to cough and splutter as I choked on the sweet and oddly pleasant-smelling fumes. I tried to resist breathing them in, but I could not. In no time I began to feel nauseous and dizzy, until I was overcome by drowsiness.

Then I felt nothing at all.

CHAPTER TEN

Grace

I suppose it could be said that ours had been a whirl-wind romance – so much so that, while I had heard much about Crows-an-Wra Manor since first meeting Richard Trevelyan, I had never before seen it. As our carriage entered through the gates and turned on to the drive, we sat beside one another facing my window, Richard in black-and-grey morning dress with his arms around me, his hands covering my eyes so that I would not see the house too soon. The window, which had become dull from the journey, had already been lowered so as not to detract from my first impression, at the same time inviting in the warm, late-spring breeze. It set my golden spaniel curls dancing, tickling my cheeks and further heightening my excitement.

'Almost ready!' Richard said, sounding as keen to have my reaction to the house as I was to give it. His mature yet mellow voice in my ear gave me goose pimples. 'You're not peeking, are you?'

I giggled. 'No, of course not,' I said, finding myself

quite breathless with anticipation now that the moment had finally arrived.

We had had such a wonderful time in Europe following our wedding that I began to doubt whether Richard could impress me any further. Immediately after we were married, we sailed from Dover to Calais, and then travelled overland via Paris to Switzerland. I will never forget the majesty of the Alps or the pale, yet colourful, Dolomite mountains as we made our way down into northern Italy. We spent much of our time in that beautiful country – a country so rich in art and culture that one could spend a lifetime there and even then never fully appreciate it. I would have been sad to return to England were it not for the promise of the equally grand future that awaited me.

'Stop the carriage!' Richard called to the driver. 'Are you ready?' he added, leaning close to my ear.

The horses came to a sudden stop and the carriage lurched, rocking me back and forth in Richard's arms. I nodded emphatically. I was never more ready to see the house I was about to make my home. I felt Richard's body shifting beside me as he brought his face alongside mine, his sideburns brushing against my glowing cheeks. A moment later, he withdrew his hands and I blinked against the light.

'Welcome, my darling, to Crows-an-Wra Manor,' he said. 'It bears no resemblance whatsoever to your family home in Northumberland, but I trust it pleases you?'

Pleases me? I could not find the words to express how overwhelmed I was by its stately proportions. My family home was but a mere countryside cottage compared to Crows-an-Wra Manor. Despite its size, I thought it a rather pretty house, part covered with ivy here and there, and the most wonderful, gnarly old wisteria, whose delicate lilac flowers were glowing like lanterns in the early afternoon sunshine. There was a statue in the near foreground, and I wondered how I had not noticed it sooner. The carriage had stopped on the far side of the turning circle at the front of the house, and the statue was in the centre. It was a cavalry officer on horseback.

'Of whom is the statue?' I asked, supposing I would soon bore Richard to distraction with all the questions I knew I would have to ask him.

'That's supposed to be my grandfather,' Richard said. 'Can't see the resemblance myself.' He laughed. 'Once we go inside, you'll have the opportunity to meet just about all the past members of my family in one bust or portrait or another. But what of the house? What do you think?'

'I think it's going to take me an awfully long time to find my way around it,' I said, looking up at the many windows until the glare of sunlight reflected in them became too bright and I was forced to look away. Perhaps I should have laughed to myself as I spoke, because Richard did not seem to grasp my attempt at humour.

'I knew it! It's too big for you,' he said, frowning at me. 'Maybe you'd like something smaller. Somewhere closer to the sea, perhaps?'

'No, it's not too big, Richard. Really it isn't. It's lovely. I'd be happy anywhere as long as you were there with me.'

Richard's smile returned. 'I'm glad to hear it,' he said. 'Of course, I'm only showing you the best view.' He leaned out of the carriage a little and pointed to the right. 'Much of the east wing, which was destroyed by the fire I told you about, is obscured from here, but you can see it if you lean out far enough.'

'I'm sure I shall see it all in good time,' I said, keen now to go inside and to meet the servants.

But where were they?

I had expected a grand reception upon our arrival, a dozen or more servants lined up on the steps at the front of the manor, waiting to welcome us, but there was not so much as an eager footman ready to carry our luggage inside. It was not until I had reset my bonnet back into place and we stepped out of the carriage that I noticed someone approaching. It was a woman of slight build, quite plainly dressed in a pale-blue day dress and shawl, with a simple white bonnet on her head. She approached, not from the house, but along the drive, as if she had come from the gatekeeper's cottage I had briefly seen as we entered the estate, just before Richard had put his hands over my eyes. She was too distant for me to make out her face, but I would have taken her for a servant readily enough had Richard not informed me otherwise.

'Ah, here comes Mother,' he said with a smile. He took my hand. 'Come along. Let's meet her halfway. I'm sure she must be excited to see you again.'

I had only met Richard's mother once before our wedding, when she had travelled with Richard to Northumberland soon after our engagement. With some five hundred miles between us, I had offered to bring my family to Cornwall to meet her, but she would not hear of it, such was her selflessness. A more considerate mother-in-law I could not have wished for. I believe we became firm friends overnight, but I remained eager to impress her and augment our relationship further. Having inherited my father's outgoing disposition, an attribute that was not to every man's liking in a woman, I took the lead in our greeting.

'Mariah!' I called, waving to her as soon as I caught her

eye. In time I, too, would call her Mother, I was sure of it, but despite our early rapport I did not want her to think me too forward.

She did not return my smile at first, and I wondered whether something was the matter. As we drew closer, however, her smile quickly flourished.

'Welcome home, Richard,' she said as they embraced. To me, she offered her hand. 'And Grace... How lovely it is to see you at Crows-an-Wra Manor at last, and what a beautiful gown you're wearing. I've always had a liking for all things turquoise.'

'Thank you,' I said as I lightly shook her hand. 'Richard bought it for me in Paris.'

'Yes,' Richard said. 'It matches her eyes perfectly, don't you think?'

Mariah began to study me more closely. 'So it does,' she said. 'I have a jade necklace that would suit you very well. You shall have it as my welcome gift.'

'Thank you,' I said again. 'I can see that I'm going to enjoy being here with you both very much. You're so kind, and you have such a beautiful home.'

'You must think of it as your home now,' Mariah said, 'and yes, it is beautiful. At least, it was.'

She tilted her head towards the east wing, and now that I was out of the carriage I could clearly see the damage the fire had caused, rendering much of the east wing no more than a blackened skeleton of what it had once been.

'But do not trouble yourself,' Mariah added, sounding brighter. 'Crows-an-Wra Manor will be beautiful again. Now, let's go inside. Having anticipated your arrival, expecting you would stop at Launceston overnight to break the last leg of your journey from Dover, I've had a light meal prepared. I'm eager to hear all about your grand tour of Europe.'

CHAPTER ELEVEN

It was much cooler in the house than I had imagined it would be. As we followed Mariah into the main entrance hall, my eyes were immediately drawn to a grand marble fireplace, but it had not been lit. She led us to a small, informal dining room that I imagined was towards the back of the house, having taken too many turns along one corridor and another for me to be certain, but there was no sun at the windows here. There was a mahogany table in the centre of the room, accommodating only eight chairs, a wide oak dresser on the long wall that was busy with blue-and-white Meissen china, if I were not mistaken, and a number of porcelain figurines. Two wingback chairs sat at the far end, arranged to either side of a burr walnut drinks cabinet. The room seemed to me a hotchpotch of styles, as if it had been filled with things that had no place elsewhere in the house.

The small fireplace in this room had not been lit either, and I wondered why, given that Mariah had anticipated our arrival. As well as laying on a meal for us, why had she not also arranged for at least this fire to be lit so as to make the house more welcoming? I felt myself shiver a little as I sat down, facing Mariah and the window. Richard, from whom I already felt too distant, having never left his side while we were in Europe, sat at one end. I smiled at Mariah and took in the meal she had had prepared for us. It consisted mainly of cold meats, fruits and cheeses – food from the pantry, which could be brought out at short notice. I thought it more akin to a supper, but I supposed there would be finer fare, in a more appealing setting, at dinner that evening.

'We've dined like royalty this past month, haven't we, Richard?' I said, helping myself to a piece of fruit.

'Yes, indeed,' Richard said, 'and with a budget to match!' He scoffed. 'The servants alone cost a bloody fortune.'

'I did suggest we should take our own,' I said.

Richard shook his head. 'Too familiar. A temporary staff was the way to go.'

'Yes,' I agreed, 'and it was wonderful. I can still taste the culinary delights of Paris. Do we have a French chef de cuisine at Crows-an-Wra Manor? Please say we do.'

Mariah was quick to reply. 'I'm afraid you really have been spoiled,' she said. 'You'll find we have simple tastes here. Good and hearty is the food that comes from our kitchen.'

I immediately imagined plain roast meats, stews or pies every evening and lost a little of my enthusiasm. I smiled to hide my disappointment. 'Well, I'm sure it will be delightful,' I said, reaching for a piece of cheese.

I thought it peculiar that none of the household staff were there to serve us, informal dining or otherwise. I still had not seen a single servant since our arrival, nor heard the faintest hint of their presence. They were either the very best of servants, making their presence known only when called for, or something was not quite as it seemed. My naturally inquisitive mind called for explanation.

'How many servants do we keep at Crows-an-Wra Manor?' I asked, slipping easily into my new role as lady of the house. 'I'm surprised I've not yet seen anyone.' I looked first to Mariah, who by my measure seemed to have the reins of the household firmly in her grasp, and then to Richard, who I supposed must also have known the answer, whether such matters interested him or not.

Richard met my gaze with a furrowed brow. 'Yes, Mother, where is everyone? The old place is as quiet as a mortuary.'

For reasons I did not yet understand, I thought the question made Mariah look a little uncomfortable. She stopped chewing her food instantly and just stared at Richard as if thinking on her answer. 'I decided to make a few changes while you were away,' she said. 'I'll explain later. It's nothing to trouble yourself with so soon after your return. I'm sure you'll understand.'

I was hanging on Richard's reply, hoping he would insist on hearing the explanation now rather than later. He looked as if he was about to say something, but he stopped short and began to fiddle with his sideburns. The creases in his brow relaxed at once and he simply nodded back at Mariah, as though he already understood the matter.

'Grace, do tell me more about Italy,' Mariah said, and I could have sworn she did so purposely to change the subject. 'How was Rome?'

We must have talked about our grand tour of Europe for at least an hour before the conversation naturally arrived at the opera ball we had attended at the Hofburg

Imperial Palace in Vienna. It set me wondering.

'Perhaps we could have a summer ball here at Crows-an-Wra Manor,' I said. 'It would give me the perfect opportunity to meet more of your friends and family, Richard, and I'm sure you'd like to show me off now that I've officially arrived, wouldn't you?'

'Of course, my darling,' Richard said, but his tone lacked conviction. 'It's just that...'

He trailed off, as though unable to articulate what he wanted to say. Mariah seemed to know. She finished his sentence for him.

'It's just that with the fire damage still to be repaired,' she said, 'we don't feel that the house is yet ready for such exhibition. Isn't that what you were going to say, Richard?'

'Why, yes,' Richard said, stammering a little, but speaking with such confidence that I did not doubt it was exactly what he was about to say. 'You've not seen the half of it yet, Grace. It would do your beauty no justice to show you off, as you put it, before the work in the east wing is completed.'

'I trust the plans for its restoration have already been drawn?' I said, wondering how long it would be before I could have my ball. 'From what you have told me, it has been some months now since the fire.'

The question made Richard look uncomfortable. He began to pull at his sideburns again as he glanced at his mother, perhaps expecting her to answer this question for him, too. I was glad she did not.

'No,' Richard said a moment later. 'There are as yet no plans. After the fire, I was in no good frame of mind to attend to the matter. You understand, surely?'

I did understand. I felt my cheeks flush with embarrassment as I recalled Richard telling me all about the fire and the tragic loss of his first wife. I could still see the tears in his eyes as he spoke of her death. Yes, ours had been a whirlwind romance, so much so that it had allowed Richard little time to grieve for the loss of his first love, let alone make plans for the restoration of the place of her death. Before I could offer my apology, Richard continued.

'And then I met you,' he said, 'and I was so pleasantly distracted from my responsibilities here at Crows-an-Wra Manor that I did not wish to return to them.'

I leaned across the table and placed my hand on the back of his. 'I'm so sorry, Richard. It was insensitive of me to bring the matter up. My ball can wait – of course it can.'

Mariah gave a sudden and deliberate cough, drawing my attention. Her eyes were on my outstretched hand, letting me know that she considered such intimacy inappropriate at the dining table. I withdrew it at once.

'The matter is best left alone,' Mariah said. 'Tell me, Grace, when is your own maid due to arrive at Crows-an-Wra Manor? You mentioned before your sojourn to Europe that you would be sending for her. Have you done so already?'

'Yes, everything was arranged before we left.'

'Before you left?' Mariah said, surprised. 'It would have been good of you to inform me.'

'I'm sorry, I didn't think.'

'No, clearly you did not. And what is her name?'

'Lucy,' I said. 'She's the daughter of one of my father's servants. We grew up together.' I gave Mariah an awkward smile. 'She should arrive in two days – three at the most.'

'Then I shall see to it that a room is prepared for her,'

Mariah said. 'Speaking of which, if you've eaten enough, I'll show you to your room and help you to get settled in.'

'My room?' I said, laughing a little at the suggestion that Richard and I were to sleep apart. 'Thank you, Mariah,' I said, 'but I'm sure Richard and I can manage. After all, we've been inseparable since our wedding, haven't we, Richard?'

Richard did not reply. Instead, he gave me a sheepish look that was as much to say that he already knew of this arrangement. I looked questioningly at him for several seconds, willing him to stand up to his mother and tell her otherwise, but he did not. The whole idea was incomprehensible to me.

'Will we not then be sharing a room, Richard?' I asked, by which of course I meant a bed, but I did not wish to be so blunt or so crude. I had just witnessed Mariah's disapproval of the open display of physical closeness, and I did not need another reminder so soon.

Mariah answered for him, another of her traits that I was quickly learning. 'Of course you shall,' she said, 'but only from time to time, surely?' She looked more serious than I had so far seen her. 'You understand my meaning, do you not?'

'No, I do not,' I said, entirely confused. 'Please speak plainly so there can be no misunderstanding between us.'

'Very well,' Mariah said with a sigh. 'I mean that you will share a bed only during such times as you are receptive. Could I be more plain?'

'No, you could not,' I said, beginning to dislike the control Mariah seemed to have over Richard and now, through our marriage, over me.

'Unless,' Mariah added, pausing briefly. She smiled to herself. 'Unless you are already—'

'No,' I cut in, fully understanding what she meant this time. 'I am not yet with child.'

'Can you be certain?'

'I assure you I can,' I said, not wishing to state so bluntly that I had begun my period of menstruation. Thankfully, she also seemed to understand my meaning.

'This certainty,' she said. 'Was it recent?'

I nodded. 'This very morning.'

Mariah stood up. 'Then come along with me,' she said. 'I'll show you to your room and introduce you to Jenken. He'll bring your cases up. As for a maid, while we await the arrival of your own, I have hired someone who can fulfil many of her duties, but her time is already stretched. I must ask you to take no more of it than is absolutely necessary.'

'Of course,' I said, feeling a little bewildered as I followed Mariah's lead and got to my feet. It seemed that I was to be the lady of the house in name only, at least while Richard refused to be its master. It was apparent that, until then, neither of us would have any say in anything that was not Mariah's will.

CHAPTER TWELVE

My room occupied a corner position on the second floor of the west wing, with views to both the front of the house, facing the carriage drive, and across a pretty parterre garden to the west, from where I imagined I would see the most spectacular sunsets. I gravitated towards the west-facing window as soon as I entered the room, Mariah in my shadow, and through the leaded lights, out over the fields and trees beyond the estate, I was even able to glimpse the dark horizon of the sea.

'The Atlantic Ocean,' Mariah said, standing close behind me.

My knowledge of geography was poor at best, so I was grateful for the information. I gave her a smile as I turned back into the room and continued to take everything in, noting that the largest of my trunks had already been brought up from the carriage. It was a large and pretty room, predominantly yellow and white, with gold stucco work on the ceiling and wall cornices.

'I trust the bed is to your liking?' Mariah said, indicating the large four-poster against the wall we had entered by.

'Yes, it looks very fine indeed,' I said, studying the intricate oak carvings on the posts and along the head-rail. The bed itself was draped in a pale-blue bedspread that shimmered in the light from the windows and went beautifully with the yellow decor. At the foot of the bed was a velvet chaise in a similar shade of blue.

I wondered whether Richard's first wife had chosen the colours, and whether she had also slept in this room – in this very bed, for all I knew. I wanted to ask Mariah, but something stopped me. To own the truth, I did not wish to know the answer, choosing instead to believe that she had not.

A knock at the door distracted me.

'Enter!' Mariah called, and then to me, she added, 'Here's Jenken with the rest of your luggage.'

With a case in each hand, and another tucked beneath each of his sizeable arms, Jenken could barely fit through the door. I watched him turn to his side as he entered, taking his time, being careful not to drop anything as he worked himself through the doorway. When he saw me he gave me the most endearing smile, which I found quite childlike, as if seeing me for the first time held a curious sense of wonder for him. He had unusual eyes. They seemed to protrude from his moon-shaped face as he stared at me for several seconds, as if waiting for Mariah to give him further instructions. For any other man my luggage might quickly have become a burden, but Jenken could have been holding empty cases for all the bother they appeared to cause him. He looked strong enough to lift a horse, and with the largest hands I had ever seen I did not doubt that he could.

'Jenken,' Mariah said, 'this is your new mistress.'

'Delighted to meet you, madam,' Jenken said, and when he spoke, I found his voice somewhat contradictory. It was far softer than I expected a man of his size to possess.

Mariah pointed to the other end of the room, where two large wardrobes waited to be filled. 'Put the cases down with the trunk beside the dressing table, Jenken,' she said, speaking in a manner that was a little more clipped than usual. 'And open the window, will you? It's a little stuffy in here.'

I hadn't noticed, but with so much to take in, my senses were already quite overwhelmed.

'Thank you, Jenken,' Mariah said once he had set my luggage down. 'You can leave us now.'

'Yes, thank you, Jenken,' I repeated with a smile, feeling that as the lady of the house, the thanks were now mine to give.

As soon as Jenken was gone, Mariah said, 'He's rather slow-witted, but he's dependable, nonetheless. Just be sure to speak slowly and clearly and he'll understand your meaning.'

'I will,' I said. 'Has he been long in service at Crows-an-Wra Manor?' I imagined he must have been or why else keep him on when it appeared that, for reasons which were as yet unclear to me, so many of the other servants had been let go?

'He was born here,' Mariah said. 'Thirty-one years ago. My late sister, God rest her soul, died giving birth to him – the result of an indiscretion with her own cousin.' She paused and went over to the bed. 'She died in this very room,' she added thoughtfully. 'In this very bed.'

That was information I would most certainly have rather been spared, but it was thirty-one years ago, and it gave me some comfort to know that when Richard came to me it would not be to his first wife's bed, as I had previously imagined. I didn't know what to say in reply, so I said nothing. Thankfully, Mariah did not dwell on the subject.

'I'll send the maid to you at once,' she said, heading for the door. 'Her name is Ada Cobb. She'll unpack your things and put them away for you. There's a bell pull there beside the bed. Once you're settled and ready to dress for dinner, use it to signal for her and she'll come to assist you.'

My eyes followed hers to the bell pull, a wide tapestry tape with a gold tassel that extended from a lever higher up. I nodded and smiled politely as she turned to leave. Then I stopped her. 'What time will dinner be served?'

'Dinner is served promptly at eight,' she said. 'There are drinks in the drawing room, if you would care for something beforehand.'

'Thank you, Mariah,' I said. 'There was just one more thing before you go.'

Mariah, now having stepped out into the hallway, stopped and turned back to me. 'What is it?' she said, and I sensed her impatience to be elsewhere.

'It's just that I was wondering where Richard's room is.'

'Richard's room need not concern you for the time being.'

'Then where is your room?' I asked. 'Should I need anything until I'm better able to find my way around.'

'Should you need anything,' Mariah said, 'as I have just told you, you have the bell pull beside your bed. As for my room, I have none. I live in the gatekeeper's cottage.'

'I hope not on my account,' I said. 'You will always be welcome here.'

Mariah gave me a thin smile. 'It is my choice,' she said, adding no further embellishment as to her reasons. 'Now, if you'll excuse me. I must find Ada Cobb for you.'

'Of course,' I said, and as she set off along the corridor I retreated into my room and closed the door.

There was a very fine bookcase in my room, with a cherry-wood veneer inlaid with pale marquetry that I imagined was of birch. The patterns it traced over the entire cabinet were in the manner of an abstract drawn from nature. There were trees and other flora, and any number of exotic birds hiding here and there among it all. I must have passed ten minutes or more trying to count them all as I waited for Ada Cobb to come to me, and I did not doubt that I would count them again during some idle afternoon when the rain was at my window.

As I waited, my attention wandered to the books themselves. There were several novels written by Jane Austen – and more than one copy in some cases. There were others by the Marquis de Sade and Sir Walter Scott, Victor Hugo and Ann Radcliffe. It was, for the most part, an eclectic collection of works of fiction, spanning all genres, but I noticed there was also some poetry among the titles, which I looked forward to reading. I had taken down The White Doe of Rylstone, a narrative poem by William Wordsworth, and had read no further than the second page when there came the expected knock at my door. I put the book back at once, foolishly thinking that I should not be reading it, that it was not now my own book to do with as I pleased.

'Come in!' I called, turning to the door.

It opened quickly, and a broad-figured woman stepped into the room, giving a small curtsey as she did so.

'Ada Cobb, madam,' she said, bowing her head slightly.

If her manner was as efficient as her tone, then I was not surprised that Mariah believed the house could be run with fewer staff.

'Come in,' I said, smiling warmly, although I already sensed it was wasted on Ada Cobb.

Her smooth, pinkish face held a dour expression that did not change in the slightest as she approached me. I put her age at no more than twenty-five years to my twenty-one, but her appearance and general demeanour made her seem much older. She wore the typical black-and-white livery that was commonplace among household maids.

'I'm pleased to meet you,' I said, still smiling, hoping to encourage conversation, but she simply gave another nod and a curtsey and waited in silence for my further instructions. She did not seem the shy type, however. Merely keen to go about her work without delay, which was all well and good, but she already had me wishing for my friend Lucy to arrive without a moment's delay.

'My luggage is there by the dressing table,' I said, indicating the cases Jenken had stacked neatly on the floor beside my trunk.

'Very good, madam,' Cobb said as she went to them.

'You can put it all away,' I said. 'I had everything laundered in Calais before we left for Dover. There's more to come in a few days,' I added, thinking of Lucy again, and hoping she had remembered to pack everything I had asked for.

Cobb did not say anything in reply. She went about unpacking my clothes with such speed that I grew dizzy watching her. I went to the armchair beneath the window that faced the front of the house and sat down, determined to engage her in conversation if it drained all my strength to do so.

'How long have you been in service at Crows-an-Wra Manor?' I asked, expecting, as with Jenken, for it to have been a good many years, but I could not have been more wrong.

'Almost a month now, madam,' Cobb said.

'Really? As little time as that,' I said with surprise. 'Were you born nearby? That is to say, do you have family in the area? Penzance, perhaps?'

'No, madam. I'm from Bodmin.'

'Bodmin?' I repeated. 'Ah, yes, I recall we passed through Bodmin on our way here, after we left Launceston. Do you come from a large family?'

'No, madam,' Cobb said again. 'Got no brothers or sisters. My father left when I was born.'

'And what of your mother? Does she live and work in Bodmin? It must be a strain for you, being so far apart.'

'My mother's in the debtors' prison. I'm working to pay her debt.'

'I'm sorry to hear that,' I said. 'It's very commendable of you, but I wonder, could you not have found a placement closer to Bodmin?'

'Not at the rates I'm paid here,' Cobb said, never once slowing down or turning to look at me as she spoke.

I watched her in silence for several minutes as I wondered what else to say. Then my thoughts turned to the reason she had been taken on at all. Mariah must have gone to considerable trouble to employ someone from so far away. Surely she could have found a servant from a neighbouring village or nearby Penzance, or kept on another of the existing servants, for that matter. Perhaps Ada Cobb's reputation somehow preceded her.

'Tell me, Ada,' I said, 'were your services in great demand in Bodmin?' I assumed they had to be.

Cobb shook her head. 'Can't say so, madam.'

'Your previous position, then – was it with a particularly well-connected family?'

'No, madam,' Cobb said, pausing and turning to me at last. 'My previous position was at the Cornwall County Asylum. Mrs Trevelyan senior found me there. Offered to double my pay, she did, so I do as I'm told and make no fuss about it. Twice the pay means I can get my poor mother out of that place in half the time.'

She went back to her work and seemed to unpack and fold away my things even faster than before. My initial appraisal of her was that she was certainly efficient, if not the most personable of God's creations, but her heart was clearly in the right place. I began to ruminate on her former position at the county lunatic asylum. I had no idea as to her duties there, but it struck me as a very odd résumé for a household maid, although I thought it went some way towards explaining her manner.

Cobb was finished in next to no time.

'Will that be all, madam?' she asked, standing to attention before me.

'Yes, for now,' I said. 'Thank you. Will you return at six to help me get ready for dinner?'

'Very good, madam,' Cobb said, and then she turned on her heel and left.

◆ ◆ ◆

Dressed in blue satin, in one of my less creased gowns, I went down to dinner half an hour early that evening, having taken instruction from Cobb on how to find my way around. I was hoping to catch Richard alone in the drawing room beforehand so that we could hold one another and talk together, just the two of us, as we had in Europe. I hadn't seen him since I was shown to my room, and I was keen to ask him – without Mariah's interference – what he thought about our sleeping arrangements.

I was to be disappointed.

I could hear them speaking from halfway across the hall. The drawing-room door was ajar, their voices rising and falling in waves, as if they were trying to be quiet but could not contain their emotions. Was it anger I heard in Richard's tone? He certainly sounded upset about something. I reached the door and paused outside, listening.

'Giles will bloody well stay away from Crows-an-Wra Manor if he knows what's good for him,' Richard said. 'The nerve of the man!'

'You need to see him, Richard,' Mariah said. 'Who knows what will happen if you do not?'

The room fell silent for a few seconds. Then Richard gave a loud sigh and said, 'You're right, of course. I'll speak with him – see what he wants.'

I sensed the conversation was drawing to an end, and in truth my conscience was getting the better of me. I could not stand there eavesdropping like a chambermaid. It was hardly fitting behaviour for a lady, especially in her own home. I coughed loudly into my hand to make my presence known, and then I entered. I was immediately struck by Richard's appearance. He looked so handsome in his black evening suit and low-cut waistcoat, his wavy hair combed slightly forward. I thought

Mariah, on the other hand, looked rather dowdy. Black for the evening was all very well for gentlemen, but for the ladies I expected to see a show of colour, or at the very least the sheen of silk or satin and a few embellishments. Mariah's dull gown had neither. It seemed to me more fitting apparel for a housekeeper, but then perhaps that was the role Mariah had now taken up, given that so many of the servants had been dismissed.

'Good evening, Richard,' I said as soon as our eyes met. 'Mariah,' I added with a smile. 'Is everything all right?'

I could not pretend that I had not overheard a word of their conversation, as loud as it was at times, any more than I could fail to notice the crimson flush that was still evident in Richard's cheeks.

'Yes, yes, of course,' Richard said, all too impatiently for me to believe him. 'Someone I'd rather not speak to wants to see me, that's all it is. It's nothing to trouble your pretty head over.'

'Who is he?' I asked. 'I couldn't help overhearing you mention someone called Giles.'

Richard glanced at his mother before replying. 'He's my brother,' he said. 'It's nothing, really.'

'Your brother? But you've not mentioned him before. Until now I had thought you an only child.' I turned to Mariah. 'I had no idea you had two sons.'

Mariah scoffed. 'Giles Trevelyan is no son of mine, I can assure you. His mother died soon after he was born. When I married his father, I was charged with his upbringing, of course, but that boy would never listen to a word anyone told him.'

'You must tell me more about him.'

'I'd sooner not talk about him,' Richard said. 'I don't very much enjoy his company, and I'm afraid if I don't put him out of my mind soon, I shan't enjoy my dinner. What do we have this evening, Mother?'

'Calves' feet and brown butter,' Mariah said. 'I had the cook prepare your favourite to welcome you home.'

Richard laughed to himself. 'I'm glad to hear she's still with us. How is old Mrs Pengelly?'

'Still half deaf, and as blind as a mole,' Mariah laughed back, 'but she cooks as well as ever.'

How adroitly, I thought, Richard had managed to change the subject. My inquisitive mind was keen to learn more about his brother, and to understand why Richard appeared to dislike him so much that he had not once before mentioned him to me. While my curiosity was far from satisfied, however, I thought it best to let the matter go for now.

'Calves' feet?' I said cheerily. 'I don't believe I've tried that dish before.'

'Then you're in for a treat,' Richard said. 'Would you like a glass of sherry?'

'Thank you,' I said, and as I watched him pour my drink into one of the tiny glasses, I noticed that his hands were trembling. It was slight, but there nonetheless. Had Richard's news of his brother wishing to see him affected him more than he was letting on? I imagined it had. As a result, I looked forward all the more to meeting Giles Trevelyan.

I took the proffered glass of sherry from Richard, drawing no attention to the fact that I had noticed his anxiety, and, turning to Mariah, I said, 'Did your sister like to read?'

Mariah's face took on a puzzled expression. 'Not particularly. Why do you ask?'

'The bookcase in my room,' I said. 'It's crammed full of

works of fiction. As it was once your sister's room, I wondered whether they were her books.'

'No,' Mariah said. 'Had you looked more closely you could have satisfied your curiosity in that regard. Many of those books were published after my sister died, which you will no doubt recall was thirty-one years ago, when Jenken was born.'

'Then perhaps they are yours, Richard?' I said, turning now to him. I smiled playfully. 'Is fiction another of your little secrets?'

'It most certainly is not,' Richard said, sounding more agitated than I thought the question called for. 'Those are my late wife's books. She used to enjoy reading in that room, by the window, of an evening. She said the light was agreeable to her.' Richard looked at his mother. 'I thought I gave instructions to have that bookcase removed.'

'I've been very busy, Richard,' Mariah said, raising her eyebrows at him with a look that was as much to say, as you well know. 'I'll have Jenken remove the books tomorrow.'

'No, please don't,' I said. 'I'm sure I can make use of them. That is, if you don't mind, Richard?'

I was sensitive to the fact that I had, albeit inadvertently, reminded Richard of his first wife again, and I thought it only proper to ensure that the presence of her books in my room would not cause him distress.

Richard, who had poured himself another drink, knocked it back and firmly set the glass down on the drinks table. 'I suppose it's all right,' he said. 'Now, shall we go and have some dinner before I really do lose my appetite?'

CHAPTER THIRTEEN

My first three days passed somewhat drearily at Crows-an-Wra Manor. I do not quite know what I had expected of my life in Cornwall as Richard's wife, but I had hoped for a little more excitement, or at least the promise of more stimulating times ahead. Thus far, however, I had found myself with little to look forward to. Perhaps Europe had irreparably spoiled me, and I would simply have to adjust to my new life now it had begun in earnest. I just had to give it time.

It had not helped that Richard had been away so much, leaving early on estate affairs, as he called it, and not arriving home again until quite late; nor that Mariah had seemed so preoccupied and aloof. I suppose it was to be expected, though, given that, with so few servants left, she was forced to fulfil at least some of their duties, affording her little time for strolls in the grounds and idle conversation with me.

I saw more of Ada Cobb than anyone else, but her cool company invariably left me craving my own again, which was just as well, because Cobb was always in such a hurry to move on to her next task. With so little to do and so few people to talk to, I found it no surprise that my predecessor had been disposed to reading so many works of fiction to pass the time, although I expected things were a little different for her. She would undoubtedly have had friends and family in the area, whereas I had none.

At least, not yet, but that was soon to change, and in more ways than one. I had received a letter, bearing a London postmark, which stated that the personal items of clothing I had arranged to be sent to me were due to arrive this very day, and of course my personal maid and very good friend Lucy along with them. I had been looking out of my bedroom window most of the day, and at other times pacing around the turning circle outside, willing her carriage to arrive.

Imagine my joy when at last it did.

It was late afternoon, the day dry and bright, if a little windy for my liking, which again was something I supposed I would have to get used to, given the flatness of the land and the estate's relatively close proximity to the sea. I was sitting in my room when I heard the carriage on the drive. I had taken one of the books from the bookcase to read, in an attempt to distract myself and quell my excitement at seeing Lucy again, and I could not put it down fast enough. I glanced out of the window briefly to be sure my ears had not deceived me, and knowing at once that they had not, I lifted the hem of my plain white day dress and ran to greet her. I was smiling long before I saw her.

'Lucy!' I called, just as soon as I was outside.

The loose gravel beneath my shoes forced me to slow

down. I saw that Jenken was already there ahead of me, come to help the driver with the numerous trunks that were piled up on top of the carriage. First, though, he went to the carriage door. I watched him open it as I approached, and there from within its shadowy interior emerged my good friend, Lucy.

I laughed at the sight of her. Summer was almost upon us, yet despite the warm sunshine she was covered from head to toe in a thick green travelling cape and hood. She had always been a petite girl, with barely an ounce of fat on her bones. As a result she was often complaining about the weather and how cold it was, even when I felt hot. I feared she would find the wind at Crows-an-Wra Manor even less agreeable than I.

As Jenken helped her down, I tried to glimpse her face, so that she would in turn see mine; she had clearly not heard me calling to her. It was not until she was fully down from the carriage and began to lower her hood back over her bonnet that she saw me at last. I made no attempt to hide my delight. I ran to her and embraced her, not as my maid, as improper as that would be, but as my good friend.

'Lucy! How wonderful it is to see you again,' I said. 'I trust you had a good journey?'

Lucy's cape began to flap in the wind. She pulled it more tightly around her. 'As good as can be expected,' she said, giving me a small curtsey as she tried to tuck the loose strands of her short brown hair up into her bonnet. 'Although I fear I shall need a balm for my backside now I've arrived.'

I laughed. Lucy never failed to put me in good spirits. 'And a good hot bath, no doubt. Then you'll be right as rain.'

'Please don't mention rain, miss. I've never seen such a deluge as when we came through Exeter.'

I was glad that Lucy had not taken to calling me madam now that I was married. Whenever Ada Cobb or Jenken addressed me as such it made me feel old beyond my years, but I supposed that was something else I would become accustomed to in time. For now, however, there was no rush. In truth, I found Lucy's familiarity pleasantly comforting.

'Come on,' I said. 'Let's get you in out of this wind.'

We began walking towards the house, Lucy gazing this way and that with the same look of wonderment on her face that I had possessed upon arriving at Crows-an-Wra Manor.

I smiled at her. 'Oh, but it is good to see you again,' I repeated. 'Did you pack everything I asked for?'

'Of course, miss,' Lucy said, still looking around her, taking everything in. 'Who's that, then?' she added, looking up at one of the windows.

My eyes followed her gaze and I saw Mariah looking down at us, still as a statue, her face without expression. I had thought her at the cottage where she spent most of her time, so I was surprised to see her.

'That's Richard's mother, Mariah,' I said, wondering why she had not come out to meet Lucy.

I imagined two possible reasons: one was that Lucy, however close to me, was a servant after all, and it was therefore beneath Mariah to afford her any special attention. The other, which I preferred, was that she very kindly wished to leave us alone to our reunion. We did, after all, have much to talk about, little of which would be of any interest to Mariah.

'How are things at home?' I asked, wondering how

long it would be before I truly regarded Crows-an-Wra Manor in the same way. 'How were Mama and Papa when you saw them last?'

'Both well, and they send their love,' Lucy said. 'They told me to say they hope to visit with you soon, once you've settled in, that is.'

The news filled my heart with joy. I missed them both terribly and wished they had made the journey with Lucy. 'I shall write to them this very evening,' I said. 'I'm sure I'll be settled enough by the time my letter reaches them, and more so by the time they arrive.'

We entered the house, Lucy still looking around her like a lost child as we made our way across the parquet floor in the entrance hall. It was filled with colourful stuffed birds of all kinds, and myriad other animals here and there behind glass cabinets. Richard had not said as much, but I imagined one of his ancestors must have been fascinated with taxidermy.

'Mariah has had a room prepared for you,' I said as we reached the staircase. 'She wanted to put you in the servants' quarters, but with so many lovely rooms close to mine, I insisted she had one of those made up instead.'

Lucy looked alarmed at the idea. 'I don't want any special treatment, miss. The other servants won't take to me if I'm treated any better than they are.'

'But you are special, Lucy,' I said. 'And besides, there really aren't many servants here to worry about.'

'There's not, miss? In a big house like this?'

I shook my head. 'I still cannot fathom why, but I'm afraid it means you'll have your work cut out for you. You're to be my maid first and foremost, of course – I was also insistent on that – but there will be other duties to perform as and when called for.'

'I've never been shy of work, miss.'

'I know you haven't. It's just a pity, that's all.'

'How do you mean?'

'I mean, I had hoped to have you here as much as my companion as my maid, but with so few staff, I'm sure necessity will dictate that you're kept from me far more than I'd like.'

We reached the top of the stairs and turned to our left, heading along the wide main corridor into the west wing, where portraits of past family members lined the walls. As we continued, I thought back over something Richard had told me at dinner the night before. Someone else was coming to Crows-an-Wra Manor – or rather, returning to the manor – whom I very much hoped to befriend.

'That's not all,' I told Lucy. 'You're to have another specific duty – a charge, if you will.'

'A charge, miss?'

'Yes, I'm informed that Richard's daughter, Sophia, will be arriving home next week. You're to see to her needs as well as mine. The poor thing was sent to live with her cousin in Truro after her mother died. We must do all we can to comfort her.'

'Of course,' Lucy said as we arrived outside her room.

'Here we are,' I said. 'I'll leave you to get settled in. I'm sure Jenken will be along with your bags shortly. He's very sweet. I expect you'll take to him at once, as I did. My door is at the end of the corridor.' I gave her a smile. 'Come and see me as soon as you're ready and I'll see about introducing you to Mariah. I'm afraid you won't be able to meet Richard until this evening.'

I opened Lucy's door for her and invited her to go inside and wait for Jenken to bring her things. As I went back to my room I thought about Sophia, and as much as I wanted to meet her, I wondered whether it would have been kinder to leave her with her cousin until the damage to the east wing had been repaired. After all, it would be a constant reminder to the child of the night her mother died, and Sophia was so very young, barely past her sixth year. I wondered whether it was because Richard had missed her too much and wanted her home, but was it selfishness on his part to bring her back so soon? For my part, perhaps somewhat selfishly, too, I thought her return might at least give Richard the impetus he needed to begin the much-needed repairs, for the charred remains of the east wing were also a constant reminder to me. I thought of Sophia's mother every time I saw them, and until the house was fully restored, I knew her presence would continue to haunt me.

CHAPTER FOURTEEN

Lucy soon settled into her duties at Crows-an-Wra Manor, and before long it was almost like old times between us. Almost, because Mariah found countless ways to keep her from me, frequently sending her to assist Mrs Pengelly in the kitchen, and even to work with Jenken in the grounds from time to time. I was glad to know, however, that even when she was not with me she was close by, and I was equally happy to see less of Ada Cobb as a result. Cobb had proved to have no more skill with a hairbrush than a blacksmith with a sewing needle, and her conversation, as poor as it had been from the first day of our acquaintance, had rapidly diminished to little more than a 'yes, madam' here and a 'no, madam' there. So much so that I had now completely given up any attempt to engage in general conversation with her. I had thought her aloof behaviour towards me merely the result of her wishing to perform her duties as efficiently as possible and stay out of trouble – to know her place, avoiding overfamiliarity – but she had no more ingratiated herself with Lucy.

It was late one morning, a few days after Lucy's arrival, that I found myself sitting in my room, thinking of legitimate ways to bring Lucy back to me, if only to sit and talk and relieve my boredom. I had not seen her since she was sent to the kitchen to help clean up after breakfast, and I surely could not be expected to wait until she came to dress me for dinner before we could talk together again. I knew, however, that to call Lucy to my room for no greater purpose than idle conversation would not please Mariah, so instead I decided I would have to speak with Mariah about the matter first. Lucy was my maid, after all, and more importantly she was my friend. As such, I would insist that Mariah allow her to spend an hour with me each day outside of her duties, if for no other reason than my sanity while Richard was so preoccupied with the estate. I had not expected it to keep him so busy, but it was a very large estate and I knew little of the attention required to run it properly. As was the case most days, it meant I would likely not see him again until dinner.

Mariah, on the other hand, I would see right away.

I stood up and went to the door, wondering where she was. In such a big manor house, I thought it might be difficult to find her. That was if she was in the house at all. As the weather was fine, I thought she might be out in the grounds, or most likely in or around her cottage, perhaps tending to her little rose garden. As I stepped out of my room and made my way along the corridor towards the main staircase, I thought it practical to at least see if she was in the house first.

'Mariah!' I called as I went down the stairs, my fingers gliding over the well-worn oak handrail.

The entrance hallway was such a large space that my voice echoed around me. It made me mindful not to call out too loudly in case Richard was in his study, as I did not wish to disturb him.

'Mariah,' I called again, more quietly this time.

I received no reply, so I continued into the heart of the house, turning back on myself and taking the corridor to my right. I had familiarised myself with most of the main rooms and passageways at Crows-an-Wra Manor by now, but at Richard's insistence I had not ventured far into the east wing. I cannot say what drew me towards it now – sheer curiosity I suppose, because I knew Mariah was unlikely to be there. For a while, the east wing seemed as a mirror image of the west, both in its layout and decor, with the same predominantly dark green walls and buff carpet runners lining the corridors, a piece of mahogany furniture here and a few paintings and ornaments there. Before long, however, the layout changed and I came to an unfamiliar staircase. My conscience told me to turn back, that I should go to the cottage to look for Mariah there. I had already ventured into parts of the house where I knew I should not go. I turned around, thinking that she was in all likelihood at the cottage anyway, but the staircase had piqued my curiosity. I stopped and turned back to it. Then I chose to ignore my conscience and climbed the stairs regardless.

The sight that met me at the top caused me to gasp. It was as if some dark sorcery had transported me somewhere else entirely. To all intents and purposes, I had left Crows-an-Wra Manor and was now in a place only visible in nightmares. I was standing in a small hallway, the colourless walls and ceiling blackened by smoke, the paint on the doors peeling. Corridors led off in three directions, and I imagined that if I continued along any one of them I would soon find myself at a boarded-up door, or the charred, skeletal ruins themselves. I peered along each dark passageway for several seconds until I thought my eyes had begun to play tricks on me. Through the darkness something golden had caught my eye. I stepped closer to be sure of it, and there on the wall was a painting, its gilt frame still bright in places. I went to it and saw that it was a portrait.

Oddly, the woman reminded me of Lucy. Not in the colour of her hair, because this woman's hair was the colour of copper to Lucy's brown, but in her slight features and pale complexion, and about her eyes, which, although pale green to Lucy's blue, appeared similarly large on account of her small face. My eyes drifted lower, to her slender neckline, and there I saw something that caused me to gasp and take a step back. The woman in the portrait was wearing a necklace that was familiar to me. It was the same jade necklace Mariah had given to me soon after my arrival. I was sure of it. I leaned closer and was in no doubt. I wondered who the woman was and looked for the answer. There was a nameplate along the bottom edge of the frame. Like much of the frame it was covered in soot, so I licked my thumb and ran it over the brass work. I was about to read it when a voice behind me startled me so much that I could have jumped out of my shoes.

'What are you doing here?'

I spun around and saw Mariah standing at the top of the stairs. She was staring wide-eyed at me with the most serious expression on her face. I placed both my hands over my heart and laughed nervously.

'Oh, Mariah!' I said. 'You gave me quite a scare.'

'You shouldn't be here,' Mariah snapped. 'It's danger-ous.' She stepped quickly towards me, her eyes on the painting as if keen to see what had caught my interest.

'I was going to the cottage to look for you,' I said. 'I just wanted to see what was at the top of this staircase first.'

'The cottage?' Mariah said, her eyes on me now. 'You're not to go to the cottage either. Didn't I tell you I like my privacy?'

Mariah had told me. On my first morning at the manor she and Richard had gone over several house rules with me. 'Yes,' I said, 'but—'

'There is no but where my privacy is concerned,' Mariah cut in. 'Is that understood?'

I suddenly felt like a scolded child who had misbe-haved once too often. Whatever had got into Mariah today? She seemed unusually tense, and surlier in her manner than I cared for.

'I'm sorry,' I said, hoping a simple apology would ap-pease her. Before she could speak again, I quickly turned our conversation to the painting. 'I was wondering of whom this portrait was.' I glanced at the nameplate, the brass now shiny and fresh. 'Rosen Trevelyan,' I said as I read it. 'My goodness.'

Although Richard did not speak his first wife's name often, he had mentioned it once when referring to her tragic death, and again in Europe when he had cried out in his sleep. It was, however, the first time I had seen her, or at least a likeness of her, and it made me want to know more.

Mariah stepped closer. 'This painting should not be here, either,' she said, studying it with me. 'Richard gave instruction to have all Rosen's portraits taken down be-fore he left for Europe.'

'Because they would remind him of his loss?'

'That, yes, and because he felt it unreasonable that you, his new wife, should have to look upon her and constantly be reminded that you were not the first.'

'It was very thoughtful of him.'

Mariah nodded. 'Do accept my apology. I'll have Jenken remove the portrait at once.'

'There's really no need to on my account,' I said. 'I shan't come back here.'

'But my son might,' Mariah said, 'and I would not wish him to see it.'

'No, of course not.'

I continued to study the portrait in silence for several seconds, and my eyes were immediately drawn back to Rosen's necklace – now my necklace. I told myself that she had perhaps only borrowed it from Mariah to wear while her portrait was being made, because I had already worn it in Richard's company and it did not seem to upset him, but it did not help to settle the immense disquiet I now felt at having seen it around Richard's late wife's neck. I knew I was being silly so I sought no clarification from Mariah, but I doubted I would ever feel comfortable wearing it again. I looked into Rosen's eyes, and I found myself wondering, not for the first time, what she was like, and whether her relationship with Richard was very different from my own.

'I suppose Richard must have loved her very much,' I said, fishing for clues.

'That is not for me to say,' Mariah said, giving nothing away.

'What will become of the portrait?'

'Jenken will burn it,' Mariah said. 'Just as he burned all the rest.'

'Burn it?' I repeated, scarcely able to believe anyone could do such a thing. It seemed very harsh to wilfully destroy something so beautiful, however much emotional pain it might cause someone.

'You shall have your own portraits made,' Mariah said. 'When the repairs to the east wing are completed, your image shall hang on these walls.' She turned away as if to leave. 'Now come along,' she added. 'I heard you call for me. What is it you want?'

I followed Mariah back to the staircase and we began to descend. I had completely forgotten about the reason I had set out in search of her, and in truth I no longer felt the urge to press the matter of Lucy's duties while Mariah was in such an unfavourable mood. I quickly decided it could wait.

'One of the windows in my room is stuck,' I lied. I knew it was a lame reason to bother Mariah, but it just came out.

'You have a bell pull in your room, remember?' she said. 'You had only to pull it and either Ada or Lucy would have come to you.'

'The bell pull, of course,' I said, as if I had only just remembered it now that I had been prompted. 'How silly of me not to have thought of it.'

'Yes, well,' Mariah said, looking back at me as we walked with what I took to be a good measure of disdain. 'Now that you have found me, or rather I have found you, there is something I meant to tell you at dinner this evening, but it need not wait.'

'What is it?' I asked as we came to the main hallway.

Mariah stopped beside one of the newel posts at the foot of the staircase. 'You recall that Richard's daughter, Sophia, is soon to return to the manor?' she said, as if I had likely forgotten that, too.

I nodded. 'Of course.'

'Well, she will be here a little sooner than expected.'

The thought brought a smile to my face. 'How soon? I'm impatient to meet her.'

'Tomorrow,' Mariah said. 'The room opposite yours is to be prepared for her. Richard thought it might help her to settle in again, knowing you were nearby. It is his hope that Sophia will soon come to call you Mother.'

'As it is mine,' I said, my voice full of eagerness. 'It has been my hope since first hearing her name.'

'Very good then,' Mariah said, and with that we parted company.

As I went back up to my room, thinking I would change my shoes and take a turn in the grounds, I felt a ripple of excitement run through me at the thought of seeing Sophia for the first time. What was she like? If she were anything like her mother, then judging from the portrait I had just seen, I expected she would be the quiet type, as timid as a mouse. If she were more like her father, on the other hand, then she would be as assured as any six-year-old girl could be. Either way, I was determined to make the very best impression on her.

CHAPTER FIFTEEN

I awoke the following morning full of anticipation, for the day ahead promised much. Not knowing precisely when Sophia's carriage would arrive at Crows-an-Wra Manor, I had asked Lucy to come to my room earlier than usual to remove any possibility that I would not be fully ready.

'Hold still, miss,' Lucy said, pushing a pin into my hair.

I was sitting at my dressing table, watching her in the mirror while she set my ringlets and arranged my centre parting just how I liked it.

'Thank goodness you're here,' I told her for the umpteenth time since she'd arrived. 'I'm afraid Ada Cobb was quite useless when it came to my hair. Her fingers are altogether too clumsy for such delicate work.'

'Don't be too hard on her, miss,' Lucy said. 'I'm sure she means well.'

'Yes, I'm sure she does. I know I criticise the poor thing far too often, but it's easy to do so when all I have to compare her with is you.'

Lucy laughed to herself. 'It's very kind of you to say so, miss, but she's worth three of me when it comes to the more physical duties I've seen Mrs T senior set her to.'

'Mariah?' I said with a smile. 'And I suppose you think of me as Mrs T junior now, do you?'

Lucy blushed and continued to add the finishing touches to my hair. 'There,' she said a moment later. 'All primped and primed ready for a royal ball, I'm sure.'

'Thank you, Lucy,' I said, spinning around on my stool to face her. 'Do you think Sophia will like my dress? Yellow always looks so cheerful, don't you think?'

'Yes, miss,' Lucy said. 'Very cheerful indeed. I'm sure she'll like it very much.'

'Good,' I said, thinking ahead to our meeting. I wondered what kind of temperament Sophia had, and I hoped she would be kind to me and not see me as someone who had all too eagerly stepped in to fill her mother's shoes so soon after her death. What would a six-year-old girl make of such things?

'Do you remember when we were six?' I asked Lucy.

'Some bits, miss. I remember the day you dressed me up in your fine clothes and sent me outside in your place. There was a garden party of some sort. I think we must have been around six then.'

'Yes, I remember,' I said with a smile. 'It was Mama's birthday party. You had everyone fooled for hours, running around on the lawn, never getting close enough to anyone for them to know it wasn't me.'

'Do you remember what you were doing?'

I giggled. 'I remember very well. I was spying on everyone through my grandfather's spyglass.'

We both began to giggle, and then I recalled another memory from that time in our lives.

'I was six years old when Napoleon died,' I said. 'You remember him, surely?'

'Of course I do, miss – the most adorable wheaten terrier there ever was.'

I nodded as I continued to think about him, and about Sophia again. 'A dog cannot be compared to anyone's mother, of course,' I said, 'however adorable the dog, but I had loved Napoleon as well as any six-year-old might love anything. I was heartbroken when he died.'

'I'm sure you was, miss.'

'Now, here I am to replace Sophia's mother,' I continued. 'Just as Napoleon was so quickly replaced. Did we love the new dog as well as we loved Napoleon?'

'Perhaps not to begin with,' Lucy said, 'but these things take time, don't they?'

My gaze had wandered absently away from Lucy while we were talking, as I tried to recall how I felt at seeing another dog in Napoleon's place so soon after his death.

'Yes, it takes time,' I repeated with a little sigh, hoping that Sophia would take to me far more quickly than I had taken to accept, and later to love, Napoleon's replacement.

'Will that be all for now then, miss?' Lucy said, breaking into my thoughts. 'Only, I've been asked to help Mrs Pengelly with the breakfast this morning.'

'It's not fair that you have to do all these other things,' I said, selfishly meaning that it was not fair on me, 'but get along with you then. I wouldn't want Mrs T senior to have to scold you on my account.'

Lucy gave a small curtsey, and then she very improperly winked at me. 'Don't you worry yourself, Gracie,' she said, addressing me now as my friend rather than my maid, in the same manner as when we were children. 'Little Miss Sophia won't need more than a day to warm to your kind heart, you'll see.'

I gave Lucy a smile for her encouragement. 'I do hope you're right,' I said, and as she left my room I supposed that, come what may, I would soon find out.

As it happened, I need not have been so eager to ready myself for Sophia's return to Crows-an-Wra Manor, because her carriage did not arrive until late in the afternoon. At Richard and Mariah's insistence I was in my room, watching from one of the windows to allow them time to greet Sophia before I was introduced. Familiar faces would put her at ease, Mariah had said, and I fully understood. I did not wish to overwhelm her.

She arrived in a little red brougham, drawn by a striking pair of greys. As it turned in front of the house and came to a stop, I instinctively moved to one side of the window so that I could not be seen. It seemed entirely improper for the lady of the house to have to peep down on the proceedings like an overly inquisitive housemaid, but I thought it was nonetheless justified on this occasion, and it would not be for long.

As the driver began to climb down from the carriage, other movement caught my eye. Richard and Mariah had come out from the house and were pacing eagerly across the gravel. I had not seen Richard with such a spring in his step since we returned from Europe. Even Mariah, whom I had never seen move with any great urgency, was doing her best to keep up with him. Although their backs were now to me, so that I could not fully see their faces, I could picture their broad smiles as they stepped up to the carriage and Richard opened the door.

Sophia did not step down to meet her father. Instead, as soon as the door was open, she flung herself at him like a jack-in-the-box unleashed. Richard caught her in his arms and spun her around so fast that her pale green knee-length dress and white-stockinged legs became a blur. They must have both been dizzy by the time he stopped, at which time he lifted her high above his head before drawing her back down into his embrace. I watched Mariah go to Sophia then, squashing the poor child between herself and Richard until all three were as one, and how I longed to join them in their happy reunion.

When at last they separated, they turned towards the house. Words were exchanged – smiling words that were full of gaiety and happiness. I wished I could hear what was being said, but I was too distant. It didn't matter. In a short while I would be introduced to Sophia, and I could already feel my palms becoming clammy with anticipation now that the moment had all but arrived. It did not help that I had been clasping them tightly together while I stood there waiting for my cue, but Richard had not yet moved away from the carriage. The conversation continued as the carriage driver lifted Sophia's luggage down from the roof and set it all in a tidy pile on the gravel. Then he took up his seat once more, and a moment later he flicked the horses' reins and the carriage moved off.

I caught Richard's eye then as he glanced up at my window, and I drew a deep breath as I watched him make his way towards the house with Sophia's hand in his. My cue had arrived. I went to my dressing table and quickly practised my smile in the mirror. Then I laughed at myself for being so nervous and went down to join them. I could not reach the top of the stairs quickly enough. I heard them enter the main hallway, Richard still holding on to Sophia, with Mariah in tow. Sophia was talking excitedly as I began my descent. I imagined she was telling her father all about her time spent living with her cousin, and of the adventures she had had. Whatever she was saying, she stopped the instant she saw me.

I suddenly felt the weight of everyone's eyes on me. It caused me to pause momentarily. I drew a breath and put on my smile to hide my nervousness as I continued. My eyes were on Sophia all the way to the bottom of the stairs. I thought she looked just like her mother – as I had seen her in the portrait I had come across in the east wing the day before. Although Sophia's hair was shorter, it was of the same copper colour, and her complexion was just as pale, although in Sophia's case it was covered with the cutest freckles. As I reached the last step, Richard brought Sophia closer to me. She was no longer smiling.

'Here she is,' Richard said. Turning to Sophia, he added, 'My darling daughter, I should very much like to introduce you to my wife, Grace. Grace, this is Sophia, about whom I've told you so much.'

Sophia did not speak, but she gave me the most charming little curtsey I had ever seen.

I bowed my head. 'I'm very pleased to make your acquaintance, Sophia. I hope we shall soon become the very best of friends.'

I held on to my smile in anticipation of at least a few words in reply, but when none came my smile began to falter. I gave a small laugh and turned to Richard.

'She's adorable, Richard,' I said, 'and even prettier than you led me to believe.'

I thought my compliment might at least have raised the hint of a shy smile from Sophia, but she just stared at me, completely devoid of expression. I noticed something in one of her hands then. It appeared to be a handkerchief, sewn with colourful embroidery. I pointed to it.

'May I see?'

Sophia shook her head and immediately put her hand behind her back so I could no longer see what she had.

I laughed again, looking to Richard once more, but this time my eyes were seeking explanation for his daughter's curious behaviour. Before he could answer, Mariah stepped up beside Sophia.

'I would refrain from pursuing the matter,' she said, as if she had read my intentions. 'It is a comfort – something the child's mother made for her. Perhaps Sophia will show it to you in time.'

Richard surprised me then.

'I won't have this nonsense,' he said. 'It's an unsanitary piece of cloth, long in need of a wash, and it is no excuse whatsoever for rudeness.' He looked down at Sophia. 'Show it to your mother.'

Sophia shook her head again. 'She's not my mother!'

'Show it to her,' Richard said, punctuating his words.

Sophia backed away, but Richard caught hold of her. He grabbed her arm and pulled it around in front of her, and then he ripped the piece of cloth from her hand.

'Here it is,' he said, sounding angrier than I had ever heard him, and over something as silly as a little piece of cloth with animals embroidered on it. I looked at them briefly, feeling for Sophia, who I thought had every right to keep such a precious thing from someone who was, after all, a total stranger to her. I began to shake my head, condemning Richard's sudden and most unexpected outburst. I was about to voice my opinion on the matter, but before I knew it, Sophia grabbed back the piece of cloth and ran up the stairs with it.

'I hate you!' she yelled back, and I could not be sure whether she meant she hated her father or me. I suspected it was me she hated for asking to see her embroidered comfort in the first place.

Mariah quickly followed after her. 'I'll take her to her room and calm her down,' she said, and in a matter of seconds they were both gone, my introduction to the young Sophia Trevelyan well and truly over.

'Was that really necessary, Richard?' I asked him. 'The matter was unimportant to me – I was merely curious to see what Sophia had in her hand. I thought it might spark a conversation between us, that's all. I'm sure she would have shown it to me in time, as Mariah said.'

'The matter was important to me,' Richard said, still sounding angry. 'You're her mother now. I won't tolerate her being rude to you like that.'

'Her mother?' I repeated. 'I'm afraid that is a right I must earn. Now I fear my task has become all the more difficult.'

'I'm sorry for that,' Richard said, his tone calming at last. 'It was not my intention. The girl must know her place, however, and learn her manners. The woman who embroidered those animals on that piece of cloth was far too lenient with her, stuffing her head full of stories and silly games when she should have been giving more care to her conduct.'

'Rosen,' I said, trying without success to make eye contact with Richard. 'Can you not speak her name?'

He turned away. 'No, madam, I cannot,' he said, 'and I beseech you never to mention it again.'

'I'm sorry,' I said, stroking his arm. 'The day has not

turned out at all how I'd hoped it would. Perhaps tomorrow will be better.'

Richard turned to face me again, and in a quiet voice said, 'Perhaps the sooner you're a real mother yourself, the better things will be for all of us. Then at least my mother will stop pestering me for a grandson, and I'm sure Sophia would enjoy having a little brother to look after.' He paused and gazed into my eyes. 'You know how much I yearn for a son.'

'Because your mother wishes it?' I asked, mindful of Mariah's apparent influence over Richard. 'Are you certain that your desire for a son is not merely driven by your need to appease her?'

Richard was shaking his head even before I had finished speaking. 'No, of course not,' he said. 'What if I were to die without an heir? Who then would inherit my ancestral home? My brother?' He gave a humourless laugh. 'Giles has always felt that Mother and I cheated him out of his rightful inheritance as our father's firstborn son. It's utter nonsense, of course, but I doubt there's much he wouldn't do to set things right, as he sees it. In truth, our father plainly saw him for the wastrel he is.' He paused, shaking his head. 'No, without a son and heir to leave Crows-an-Wra Manor to, there's every chance that Giles may some day get his hands on it. I cannot allow that. You understand, don't you?'

'Yes, I understand,' I said, giving him a coquettish smile. 'That I am not already pregnant has not been for the want of trying. Come to me tonight,' I added, eager to please him.

I waited for his answer, but it did not come. The sound of another carriage on the drive suddenly drew his attention away from me.

'Who the blazes can that be?' he said, going to the main doorway, which was still open.

I followed after him and stood beside him on the threshold as the unexpected carriage made its turn on the drive before us. The door opened almost before it stopped, which it did suddenly, as if in haste. I saw a black and tan calf-length boot extend out from beneath a black frock coat as a heavy-looking man stepped out, a top hat on his head and a cane beneath his arm. I had no idea who he was. I had never seen him before, but Richard, to his dismay, clearly had.

'Giles,' he said under his breath. 'Grace, you must go to your room at once. Do not come out again until I send for you.'

CHAPTER
SIXTEEN

Rosen

How long had I slept? I do not know. The last thing I recall with any clarity is the sweet smell of ether and Mariah's hand over my mouth.

And Giles Trevelyan.

The scoundrel had constrained me. Yes, I recall that as vividly as if it were yesterday, although I expect it was not. How long had Mariah kept me in a state of half-sleep with her drugs and potions? That is the better question. If my dreams were any indicator, then I should have to conclude that as much as a month may have passed, for they had been many – as many as the headaches that came and went as I drifted in and out of consciousness.

I sat up in my bed, feeling no headache today. Perhaps my punishment was over, for now at least. I rubbed my eyes and my blurred vision began to clear. There was bright sun at the skylight, the air in my room pleasantly warm. It was summer at last, of that much I was sure, and I was glad of it. I feared the cold. Were I still here when winter returned, I knew I would not survive it without a fire to warm me. I withdrew my hands from beneath the bed sheets and gasped at the sight of their frailty. They were already little more than skin and bone.

My dreams, the only means of escape I had from this room, began to come back to me. Most had already faded, but one was so repetitive that I could recall it quite clearly now in waking. I was at a masquerade ball, looking for Richard, but every mask I lifted revealed the face of another woman – the same woman, over and over again. I tried to picture her face, but it was not clear to me, although I knew well enough who it was. It was Richard's new wife. It should have been a nightmare, but I cannot say that it was because the ball never ended. There was no sudden shock to pull me out of it, just the myriad masks and the same face beneath them.

I folded back my bedcovers and dragged my weak legs out of bed. My pale feet caught the chamber pot and set it clattering across the floor. It was thankfully empty, or I would have drawn Mariah's wrath again. I tried to stand and had to steady myself. Where were my books? I could see none. The rest of the room was otherwise as bare as it had been on the very first day I awoke here. Staggering to the chair by the window, I began to weep at my pathetic existence. I did not wish to be punished in this way again. I had to be compliant, at least until Mariah gave me my silks so that I could use them to embroider my cry for help into the laundry and hope to chance that someone other than she would see it.

As I sat down, I recalled another of my dreams. More recently, my sleep had been haunted by a child's laughter.

But was it a dream? It seemed so real to me that I now found myself questioning the matter. I began to think hard on when I had heard it, and of the circumstances of the dream that surrounded it, if that is what it truly was. My mind was so foggy, however, that nothing was clear. Of course, I wanted to believe that it was my Sophia I had heard, but I did not now hold much hope in that. I thought to go to the window then, to look out through the slat I had broken, but I did not have the energy for it, which was just as well, because a moment later the upper hatch in the door shot open and Mariah pushed her face in to see me. Her eyes squinted sharply around the room, noting the upturned chamber pot that must have drawn her. Then they settled with all their usual spite on me.

'Noise!' Mariah said, stabbing the word at me. 'Have you not by now learned your lesson?'

'I – I'm sorry,' I stammered, keeping in mind my need to be compliant. 'It was an accident. I had no idea it was —'

'Enough of your excuses,' Mariah cut in. 'I've brought you some water and a heel of bread, which is more than you deserve for the trouble you're causing me.'

'I'm sorry,' I said again. 'I'll be good from now on. I promise.'

A thin smile creased Mariah's lips. 'You had better be,' she said. 'And if you hold true to your promise, I shall let you have back one of your books.'

'Could I not have my silks?' I asked. 'I do so miss my embroidery.'

Mariah studied me for several seconds without answering. 'Perhaps,' she said at last. 'But you need to prove yourself first, remember?'

'I will,' I said. 'You'll hardly know I'm here from now

on, and neither will anyone else,' I added, knowing that was what Mariah wanted to hear.

'That is as it should be,' she said. 'But we'll see.'

With that, Mariah closed the hatch. A moment later, the lower hatch opened and my bread and water were passed through.

I stood up to fetch it, my mouth parched from our conversation, albeit brief. 'Before you go,' I asked, 'can you tell me how Richard is?'

The upper hatch opened again. 'Do not pretend to care anything for my son now,' Mariah said. 'Not after all he has done.' She paused and began to study me questioningly. 'What are you really asking me?' she added, as much to herself as to me as she calculated the answer. 'Ah, yes. Of course. You really want to know how Richard is faring with his new wife, don't you?'

I nodded. 'Yes, I suppose I do.' I also wanted to satisfy my earlier supposition about where Richard and Mariah had gone when they left me at home with Sophia, not long before the fire. 'All those trips Richard made to London,' I added. 'They were to see her, weren't they?'

Mariah nodded.

'And did you really go to see your brother in Bristol?'

This time, Mariah shook her head. 'I cannot say I ever cared for his company.'

'I knew it,' I said. 'You went with Richard to meet his prospective new wife, didn't you?'

'Correct again,' Mariah said. 'I see your mind is not yet so addled that you have lost your power of reasoning. We did not, however, travel to London.'

'Where then?'

Mariah smiled cruelly at me, and I was wary of what she would say next. 'We travelled to Northumberland,' she said, 'to attend the engagement of their marriage. Her name is Grace, and she is everything you are not. Need I say more?'

I stared expectantly at Mariah, knowing she was about to, whether I wished it or not.

'Oh, I suppose I must,' she continued. 'Grace is quite tall and very beautiful. More importantly, she is fertile. She will soon give Richard the son you could not. She may be a touch too inquisitive for her own good, but I'm prepared to overlook her shortcomings for the time being.' She paused and raised an eyebrow at me. 'Do not expect her curiosity to bring her here, though. I have already warned her never to do so.'

I did not doubt it. 'Richard loves her then?' I said, keen to understand the depth of his feelings for his new bride.

Mariah gave a sharp harrumph. 'Love, love, love,' she said with impatience, shaking her head as she spoke. 'What does that matter? Love or not, my son could not be happier with his new bride. Is that what you want to hear?'

Again, Mariah did not wait for me to answer. Thoughts of her son's happiness had evidently turned her mind to other things.

She scoffed. 'Richard's brother, on the other hand, is another matter altogether.'

'Giles has been back to Crows-an-Wra Manor?'

Mariah nodded. 'And I saw to it that Richard knew why he'd come. He was soon sent on his way again.'

'With a tidy sum for his silence, no doubt.'

Mariah's lips creased into an unpleasant smile. 'Tidy enough to keep him quiet about you, if that's what you're wondering. Now eat your bread and be quiet. I have chores to attend to, no thanks to you.'

The hatch slammed shut with a thud and I was alone again, feeling all the better for it. Mariah's company, though necessary at times, was anathema to me, and I could only bear it in small doses. I picked up my bread and water and took it to the fireplace, where I sat to one side and listened at the chimney for my collared doves. A moment later, I concluded that either the chicks were unusually quiet today, or I had been in and out of sleep for so long that they had by now fledged. As I sipped my water and nibbled delicately at my bread to make it last, I suspected the latter.

'Coo-coo-coo! Are you there?' I asked. I received no reply. My doves had gone, and I was sorry for it because I had enjoyed their company while it lasted. 'Giles will be back for more money,' I added, knowing full well that I was now talking to myself, but I could pretend, couldn't I? 'Richard will not have everything his way, you'll see,' I told my new, imagined friends, and the thought lifted my spirits. 'He will torment Richard and bleed him dry before he's finished with him, and what then? Why should Giles keep his silence over me when he has nothing further to gain from it? Besides, one word to my brothers and Crows-an-Wra Manor itself could be his.'

It was a dark thought, necessitating Richard's murder at my brothers' hands for what he had done to me. Now that I had given word to it, however, I nonetheless found myself dwelling on the matter. If only I could somehow find a way to put the idea into Giles's head.

Then again, perhaps it was there already.

CHAPTER SEVENTEEN

The following afternoon I was sitting in my armchair, reading the book Mariah had said she would bring to me. I shall never know whether she chose it at random from the many books in my collection, or because of my reference to love the day before, but I suspect there was at least some calculation in the choosing of the material. It was a copy of A Sicilian Romance, one of Ann Radcliffe's novels, which had arrived with my second meal of the day, if the meal I received with my book could justly be described as such. It had consisted of little more than a few greying pieces of boiled potato, swimming in a mutton and pea broth. The former comprised little more than a few stringy slivers of meat, and the latter I could count on one hand. I suppose it was a step up from the bread and water I had received earlier that day, and again on this, but I was convinced Mariah was trying to starve me to death to relinquish herself from the burden of being my jailer.

I hadn't read the book in years, which was a treat in

itself, and was making good progress. I had arrived at the part where the protagonist, Julia, having fled into the secret tunnels of the Mazzini castle, discovers her imprisoned mother, whom she had previously thought to be dead. I had to allow myself a knowing smile as I was reminded of the scenario, being in no doubt whatsoever now that Mariah had gone to some lengths to find this particular novel for me. I began to turn the page, feverishly reading on now that I was once again able to, but just as I did so I heard a sound that caused me to stop instantly. I even held my breath for a moment, keeping completely still and silent as I waited with hope for the sound to return. I had to be sure that my ears had not deceived me. It was a child's laughter. I was sure of it. The same laughter I had heard in my dreams, only now I knew I was not dreaming.

When several seconds had passed and the laughter did not return, I began to question my sanity. A moment later, I put my book down and went to the fireplace, where I leaned my ear so close to the opening that my head was almost up inside the chimney. I could smell the soot. I could hear the wind, punctuated now and then by the cry of a gull. But what of the laughter? Had I only imagined it, or was it a gull I had heard? Perhaps I really was going mad. I listened until my legs began to shake and they became too weak to hold me there any longer. Then, just as I was about to return to my book, I heard the sound again. It was faint on the wind, but I was certain no gull had made it.

I rushed to the window and worked the broken slat free so that I could look out, perhaps to see for myself who was there. It was a bright afternoon. At first I had to blink and squint in order to see anything. Then, as my eyes became accustomed to the brightness, I began to see more clearly. I picked out the carriage drive and followed its stony grey course towards the manor. I heard the laughter again. It sounded closer this time and my eyes were drawn down to the footpath that led up to the cottage. The sound was not that close, but there were trees just beyond, a small copse and a clearing where my Sophia used to enjoy playing. I could barely see the edge of it. I pressed my eye closer and a little more of the copse became visible to me. I saw a figure then, running in and out of the trees. I was sure it was Jenken. I hadn't seen him running about that copse since...

I paused and drew a sharp breath. I had only ever seen Jenken behave in such a manner when he was out playing with Sophia. Playing chase between the trees in the copse was one of Sophia's favourite games. She would make Jenken chase her until he was giddy with exhaustion. Now I pressed my eye so hard to the gap in the shutter that my head threatened to burst through it.

'Sophia!' I shouted, desperate to catch even the slightest glimpse of the girl whose laughter I had heard – of the girl with whom I knew Jenken had to be playing chase in the copse.

My breathing became rapid. Were it not summer, I would have quickly steamed up the window. I cursed the shutters and began to bang on them until I thought more of the slats might break, and so what if they did? I wanted to smash the window so that I could lean out and cry her name.

'Sophia!' I yelled again as I began to cry through my frustration. Then a sound beyond my door brought me sharply to my senses.

Mariah was coming.

I was in such a panic that in my haste to replace the broken piece of slat I began to fumble with it, much as I had previously when Mariah came close to discovering my secret. I managed to slot it back in this time. Then I leaped into my armchair, grabbing my book as I did so, just as the upper hatch shot open.

Mariah narrowed her eyes on me. They remained full of suspicion as she glanced about the room, first to my bed, and then to the fireplace, before drifting past me to the window.

'I heard noise,' she said, settling her eyes back on me. 'I heard you calling for your dead daughter. Did you have another dream?'

'No,' I said. It would have been far easier to simply say yes – that I had fallen asleep reading my book and that I had awoken calling Sophia's name – but I had not been dreaming. I really had heard a child's laughter. 'Sophia is alive, isn't she?' I added, challenging her to deny it now.

Mariah gave a sigh. 'Sophia is dead, Rosen,' she said, feigning a measure of sympathy for my benefit. 'You know this to be true. Why can you not accept it?'

'Then whose laughter did I hear?'

'Grace has a friend visiting,' Mariah said. 'She has a daughter about Sophia's age. It was her you must have heard.'

I felt my heart beginning to sink, draining what little colour was left in my cheeks. It was entirely possible, of course. Why should Jenken not play chase with other little girls as he had with Sophia? I didn't know what to say.

'You'll have no more books for a week,' Mariah said, 'and you can forget about your silks for the foreseeable future. You will learn to keep quiet.'

Without another word to me, Mariah shut the hatch

again. A second later I heard her on the stairs, muttering to herself as she descended them, leaving me once more alone with my thoughts. When I was sure she was gone, for now at least, I went back to the window, and to my horror I saw that there was a slight gap in the shutter where, in my haste, I had not fully replaced the broken slat. The crack that was left was quite bright from the light beyond. The threat of discovery set my pulse racing momentarily, but I quickly convinced myself that even if Mariah had noticed it, it had drawn no suspicion. If it had, I am sure my punishment would have extended to more than the denial of reading material for a week. Still, I would have to be more careful in future.

Removing the slat again, I looked out as before. I do not know what I was hoping to see – the girl, I suppose, because I found myself wondering whether she was anything like my Sophia. I must have stood there for an hour at least, watching the edge of the copse, but in that time no movement drew my eye save the wind in the trees. No sound gave me cause for further excitement.

CHAPTER EIGHTEEN

I am such a fool!

Should I not know Mariah and her duplicitous ways well enough by now? I awoke the following morning with a most violent headache, which, as I had learned, was a clear indication that Mariah had had cause to enter my room while I slept. It did not take long for me to discern the reason, and it was not for anything as trivial as clean bed sheets or scrubbed skin. Neither had Richard come to me again to satisfy his carnal urges, but then what use was I to him now that his new wife was at Crows-an-Wra Manor?

During the several months of my confinement, I had become quite adept at calculating the time. The shadows cast into the room through the skylight told me it was close to midday. When I first sat up, I saw my usual cup of water on the floor by the door's lower hatch, but there was no bread today. I knew then that I was being punished for something, and it was only when I looked across to the shutters at the window, wondering what I might glimpse of the outside world today, that I knew what it was.

My jaw dropped.

I swung my legs out of bed and went to the window in utter disbelief, and yet I should perhaps not have been so surprised. Mariah had discovered my little secret after all. The slit of light where I had not fully replaced the broken slat the day before had betrayed me. There was now a larger piece of wood nailed over it, and if that were not enough to prevent me from removing the broken piece ever again, several longer lengths of wood had been nailed vertically at intervals along the entire width of the window. Now I thought my jail truly complete, with bars and all. I do not know why, but I suddenly found myself laughing at the situation. It came from the madness that was growing within me, I suppose, because there was nothing remotely humorous about the matter. My eyes had once more been closed to the outside world. Now I had only my ears again.

I had to get out.

Collecting my water, I went to the armchair and sat down to think. I could not wait for my silks in the hope that Mariah would some day be kind enough to give them to me. Mariah was not a kind woman. And what were the odds that the right person would see my plea for help, anyway? For all I knew, the entire household was complicit in my incarceration. The thought filled me with dread. Surely it was not possible. I was aware by now that most of the servants had been made to leave the manor, and I had seen one other brought in, presumably to help replace them, but who among the old servants remained? I could not know, but I am sure Mariah would have seen to it that there would be no one left whom I could trust, perhaps with the exception of Jenken. But what business did a groundskeeper have with dirty laundry? I thought the new lady of the manor would surely know nothing of my husband's fiendish plans, but the same was true of her, if not more so, when it came to dirty laundry.

I needed an entirely new plan.

I sipped my water slowly until my headache began to subside. Then I turned my thoughts to how I might accomplish this seemingly impossible feat. I could not sit around and wait for some form of change to come, that much was certain, because nothing ever changed for the better in my little room. I had to use what I already had, which at this juncture was very little. An hour quickly passed, then another more slowly, and in that time nothing occurred to me. My thoughts just kept returning to my need to get a message out, but how? The only thing that ever left my room was my cup and bowl, and my dirty bed sheets. It crossed my mind that rather than waiting for my silks to sew my message into my sheets, I could cut myself and write it in my own blood, but I thought it would be messy at best and would stand out far too much. Mariah would see it straight away, and besides, I had not so much as a pin with which to prick myself.

I was about to determine the matter quite hopeless when another possibility popped into my head: instead of getting a message out via my laundry, perhaps I really could get out myself. I do not mean among the laundry, as that would be quite impossible, but on laundry day my door is opened. I, of course, am drugged and oblivious to Mariah's presence as my bedding is changed and my skin is scrubbed, but what if I were not? What if I were only pretending to be unconscious? Then the door would be open, and perhaps without the threat of me waking up it would be left ajar, or at least left unlocked long enough for me to slip out while Mariah went about her duties. Of course, for this to work I must not be in a drugged state, and the only way that was possible was if I did not eat any more of my evening meals, or drink the water that accompanied them.

It would be difficult. I would have to find a way to hide my food, and the smell of it if too many days passed. I would go hungrier than usual, and thirstier than ever, but I would still have my first meal and water each day as usual. Now that the idea had come to me, I knew I had to try it, even though I did not dare to contemplate Mariah's retribution if my attempt to escape failed.

CHAPTER NINETEEN

Four days passed. During that time I thought I had coped commendably well with the preparations for my plan to escape my accursed prison. That is, until now. On the evening of the fourth day, having taken only the bread and water Mariah brought to me each morning, I found that a new kind of torture was upon me. One cannot fully understand how difficult it is for someone so hungry and so constantly thirsty to look at a meal, however meagre, and a cup of water, however small, and then discard them both. I missed the water most of all, but, as innocuous as it appeared, I could not trust it, for I had no way of telling how Mariah's sleep-inducing drug was being administered.

I was sitting on the floor by the door's lower hatch, staring at the water now, contemplating a sip – just one tiny little sip with which to wet my tongue and my dry, cracking lips. Mariah's sleeping draught was certain to be in my food, I told myself. Why risk me discovering it in a simple cup of water when the flavours and colours of my broth could so easily hide its presence? I picked up the water and raised it to my nose. I sniffed it and smelled nothing unusual. I put the cup to my lips, hovering it there until my hand began to shake. Then I stood up and went to the fireplace with it, where I began to pour it very slowly over the exposed brickwork. I could have cried to see it go. I had discovered on the first night after hatching my plan that the bricks were quite porous. As the liquid ran down over their rough red faces, it was quickly absorbed. By morning there was never a trace. The same could not be said of my broth.

I had been hiding it in the chimney each evening and it was beginning to give off an unsavoury odour, made worse by the summer heat that had been building these past few days. The fireplace was wide enough and high enough for me to reach up inside it, where I had discovered shelves to either side of the opening where the flue widened. There I had poured my bowls of broth, and for the most part the smell had been carried up and out through the chimney pots, but every so often a back-draught would bring the smell down into the room. I doubted Mariah could have smelled it from her hatch in the door, but now that it had become more pungent, I was aware of it just standing there. A few more days and it would not go unnoticed by Mariah's keen senses. I collected my broth and had to pinch my nose as I reached up into the chimney to dispose of it, praying as I did so that my bedding would be changed soon or my plan to escape would be undone.

Setting the empty cup and bowl back by the lower hatch so that Mariah would know I had taken it, I went to my bed and waited, trying hard not to sleep as I listened for Mariah's footfalls on the stairs.

I cannot say with any certainty how long I waited for Mariah to come, unsure even if she would. The light at my window in the ceiling above me was fading as I went to my bed, and as I lay there, willing my heart to stop racing with anticipation, I watched the light gradually turn to black. I counted the stars, as I often did, and I listened to every little sound, near and far, though they were few. Once the birds had finished their evening chorus, I heard little more than the wind in the chimney, which was calmer today than it had been of late. I heard familiar scratching beneath the floorboards from time to time, but it did not last, which I thought a pity, as I would have liked a mouse or even a friendly rat for company. What I did not hear was Mariah at my door – at least, not for some time.

Hours must have passed. My eyelids had become unbearably heavy and I was having the devil of a time trying to stay awake. I knew I was close to failing, but at last I heard a sound that caused me to jolt from the half-sleep I had settled into. At first, I could not for the life of me determine what had caused it. It seemed just a random sound to my sleepy senses, but it was so sharp and so loud in the still of the night that it instantly set my heart racing again. My first instinct was to sit up and listen more carefully, but I knew I could not. Nor did I need to. Now that I was fully awake, when the sound came again I recognised it at once as the coarse creaking of a floorboard. Someone was on the stairs.

'Please don't let it be Richard,' I found myself saying under my breath.

I should not have said anything, of course, and I immediately bit my tongue to prevent any further utterances. If my evening meal had indeed contained Mariah's sleeping draught then I should for the most part be unconscious, unable to speak or move a muscle, but I hoped with all my being that if I had been given it then it had not been for his pleasure. I could not endure his perversions in a sensible state.

It fell silent again. A moment later I heard a tinkling sound, which I took for a set of keys jangling on a ring. Whoever was out there was approaching my door. It was enough to make me rigid with fear, whether it was Richard or Mariah. I heard a slight but familiar grating sound then. It was the bolt that secured the upper hatch in my door. I did not hear the hatch open, but in the ensuing silence I knew it had. The intensity of the person's eyes upon me was almost palpable. I kept perfectly still and forced myself to breathe more slowly, as I would were I asleep.

As I lay in my bed, listening, with my eyes tightly shut, I pictured everything happening around me as if watching from my armchair. I heard the key in the lock, and then the door itself as it slowly opened. I knew then that it could not be Richard. If it were Richard, he would have opened my door more forcefully in his haste to enter my room, full of bestial desire. No, it had to be Mariah. That was good. She had come to change my bedding and scrub my skin. With luck, I would have my chance to flee.

I sensed the light from her lamp, and heard her heels on the floorboards in my room as she approached my bed. It caused a sweat to rise in me. The light at my eyelids intensified suddenly as she held her lamp over me, studying me to be sure I would not, or could not, awake. I heard her put the lamp down. A moment later I felt the cool night air on me as my bedding was drawn down.

I wondered whether Mariah would strip me next. I hoped she would not, although I would gladly have run naked from that room if I had to. I felt her hands on me, firm and purposeful as she rolled me awkwardly on to my side. Then she began to tug at my under sheet before rolling me back again, sighing with frustration to herself every now and then as she did so. Once she had finished, I heard her gather everything up, and then came the sound of her heels on the floorboards again, now receding to the door. She was going. Would she lock the door behind her as she took my dirty bedding out for laundering? What need would she have to do so? I felt my heart begin to race harder as I listened for the creaking of the door hinges and the key turning in the lock, but neither came. All I could hear now was Mariah's footfalls on the stairs as she descended them.

My chance had arrived.

I opened my eyes – slowly at first, to be certain I was alone – then across the moonlit floorboards I tiptoed to the door, aware that the slightest sound could bring my hopes of escape crashing down around me. There were no more skylights beyond my room. Peering out into the semi-darkness, I saw a small landing area and the top of the staircase, which held a faint amber glow from the lamplight below. There were no other doors – nowhere else to run and hide if I did not at least make it down the first flight of stairs unseen and unheard. I stepped to-wards them, mindful of the creaking floorboards. Then, keeping to the edges and treading as lightly as I could manage, I began to descend.

By the time I reached the bottom of the stairs, I was

bathed in lamplight. I saw the lamp on a half table against the wall between the staircases. There was a short corridor and a number of doors here, but I had no interest in them. I was on the first floor now and the way out of this miserable place was below me, so I continued down in the same manner as before – slowly and quietly, one careful step at a time. I wished I could go faster. It would not be long before Mariah returned to my room to wash me and replace my bedding. I had to hurry, but at the same time I could not for fear of making the slightest sound. As careful as I was, however, halfway down I heard a creak beneath my bare feet and I froze, listening. I swear I could hear my heart beating, but thankfully nothing else.

There were terracotta tiles on the floor at the bottom of these stairs, which I welcomed for their silence. Another lamp lit the hallway I now found myself in, illuminating several more doors along its wide length, and in particular the door I was interested in. Larger than the rest and painted glossy black, it was the front door – the door to my salvation. I approached it, but even before I reached it I could see that it was heavily bolted, probably locked, too, for all I knew, and why not, at this late hour? I tried the lower bolt, but it quickly began to groan in protest. Then another sound stopped my breath. One of the doors behind me was opening. I spun around and saw the glow of another lamp, its beam growing wider as the far door opened. I ran to the space beneath the stairs, and just as I reached it I glimpsed Mariah, backing out into the hallway with a heavy-looking wooden pail. I shrank into the shadows as the hallway grew brighter. Then I heard her on the stairs immediately above my head. She was going up to my room to scrub me clean.

I did not have long now to make my escape.

As soon as I felt that Mariah had begun to ascend the next flight of stairs, I ran. I took the door she had entered the hallway by, judging from the pail of water she was carrying that it had to lead to the scullery and the back door. I was not wrong. I emerged into a cluttered room full of old pots and pans and mismatched crockery, lit by a dull lamp on a small pine table. At the far end I saw the door, which I made for at once, bashing my thigh on one of the chairs in my haste. I cursed the rasping sound its legs made as they scraped across the tiles, but I did not stop. I saw my pile of bedding as I went, and the washtub beside it. I was almost there.

Then I stopped. Or rather, something stopped me.

I found myself unable to move another inch. There was a pine dresser against the wall to my right, and hanging from one of its shelves was a dress. It was not perhaps so unusual to see such a pretty little dress hanging in a scullery, where it was possibly awaiting a needle and thread. What struck me cold enough to stop me in my tracks was to whom the dress belonged. It was Sophia's dress. I approached it and touched the pale yellow fabric. I ran my fingers over the pattern at the hem – a floral pattern that I had embroidered with my own hand. What was it doing here? Why, if Sophia was dead? Her name began to rise in my throat, but I was suddenly too emotional to voice it.

If Sophia was dead.

I knew then with all certainty that she was not. She was alive, and here at Crows-an-Wra Manor. I had been right all along, but I did not have time to contemplate the ramifications of my discovery. At that moment the back door opened, snapping me to my senses, and there was Jenken's hulking figure standing in the door frame, a look of confusion hanging on his childlike face. I was shocked to see him.

'You're not supposed to be down here,' he said, letting me know at once that he was no longer as kindly disposed towards me as I had once thought. It made perfect sense now, of course. As my jailer, Mariah needed help, and from someone she could trust implicitly.

Jenken looked at the dress, clearly having seen me touching it. 'I didn't mean for it to tear,' he said, with a surprising degree of panic in his voice. 'We were playing in the copse. She caught it on a branch, and it was to be mended so no one would know. You won't tell the master, will you?'

I shook my head, replaying his words in my mind. There was no doubt he was referring to my Sophia. It was her I had heard laughing in the copse that day.

'No,' I said, still a little unsure of what to make of our encounter. Surely it was I who should be panicking, but here was Jenken, as simple-minded as he was, in quite a state over my having discovered his little secret. 'If you let me go, I swear I won't tell a soul,' I said, and I quickly learned that he feared something far greater than the discovery of Sophia's torn dress, and it was not Mariah's wrath.

'You can't leave here,' he said, the lines on his face deepening with concern at the idea. 'You'll try to harm her again if you do. I can't let you harm her. They told me to look out for her, to keep her away from the cottage, and I do – keep her away from you!'

'Harm her?' I repeated. 'Harm my Sophia?' I could not believe my ears. My eyes narrowed on his, imploring him to make sense of what he had just said.

Whether or not Jenken was about to explain why he

thought I might harm my own beloved daughter, I shall never know. The door behind me had opened. I heard the sound of Mariah's rapid heels on the tiles behind me. Then, as I turned to face her, I saw a flash of copper and felt the blow of a skillet against my head before I fell, half senseless, into Jenken's arms.

CHAPTER TWENTY

Grace

Drinks on the terrace. How lovely.

I left my room in the early evening, dressed all in white with a lace frill in my hair, feeling considerably more excited than I usually did when I went down for pre-dinner drinks. We had a guest, and as I had come to understand that a guest of any kind was a rare thing at Crows-an-Wra Manor, when I overheard Mariah telling Cobb to make up one of the many spare bedrooms I was naturally delighted. I was surprised, however, to learn who our guest was. Giles Trevelyan was back at Crows-an-Wra Manor, and by invitation this time.

His brief visit two weeks before, when I was ordered to my room like an impudent child in need of discipline, had not been an agreeable one as far as Richard was concerned. Needless to say, as inquisitively disposed as I was, I had not gone to my room as instructed, but had watched and listened on the galleried landing, out of sight at the top of the main stairs. To my disappointment, I overheard very little, but the general tone of their conversation, which was never one of cordiality, bordering on outright hostility at times, confirmed to me that Richard had not welcomed his brother's unexpected visit. So why had he been invited back, and to stay this time? I really was most perplexed by this sudden change in Richard's attitude. As I made my way down, taking one of the smaller staircases at the back of the house, I was resolved to understand why.

The ever-present wind set my dress dancing as soon as I stepped out on to the terrace, but I welcomed it today. It had been hot all week, and the evenings offered little respite. Thankfully, the terrace was in partial shade, which further helped. I saw Richard and his brother seated opposite Mariah at a small table that had been laid out abutting the low balustrade, facing far-reaching views over the lawn towards the lake and the distant trees. They were all engaged in conversation. No one seemed to notice my arrival.

'Richard!' I called, giving a little wave.

Both he and Giles turned to me at the same time, and I cannot say which of them was smiling the most when they saw me. They stood up together as I approached the table, and it was Giles who dashed around to the other side to pull out my chair.

'What an uncommonly warm evening it is,' he said as he and Richard sat down again. 'I should hate to be cooped up somewhere on an evening like this, wouldn't you?'

'Yes,' I said, unsure whether he was still addressing me as he kept glancing at Richard as he spoke. 'I'm sure it would be most unpleasant.'

'Indeed,' Giles said. 'Akin to torture, I'd say. Wouldn't you agree, Richard?'

Richard did not answer.

'Never mind,' Giles continued, laughing to himself as if something had amused him. Looking at me again, he added, 'Richard's been telling me all about you. I hear that you particularly enjoyed your time in Italy. So much so that you'd like to recreate a little piece of it here at Crows-an-Wra Manor. Is that so?'

I had so far only been in Giles's company briefly, when we were introduced upon his arrival at the manor not three hours ago. Sitting opposite him now, with Richard close beside him, I thought the resemblance between them striking, even though I knew them to have been born of different mothers. I returned the smile that hung on Giles's lips as he waited for my reply, and with great enthusiasm said, 'Yes, I should like that very much.' I looked at Richard then, adding, 'It would make for the most wonderful birthday present, and every time I saw it I would be reminded of our honeymoon.'

Giles began to laugh so much that he slapped the table. 'She's got you good and proper there, Richard!' he hooted. 'How could any man refuse such a thing?'

Richard was not laughing. He cleared his throat. 'We still have the east wing to rebuild before any consideration can be given to the gardens.'

Giles turned to his brother with a look of surprise. 'I fail to see what the one has to do with the other,' he countered. 'Surely it's as well to do both together and get all the palaver over with at the same time?'

'Oh, could we, Richard?' I said. 'Please say we could.'

'I'll think about it,' Richard said. 'Is that enough for

now?'

I nodded. 'Yes, of course.'

'Good. Now, what's keeping our blasted drinks?'

Mariah began to stand up. 'I'll go and find out,' she said, but then I saw Lucy approaching.

'Here's Lucy with them now,' I said, 'and please don't blame her for the delay. It's entirely my fault. I asked her to prepare something special for us, and as it's so hot I made her go to the icehouse.'

'Something special, eh?' Giles said. 'I do like surprises.'

'I brought it back from Italy,' I said. 'I've been waiting for an occasion to open it.'

'Have you indeed?' Giles said. 'Well, I'm very flattered, I must say. It makes me feel very welcome.'

I noticed him glance at Richard again as he finished speaking, as if to suggest that his brother had not. While everything seemed amicable enough so far for our first evening with Giles, I knew Richard well enough to understand that he remained uncomfortable in his brother's company.

I played the matter down. 'It's only a small gesture, really,' I said. 'In truth, I couldn't have waited another week to open it.' To Richard I said. 'You'll know what it is as soon as you see it. It was my favourite aperitivo.'

Lucy arrived at the table carrying a silver tray, on which was set four glasses filled with a red-coloured liquid. 'I'm sorry it took so long,' Lucy said. 'I've been chipping away at the ice in the icehouse for ages.' She served the drinks rather casually, and in no particular order, which instantly put a frown on Mariah's face.

'Have you lost you manners, girl?' Mariah asked her.

'Manners, madam?'

Mariah gave a huff. 'Surely you know full well that

proper etiquette dictates you serve the ladies before the gentlemen?'

'I'm sorry, madam,' Lucy said, setting Mariah's glass in front of her last. 'Oops,' she added as some of the drink spilled onto the table.

It was just a drop, and I thought Mariah completely over-exaggerated as she shot back in her chair to avoid getting any of the drink on her dress, which was also white to stave off the heat.

'You clumsy girl!' she said, almost shouting. 'Have you been at the drink yourself? Is that what you were really doing in the icehouse all this time?'

Lucy flushed. 'No, madam. Of course not,' she said as she began to mop up the spill with her apron.

I knew otherwise. I had told Lucy she must try one of the drinks herself, although I had not anticipated her doing so before she had served ours. She winked at me as she turned away from Mariah, confirming it. I noticed then that Giles was watching every move Lucy made, and rather more intently than seemed fitting. If he had noticed her wink, he did not let on. She gave a curtsey and slowly retreated from our table, and now Lucy had also noticed Giles's attention. We all had. It was impossible not to. He had turned in his seat to fully see her and he was smiling broadly at her, with more than a hint of fancy dancing in the corner of his mouth. I saw Lucy smile back at him briefly before she turned and left.

'What a charming creature,' Giles said, making no attempt to conceal his attraction.

Mariah was of a different opinion. 'That girl is the worst housemaid I've ever had the misfortune of knowing.'

I had to defend Lucy. 'That is because Lucy is not a

housemaid,' I said. 'What is to be expected when one tries to fit a square peg into a round hole?' I picked up my glass to discourage a reply. The drink felt wonderfully cool in my warm hand. 'Salute!' I said in the Italian way, raising my glass towards the middle of the table.

'Yes, cin cin!' Giles said.

We clinked glasses, and as we did so I looked around the table, trying to make a connection with everyone in turn such that my toast would be felt as sincerely as it was intended. Giles was still full of smiles as he nodded his head towards me. Richard looked at me, our eyes meeting briefly, but he still could not seem to manage a smile, and Mariah looked at no one. Contrary to my expectations, I was beginning to like Giles Trevelyan. His happy outlook was such a contrast to the way Richard had been since we returned from Europe, and his mother... Well, I could not say that I had yet felt truly relaxed in her company since my arrival, despite my early desire for things to be otherwise between us. Now, with Giles there, it was also a blessing to have the opportunity to engage in more varied conversation. Whatever the differences between Richard and his brother, I found Giles quite the gentleman.

'I say, that's got a bite to it,' Giles said as he tasted his drink. 'What is it?'

I took a sip and was immediately transported back to Lombardy in northern Italy, where I first discovered it. 'It's called Bitter all'Uso d'Holanda,' I said, trying my best to sound Italian.

'It's bitter all right,' Richard said with a huff. 'I can't say I really took to the stuff myself.'

'I think it's just the thing before dinner,' Giles said, perhaps just to be contrary. 'It's already got my saliva up.

What's in it? Do you know?'

'Not exactly,' I said. 'I'm told the recipe is a strict family secret. It was invented by an Italian gentleman called Gaspare Campari from a blend of herbs and spices, fruit peels and the bark from trees.' I giggled to myself. 'Who would have thought to put tree bark in a drink?'

'I can't drink this,' Mariah said, pulling a sour face as she put her glass down again. 'Lucy!' she called. 'A glass of Madeira, and be quick about it.' Under her breath, she added, 'The sooner the better, to take away this awful aftertaste.'

'It's not that bad, surely?' I said, wondering whether Mariah was refusing to drink it just to spite me.

'I'll take it off you,' Giles said. 'Mine's going down rather too well.' He picked up Mariah's drink and emptied it into what little remained of his own. Then, looking at me, he said, 'Do tell me more about your vision for your Italian garden.'

Before I began my reply, Lucy crossed the terrace with her silver tray, carrying Mariah's glass of Madeira. She was walking so fast, bless her, she was almost running. She did not speak this time, nor did she once look at Giles, but Giles's eyes were back on her from the moment she arrived. I thought it entirely inappropriate, so I tried to distract him with my answer. I pointed out towards the lake and all eyes followed.

'I thought a pergola by the lake there, with stone pillars and a balustrade, would be a good place to start,' I said as Lucy delivered Mariah's drink, this time, thankfully, without spilling a drop. 'And more statuary,' I added, noticing that I had lost Giles's attention already. 'Nothing says Italian garden more than statuary. Wouldn't you agree, Giles?' I received no answer. 'Giles?'

As Lucy left us again, Giles's attention snapped back to our conversation. 'Statues,' he said. 'Yes, definitely. The more the merrier.'

I could have laughed at him, were his affections being directed towards anyone other than my Lucy. I did not wish to see her ruined by him. Such things rarely, if ever, turned out well for the lower classes.

While we were back on the subject of my Italian garden, I turned my attention to Richard. 'Do you remember Florence, Richard?' I said. 'I was so taken with the Boboli Gardens that I thought it would also be wonderful to try to recreate a small part of it. Wouldn't that be lovely?'

Richard sighed. I thought he was about to say something negative about it, but he didn't. Instead, he smiled at me, and there in that moment I once again saw the man I had married. 'If it will make you happy, my darling,' he said, 'then yes, of course you shall have your garden. And once it is complete, I shall have a crate of this aperitivo shipped from Italy to fully recreate those happiest of days we spent together.'

'Bravo!' Giles said, somewhat spoiling the moment for me. I knew he was being condescending, but I didn't care. I could not have been happier.

'Thank you, Richard,' I said, and before I could say any more, Mariah stood up and addressed us.

'Shall we go back inside? I'm sure it's almost time for dinner.'

CHAPTER
TWENTY-ONE

Early the following morning, I was out walking in the grounds. I preferred the afternoons for my constitutional stroll, but the summer heat had this past week stolen all the pleasure from it. As the nights were uncomfortably hot, however, to the point of being stifling, I was typically awake early and in need of fresh air, so I didn't mind so much.

More and more since my arrival at Crows-an-Wra Manor I should have liked to walk by the sea, but Richard was always so busy that he had not yet found the time to take me, and although close by, the sea was tantalisingly out of reach. I would gladly have gone by myself regardless, or in the carriage with Jenken, but Richard would not entertain the idea of me venturing out without an escort and Jenken could not be spared. I supposed I would have the opportunity later in the year, when Richard was less busy with estate affairs, and now his plans to restore the east wing. He had spoken rather excitedly about them over his many glasses of claret at dinner the night before, and was now seemingly as keen as mustard to begin the work.

I must have been out in the grounds for an hour at least, first taking a turn around the lake, where I continued to imagine my Italian garden, then through a tall grass meadow that would soon be harvested for the horses' winter feed. I let my hands brush against the wildflowers as I went, thinking absently to myself about nothing in particular. At length I came to a small woodland, not far from Mariah's cottage, and there I decided to begin my return to the manor.

I immediately made for the carriage drive, thinking it the quickest route back as I had by now built up a keen appetite and did not want to miss my breakfast. I had not taken two steps towards it, however, when I was startled by the sound of laughter over the morning birdsong. I spun around, seeking its source, but although the sun was already bright and had climbed above the treetops, I could make out little amidst the shadows beneath the trees' leafy canopy. I went closer, squinting into the shadows to see better. Then I heard the laughter again. This time I thought I saw movement.

'Hello?' I called. 'Who's there?'

I was sure I saw someone then, dashing from one tree to another, and at the same time giving another little giggle.

'Sophia?' I said, now standing at the edge of the wood. 'Is that you?' I imagined it had to be. The laughter was high in pitch and the fleeting shadow I had seen was about her size. I stepped in among the trees, looking for her. 'Do you want to play hide and seek?' I added. 'Is that it?'

At that moment, Sophia stepped into view from behind one of the trees, barely six feet away. She didn't say a word. She just stood there staring at me, still in her nightgown and cap, her feet bare and dirty from the woodland undergrowth. She was no longer laughing, nor even smiling at me.

'Sophia,' I said again. 'It is you. Is everything all right?'

'It was,' she said, 'until you came along and spoiled everything.' She sounded angrier than any privileged six-year-old child had any right to.

I felt my brow begin to crease. 'Spoiled everything?' I repeated, dumbfounded. 'What did I spoil?'

'My game, of course!'

I still had no idea what she was referring to. 'Did you not just laugh to draw my attention?'

'I didn't know you were there,' Sophia said. She glanced to her right and pointed. 'Now he's found me. See!'

I stepped forward so that I could see around the large tree to my left, and there was Jenken coming towards us. 'So you were already playing hide and seek,' I said. I put my hand to my mouth, but could not hide my laughter. Sophia, however, did not see the funny side of the matter.

'Why are you laughing?' she said, raising her voice. 'It's not funny to ruin other people's games.'

'No, it's not,' I said, calming myself down again. 'I'm sorry, truly I am. I had no idea anyone else was here.'

'Good morning, madam,' Jenken said, touching his forelock as he arrived beside us. He was panting slightly. 'Miss Sophia was having trouble sleeping, so she came out and found me for a game.'

'Do you play together often?' I asked him.

He gave me a toothy smile, looked down at Sophia, and then back at me. 'Most days,' he said. 'Miss Sophia likes her games.'

'Yes,' Sophia said, 'and I don't like them spoiled!'

I thought something was spoiled all right, but it was not Sophia's silly game. Were she my own child I would have promptly dealt with her, but she was not. Conscious of the fact that she had recently lost her mother, and of my hopes to win her over some day, I bit my tongue and smiled. I offered her my hand in friendship and apology.

'Breakfast must nearly be ready,' I said. 'Shall we go back to the house together?'

'I'm not hungry.'

'Then perhaps something to drink. Surely you must have built up a thirst with all this running about?'

Sophia took a step back. 'I'll go in when I'm ready to,' she said. 'Besides, I want to play another game.'

With that, she ran around me and stopped at the edge of the wood where I had entered.

'What game is this?' I asked, still smiling at her, hoping to join in. 'Can I play, too?'

Sophia grinned. 'Yes,' she said, nodding. 'All you have to do is catch me.'

It was a game of chase then, or so I thought. The next moment, Sophia ran to the nearest tree and began to climb it. She was so fast that she was already out of my reach before I caught up with her. I looked up into the branches and still she was climbing, steadily higher and higher.

'That's not fair,' I said. 'I can't catch you up there.'

'I don't want you to catch me up here,' Sophia said, and it was only then that I realised what she meant. 'I want you to catch me down there when I jump.'

I was horrified at the thought. 'Come down at once!' I called. 'It's not safe. You'll hurt yourself.'

'Not if you catch me,' Sophia said. 'You will catch me, won't you?'

'I can't possibly catch you. Don't be foolish!'

'My mother always caught me when I used to jump off the chair. You want to be my mother now, don't you? You want me to love you as I loved her?'

'Yes, of course,' I said, wondering what kind of cruel game this was.

'Then catch me!'

I thought she was going to jump there and then, but instead she caught hold of the tree trunk and laughed at me as she leaned out.

'Jumping from a low chair is a different matter altogether,' I said, 'and I'm sure you were much smaller and lighter then.'

My rationale served no purpose. I watched Sophia sit down on the branch she had been standing on, and my heart was in my mouth as she slid herself along it until it began to bend under her weight. A moment later I heard a crack and feared the branch might break at any minute.

'This is not a game!' I called up to her. She was sitting several feet above my head and would likely suffer serious injury if she fell.

The danger, however, did not seem to trouble her.

'I'm going to count to three,' she said. 'Then I'll jump. If you love me, you'll catch me.'

'Climb back down, please,' I implored her.

'One!'

'You've made your point!'

'Two!'

'Sophia, you mustn't. You'll hurt yourself!'

'Three!'

With that I almost fainted. Sophia pushed herself off

the branch. Suddenly she was falling, and so was I. It was not from the shock of seeing Sophia fall from the tree, however, but because Jenken had abruptly stepped in, knocking me over in his haste to catch her. It all happened so fast. As soon as I recovered myself and looked up, I saw Sophia cradled safely in Jenken's arms. A moment later I heard her laughing again, and it was my turn to not see the funny side of the matter. I determined there and then that Sophia had the most peculiar sense of humour I had ever come across.

Jenken lowered her to the ground, saying nothing, and I did not blame him for knocking me down. If he had not, Sophia and I would both likely have been hurt.

'You see?' Sophia said, looking down at me. 'Jenken loves me, and I love him. He always saves me – always.'

'You've played this game before?' I asked, horrified by the thought.

Instead of answering me, Sophia ran off towards the house, and Jenken helped me to my feet as I brushed myself down.

'Pardon me, madam,' he said. 'I had no choice, see. Jenken never has a choice with that game.'

I now saw Sophia in quite a different light. She never spoke to me about what had happened in the wood. Indeed, all through breakfast she did not speak to me at all. Every now and then I would glance at her, and she at me, and from time to time she would give me a smug little smile, as if to show me how satisfied she was with the outcome of her wicked game. She had won and she knew it. No, she was not the pleasant and polite little girl

I had hoped would some day call me Mother. She struck me now as a cunning and manipulative child, who had undoubtedly matured beyond her years. I had never encountered such a cruel streak in one so young, or such apparent fearlessness. These were all adult characteristics to my mind – traits one collected through experience and nurtured prejudices. Had she been like this before her mother died? Or had Rosen's tragic death severely affected Sophia's mind? Either way, I felt more than a little concerned for her.

My own mind lingered so distractedly over what had happened that morning that I paid little attention to the general breakfast conversation – although, as Mariah did not join us, and as Richard was as quiet as I typically found him to be in his brother's company, there was nothing of any great interest to miss. I was the first to make my excuses and leave, my former hearty appetite having all but deserted me since my encounter with Sophia in the wood. Entirely unsatisfied with my morning, I decided to take another stroll, if only to clear the unpleasant thoughts that kept circling through my mind. I felt angry, which was most unlike me, angry with Sophia. No, with myself for letting a child get the better of me.

I took one step outside, however, and quickly decided that the air was already too warm for any kind of physical exertion, so I thought I would explore more of the house. I had covered much of it by now, but there were places I had not yet been – out of the way places such as the attic rooms, from where one could access the roof. Although Richard had not yet found the time to take me up there himself, he had told me of the marvellous views that could be seen, and I imagined the breeze would be stronger, the air a little cooler, up there.

Along the way, I decided to collect a book from my room to take with me. The views from the roof would likely entertain me only so far, and I desired escape – to be transported somewhere else entirely, and how better than through the pages of a book? But which one? There were so many to select from that I spent more time in the choosing than I had expected. My mood was the problem. I saw a copy of Candide, a short book that was potentially just the thing to help while away the rest of the morning, but I did not care for Voltaire's satire today. I thumbed over several of Jane Austen's books, all of which I'd read too many times before, and then I came across a book that seemed perfect for the kind of peace and solitude I was craving. It was a tatty old leather-bound copy of Daniel Defoe's Robinson Crusoe, a book I should by now have read, but somehow had not.

I gently teased it out from its place on the upper shelf, afraid that it might fall apart or turn to dust in front of me were I anything but deferential in my handling of it. As it turned out, I need not have concerned myself. When I opened the cover, I found it robust enough. Its jacket had simply become worn out from having spent more time out of the bookcase than in. I read out the title page.

'The life and strange surprising adventures of Robinson Crusoe of York.'

I turned the page and began to read, only to affirm my choice of reading material, but before long I was five pages in, then seven, eight, nine. I might have kept going right there in front of the bookcase had a sound not distracted me. It was laughter again. Had Sophia followed me to my room, bent on teasing me further? I went to the door immediately, snapping my book shut in frustration. If Sophia had come to play more of her cruel games on me, then she would find me more than a match for her this time. As I opened my door, however, quietly so as to pretend I had not heard anything, I saw Giles. He was further along the corridor with his back to me, but it was not a man's laughter I had heard.

A moment later I caught a glimpse of Lucy and realised it must have been her laughter. She was standing against the wall in front of Giles – although pinned to the wall by him would be more accurate. His hands were against the wall to either side of her shoulders and there was little space left between them. Not wishing to be seen, for I immediately felt awkward and embarrassed, I shrank back and observed.

'Lucy, Lucy,' Giles said. 'I can make things very comfortable for you here, if you'll let me.'

'Run along with you now, sir. You've had your fun,' Lucy replied, giggling again as she spoke, but I could tell now that her laughter was born of nervousness.

'You mean to say you've only been teasing me?' Giles said. There was playfulness in his tone, too, but I sensed that he was offended by the idea.

'Begging your pardon, sir, but I didn't mean to.'

'Oh, but you have.'

'Well, I didn't mean anything. Now, if you'll excuse me, I have my duties to attend to.'

Lucy tried to move out from beneath one of Giles's arms, but he lowered it, blocking her. He laughed. 'I can't let you off that lightly now, can I?' He leaned in then and tried to kiss her.

'Stop it, sir. Please!' Lucy said, moving her head from side to side to avoid him. She tried to push him away, but it did her no good.

Giles grabbed her by her wrists. 'I can also make things

very difficult for you,' he said, his tone now far more serious. 'You would do well to keep that in mind.'

'Just let me be, sir. I don't want any trouble.'

'Then you'll stop teasing me and come to my room in one hour.'

I had hoped the situation would settle itself amicably and without intervention, but I could see how distressed Lucy had become, and how intent Giles was on having his way with her. I had feared as much and could not allow it. Giles Trevelyan was clearly not the gentleman I had previously taken him for. I rattled my door handle, as if I had just opened my door, and stepped out into the corridor, looking at the pair of them with surprise, as though I had only just seen them.

As I approached, I saw now that Lucy had tears in her eyes. 'Lucy?' I said. 'Whatever's the matter?'

She looked at Giles and so did I. Giles stood back, a sheepish grin on his face. 'Nothing's the matter,' he said. 'Isn't that right, Lucy?'

Lucy did not answer. Instead, she gave a small curtsey and said, 'I'll be about my duties then.' And with that, she left in one direction, and Giles left in the other.

I sighed to myself as soon as I was alone again. My mood had now slipped into a rare melancholy, sapping my former enthusiasm for exploring the attic rooms and taking my book up to the roof. It could wait for another day, when I felt more inclined. I went back into my room and gently closed the door, having decided instead to while away the rest of the morning, or the entire day if it suited me, by an open window. There, I felt I had the least chance of encountering anyone else until I was good and ready to.

CHAPTER TWENTY-TWO

Rosen

I can't let you harm her...

Jenken's words would not let me rest. I had repeated them in my mind and out loud so many times now that it seemed to me no other words existed. What did he mean by that? How could he believe me capable of harm where my Sophia was concerned? I had to know.

I was sitting on the hearth by the fireplace with my knees curled up beneath my nightgown, gently rocking back and forth as Jenken's words continued to play through my mind. I had been there all morning and all the previous day because, as uncomfortable as it was compared to my bed or the armchair, my room had become unbearably hot and I welcomed the flow of air that was being drawn up through the flue. Through a searing shaft of light from the skylight above, I stared at the lower hatch, willing it to open so that I could ask Mariah why Jenken would say such a thing, but I knew she would not come.

I was being punished again, and this time I fully expected to be abandoned to die of dehydration for trying to escape, but so help me God, I would endure. I had to. Sophia was alive. There was now no question about it, and I would survive this, if not for my pitiful sake then for hers. I reached up and felt the lump on my head, still present and still very sore where Mariah had hit me with that skillet. I had not seen her since then, and my thirst in this heat was overpowering, but surely Richard would not let her take her punishment too far. Then again, with his new wife now comfortably ensconced at Crows-an-Wra Manor, perhaps he had abandoned me, too.

'I can't let you harm her. I can't let you harm her,' I said under my breath as I rocked back and forth, my eyes still fixed on the lower hatch.

Then something distracted me. Other words had reached my ears, or had I imagined them? Out of my need to fill my head with words other than Jenken's, was my mind playing tricks on me? Perhaps I was insane at last, but then I supposed that one would not have such thoughts, or question their sanity, if one truly were insane. I listened more attentively at the chimney, and very soon I knew that I had not imagined it. I heard a woman's voice that was unfamiliar to me. She was singing. It was a nursery rhyme – one of Sophia's favourites from Tommy Thumb's Pretty Song Book.

'London Bridge is broken down, dance over my Lady Lee. London Bridge is broken down, with a gay lady...'

At first I wondered whether it was Richard's new bride, the words having stuck in her head from already having heard Sophia sing the rhyme once too often in her company, but I quickly discovered that it was not.

'Lucy!'

The voice calling to her was unmistakably Mariah's. She must have seen Lucy, whoever she was, coming towards the cottage and gone out to meet her before she drew too close.

'Begging your pardon, madam,' I heard Lucy say, 'but I've brought these scraps up from the kitchen as I know Ada does most mornings. She was busy seeing to the rooms, see, and I thought—'

'Clearly you did not think, did you?' Mariah said, her tone curt. 'When you first arrived here, I was very explicit when I instructed you never to come to my cottage. Never!'

'Yes, madam, but I—'

'Yes, but nothing!' Mariah yelled. 'My privacy is sacrosanct. Do you understand? Ada was instructed that no scraps were to be brought here today, as yesterday. Now get back to the house. I'm sure you have duties to attend to.'

'Yes, madam. I'm very sorry. I just supposed you must have a little dog here, or a cat, and I couldn't bear the thought of it going hungry.'

'Damn your impudence, girl. There is no dog here, and certainly no cat.'

'Begging your pardon again, madam, but who are the scraps for, then? I see Ada, and sometimes Jenken, bringing them here most days.'

The conversation fell silent.

They are for me, I thought. That is, when I am not being punished. I felt the sudden urge to say so at the top of my voice. What did I care for Mariah's wrath now? If she had left me to die of dehydration then she could do no more to me, and if she wished to hit me again, then so be it. Perhaps this Lucy, who I now understood to be another new maid, was close enough to hear me and raise the alarm. I ran to the shutters and began banging on them with all the strength I could muster.

'They are for me!' I shouted, as loudly as my parched throat would allow. I coughed several times but kept banging. 'Help me!' I yelled. 'I'm up here!'

Unable to see out of my room now that my broken slat had been discovered and the shutters nailed with bars, I dashed back to the fireplace to listen again, wondering whether I had been heard.

'Whatever was that, madam?' I heard Lucy ask. 'Did you hear that noise?'

I caught my breath and smiled to myself. I had been heard. Mariah, however, was quick with her reply.

'That would be Jenken, of course,' she said. 'He's making some repairs. That's all it was.'

'But I just saw Jen...' Lucy trailed off. 'Nothing, madam,' she added. 'It's none of my business I'm sure. I'll take these scraps back to the kitchen and get about my duties.'

In my head, I finished Lucy's words for her. She had just seen Jenken elsewhere before she came here, so how could Jenken already have been engaged in repairs at the cottage? At least, I hoped that was what she had been about to say.

'I'll come with you to see that you do,' Mariah said, and now I heard a change in her tone. The anger had completely gone. In its place was an eerie calm that was laced with suspicion. It left me feeling that Mariah knew Lucy had not believed her.

CHAPTER TWENTY-THREE

The hours slipped slowly by.

After all my wailing and banging on the shutters, which I was sure had been heard by the maid, Lucy, I had expected Mariah to come to my room without delay. I had imagined she would be eager to mete out some new punishment, but she did not come. Still sitting by the fireplace, I continued to stare at the door to my room as the searing shaft of sunlight traced time across the floor and gradually faded. I sat and I stared until the moon and the stars replaced the sun, and somewhere in between I must have drifted off to sleep. I had no idea what time it was when I awoke.

I did so with a start.

As soon as my eyes opened, I reeled back against the brickwork. Mariah's face was at the upper hatch. It was lit so ghoulishly by her lamp, her sharp features casting long shadows on her face, her eyes glaring so hatefully at me through the half-light, that I thought myself caught in a nightmare. Then I saw a cup on the floor by the lower hatch and I relaxed. Had she brought me water at last? I could not imagine why, after all the noise I had made.

'I suppose you must be very thirsty by now,' Mariah said, her voice sounding as cold as I had come to expect. 'Come here and drink your water.'

I did not move for several seconds, untrusting of her as I was. Why show me this kindness? Was the water poisoned? Was there water in the cup at all, for that matter, or had she merely come to me in the night to wake me from my sleep and torture my already fractious senses?

Aware that I did not trust her, Mariah spoke again. 'The water is not from me. If you do not come and drink it this instant, I shall take it away again and tell Richard you did not want it.'

'It's from Richard?' I said, moving at last.

'Yes, who else? Were it down to me, you would not drink one drop of water ever again.'

That much I did not doubt. Slowly, I stood up, my limbs cramped and aching, as much, I imagined, from the effects of dehydration as from the hard surface and the uncomfortable position I had slept in. At first, I was afraid to go to the door – to Mariah. I cannot say that I had felt truly scared of her until now, but such apparent hatred had made me so. Perhaps it was not Mariah herself I feared, or the harm she may one day do to me, but because I now wanted to live. Before I knew my Sophia was alive, I had not cared for myself as I do now. I took a step, and then another, my eyes flitting between Mariah and the cup. Then I saw moonlight reflected in the water's surface and I ran to it, falling to my knees before it as if penitent before the Lord himself. I drank until it was all gone, and when I came up for air Mariah began to laugh at me.

'You're a wretched creature,' she said, looking down at me with disdain. 'I really cannot understand why Richard refuses to let you go, but he will. His new wife will fall pregnant soon enough. She will give him the son you could not, and he will quickly forget all about you.'

I tried not to listen to her, but she spoke a truth that was hard to ignore. Richard could not keep me like this forever. My very existence was too great a risk to him. If I did not escape soon, I could not expect to see another summer. I may have been forced to listen to her, but I did not indulge her torment. Instead, I voiced the questions I wished with all my being to know the answers to.

'Why did you lie to me about Sophia?' I said. 'Why did you tell me she was dead, and that her body had been laid to rest beside mine in the churchyard at St Buryan's?' I knew now, of course, that this hateful untruth was set to deceive me alone – everyone else having been duped into believing it was just I who had been buried that day.

'Because it was better for both of you if one believed the other to be dead,' Mariah said. 'And because you would have been far less manageable if you knew before now that she was alive, would you not?'

'Yes,' I said, unable to lie about it. If I had known without doubt that Sophia was alive when I first awoke here, while I still had my strength, I would not have acquiesced for one moment of the day or night.

'Not that you've exactly been a model guest here,' Mariah continued. 'But make no mistake – Richard's sentimentality may not save you again.'

With that, Mariah closed the hatch and I shot to my feet. 'Mariah?' I said. 'Please, I have another question I must ask you.'

Silence.

'Mariah?' I said again. 'I know you're still there. Please open the hatch.'

The hatch shot open. 'If I answer your question, will you promise to behave yourself? Will you promise on Sophia's life?'

I drew a sharp breath. I had not expected that. In truth, I had to think about it, and for longer than Mariah had patience for.

She closed the hatch again.

'Yes,' I said with haste. 'Yes, I promise.'

Mariah looked very pleased with herself when she opened the hatch again. 'Very well. Ask your question.'

'I want to know why Jenken said that I was not to harm Sophia. Why would he say such a thing? How could he believe it possible?'

'That is two questions,' Mariah said, 'but as they lead to the same answer, I'm prepared to overlook it. I must warn you, however, that you may not like what you hear.'

'I must know,' I said. 'Please tell me.'

'Very well. He would say such a thing to you because he very much believes it possible.'

'But how?' I asked again. 'Surely he knows how much I love my daughter. He has seen us together every day. He knows how close we have always been.'

'And you know how much Jenken dotes on the girl, don't you?'

'Yes, but—'

'Well then,' Mariah cut in. 'You know he would protect her with his life if he thought she was in danger.'

'Danger?' I said, perplexed. 'From me?'

'Yes, from you,' Mariah said. 'Jenken, as you know, does not think too hard on things, as others might.' She paused and studied me in such a way that made it clear she meant that I thought too much – too much for my own good. 'Jenken only had to believe you meant Sophia harm, and he would never let you near her again.'

'And why would he believe it?' I asked, wondering what lies he had been told.

'He believes it because he thinks you were so jealous of Richard's affection for Sophia over yourself that you tried to kill her the night you started the fire in the east wing.'

I put a hand to my mouth to stifle the gasp I gave at hearing that. It was the cruellest lie imaginable. I was not jealous of my husband's love for our daughter. I had not started the fire. Richard had, to pretend that it had taken my life, leaving him free to marry again.

Mariah had not finished. 'Jenken believes that you are affected by a malady of the mind, and have been locked in here for your own good and, above all, for the good of poor little Sophia. It was the perfect way to guarantee his help, and his silence.'

I began to stagger away from the door, weakened as if by the strongest blow Mariah and her cruel tongue could have dealt me. I could not bear to listen to another word.

'Go away!' I yelled as I crumpled on to my bed.

I buried my face in my pillow. Tears began to fill my eyes. I knew it to be no more than a wicked lie, but to think that Jenken, and perhaps others, thought me capable of deliberately trying to kill my daughter was abhorrent beyond measure to me.

Mariah was already laughing by the time my head touched my pillow. 'I told you that you might not like what you hear,' she said. 'You bring it all upon yourself. Now, remember your promise, won't you? I should hate to see any harm befall Sophia if you do not.'

CHAPTER TWENTY-FOUR

Grace

Having spent most of the previous day in the quiet company of Robinson Crusoe, sharing in his solitude, I awoke the following morning feeling irritable and restless. I had not slept well on account of the lingering heat during the early part of the night, and the thunderstorms that came and raged as if immediately above Crows-an-Wra Manor during the latter.

And because of Richard.

He had come to me sometime in the small hours, when the house was still and I had at last begun to settle. It was by no means the first time he had done so, and I suppose his visit might have been considered romantic under different circumstances, but his attentions on this night in particular were not welcome, not least because he was terribly drunk on wine and brandy. In truth, given the stupor he had fallen into not long after dinner, I was surprised to see him, although he did not share my bed for long. He remained only for as long as was necessary, and he spoke to me hardly at all.

I sat up in my bed and drew in the morning air to help clear my thoughts, and while I rued the thunderstorms at the time, I now welcomed the change they had brought. The breeze from the open windows was decidedly cooler. I could feel it at the back of my nose as I breathed, and on my skin as soon as I threw back the bedcovers. The hot air of the day before was now replaced by something so much fresher that, despite my restless night, I felt quite energised as I swung my legs out of bed and tugged on the bell pull for Lucy to come and help dress me.

I went to the windows with a smile on my face and began to pull each one to a little in order to calm the breeze, wondering what kind of day lay ahead for me. As much as I was enjoying my book, I hoped the day would yield greater excitement than the continued words of Daniel Defoe. A moment later, I saw something out of the window that made me think it had certainly got off to an intriguing start. The carriage was returning along the drive. I followed its rapid course towards the house, and as it drew closer I was convinced that Richard was driving it. The scene before me further stirred my senses. Wherever had Richard been at this early hour? As inquisitive as I was, I made a mental note to ask him at the earliest opportunity.

There was a knock at the door then, and I turned to it as it opened, expecting to see Lucy, but it was not. In her place stood a particularly sour-faced Ada Cobb.

'Where is Lucy?' I asked, my brow furrowing in confusion. Seeing Cobb there in Lucy's place forced me to forget the usual courtesies.

'Good morning, madam,' Cobb said with a bow and a bob, thankfully not having forgotten hers. 'Begging your pardon, but I'm all there is and I'm already rushed off me feet, so I can't spare you long.'

'Can't spare me long?' I repeated, squinting at her rather keenly as I tried to understand the situation. I went to her. 'I ask you again,' I said, my tone more curt than was intended. 'Where is Lucy? Is she unwell? Is that why you are here and she is not?'

'No, madam,' Cobb said. 'She's not here no more. That's why. She's gone.'

I found myself repeating her words again. 'Gone?' I said, shaking my head this time. Then it dawned on me. It had to be connected with the reason Richard had been out with the carriage so early. 'What do you know of the matter?' I asked, certain that Cobb, who had likely been among the first awake that morning, would know plenty.

'I don't know much,' Cobb said, to my disappointment. 'I heard the carriage pull up outside, so I took a peek. Barely light, it was, but I saw Lucy with Mr Trevelyan right enough. She had her little travel case with her – same as she arrived with.'

'Do you know where Mr Trevelyan was taking her?'

'Begging your pardon again, madam, but how should I know that? I see he's just back, mind, so he can't have taken her much further than Penzance.'

Penzance...

If I was correct to suppose that Lucy had been dismissed and made to leave Crows-an-Wra Manor with all haste, then that was as far as Richard would need to take her for her onward journey back to Northumberland. I could also guess well enough at the reason: the lecherous

Giles Trevelyan. I could feel my face beginning to flush. How dare Richard dismiss my own maid, my friend, and without first speaking to me? I made for the door, brushing past Cobb without saying another word.

'Don't you want to get dressed, madam?' I heard Cobb say as I opened the door, barefoot and still in my nightgown.

'No, I do not!' I called back as I left, sounding angrier than I had ever known myself to be. I was going to see Richard, to demand that he return to Penzance, or wherever he had been, and bring Lucy back at once.

I found Richard in his study, a room of the house in which I knew my presence was unwelcome, but I felt so incensed by his actions that I did not care. I did not even think to first knock on the door, so distraught was I over Lucy having been sent away without the opportunity to at least say goodbye. Richard was removing his boots as I entered. The look of surprise on his face, and his dark frown in particular as he looked up at me, told me that he was not happy to see me.

'Grace,' he said, sounding weary. 'Not now, please, and not here. Haven't I told you never to bother me in my study?'

'Yes, Richard, but I must—'

'Then surely it can wait,' Richard cut in. 'Whatever it is.'

'I'm sorry, Richard, but it cannot,' I protested. I had never stood up to him in this way before, and doing so now made my hands tremble a little. It was fear, I suppose, but despite the darkness in his eyes, some things had to be said. 'You know very well why I'm here. How could you do such a thing? Why did you not tell me?'

Richard sank his head into his hands and slowly pushed his hair back as he sat up again. 'Because there was nothing to be said. Lucy had to go, and quickly.'

'On account of Giles, I suppose?'

'Yes, because of Giles, and for all your maid's flirting with him. He told me what happened and I will not tolerate it. My brother is embarrassed. I promised him she would be gone by the time he rose from his bed, and that is all there is to it. But I suppose you've heard a different story from Lucy's biased perspective?'

I had to scoff at hearing that. As if Giles had not spun his brother a story to put him in a good light over my poor Lucy. 'No,' I said. 'Lucy has told me nothing. I saw it for myself, and I must tell you that you have the matter quite wrong.'

It was Richard who scoffed then. 'Wrong indeed!' he said. 'I saw the way she looked at him. If her playful flirtations could not be construed as leading a man on, then I do not know what could.'

'If Lucy was being at all playful towards Giles, then she was doing so only to be polite,' I said, growing more and more frustrated by my husband's one-sided opinion. 'When I saw the two of them together, your brother was practically forcing himself on poor Lucy. His behaviour was nothing short of monstrous. Now, you must go to Penzance and bring her back at once.'

Richard stood up, and I must confess that I cowered back a little. 'I will do no such thing, woman!' he said. 'Do you not see? It does not matter who did what between them. My brother's embarrassment remains. It cannot be undone. It can merely be eased by their separation. Simply put, one of them had to go.'

I gave a huff and turned away, no longer able to look at Richard. 'Then it should have been Giles you took to Penzance this morning,' I said, and then I left, no more satisfied with the situation than when I had arrived.

It was not as if Richard liked his brother, which made me wonder why he would take his side in the matter. And yet, for reasons I still cannot fathom, he had invited him to stay at Crows-an-Wra Manor. If Richard wanted good reason to ask him to leave again, there it was, but he had not taken the opportunity to do so. I pondered over this all the way back to my room, concluding that it was likely because of the class difference. A gentleman is never wrong, after all, or so Richard apparently believed. Or was there more to this curious relationship that existed between them? I made a mental note to be particularly observant around them in future.

CHAPTER TWENTY-FIVE

I was beginning to feel like a prisoner in my own home. I should have liked to take myself off in the carriage to Penzance, if not to look for Lucy myself, because she was in all likelihood long gone by now, then for the variety, but once again Richard would not hear of it. That aside, my solitude was in part self-inflicted, I knew, but here was yet another day in my humdrum life where I had chosen to remain in my room so as to avoid seeing any-one, for I could not bear to look upon Giles Trevelyan's face again. Neither did I much care to see my husband after what he had done.

It was the middle of the afternoon, and I was close to finishing Robinson Crusoe, at the section of the book concerning the fight between Friday and a bear, when I was disturbed by a knock at my door.

'Come in!' I called, sitting up in my chair by the win-dow to see who it was.

It was Cobb, and for once I was glad to see her – glad, at least, that it was not my husband or his wretched brother.

'Pardon the intrusion, madam,' Cobb said with a bow, 'but Mr Trevelyan sent me to ask you to come to his study.'

'His study?' I said, intrigued.

'That's right, madam. He says he has something he wants to show you.'

'Does he indeed?' I said, closing my book.

My first reaction was to send Cobb back to my husband to tell him that I could not come – that I had a screaming headache on account of the upset he had caused me – but to be invited to his study, when he had reminded me in no uncertain terms that very morning that I was not welcome in that room, had already filled me with curiosity. And whatever did he have to show me that I could possibly be interested in after he had so cruelly taken sides with his brother earlier? Of course, I had to find out.

'Very well,' I said, getting to my feet. 'I take it he means to see me this instant?'

'More or less, madam,' Cobb said. 'As soon as it pleases you was his actual words.'

I smiled to myself. It did not please me, not at all, but what choice did I have? It did please me, however, to keep Richard waiting, so I settled back into my chair and opened my book again, intent on finishing it first.

'Then I shall see him shortly,' I told Cobb. 'You are dismissed.'

'Very good, madam,' Cobb said, curtseying slightly before she turned on her heel and left.

I must confess that I was far too curious to know what Richard wanted to show me, and in his study of all places, to concentrate on the remainder of my book, so I did not keep him waiting quite as long as I'd hoped to. No more than ten minutes had passed when I closed the book again with a snap and made my way down to his study. When I arrived, however, and raised my hand in readiness to knock on the door this time, I froze. I could hear voices inside. Richard was talking to someone. I looked around me to ensure I was alone in the hallway, and then I listened more closely to determine who else was there. It was that wretched brother of his.

'I've been thinking about our little arrangement, Richard,' I heard Giles say. I thought he sounded smug about something. 'A generous monthly allowance and a roof over my head here in our ancestral home is all well and good, but it simply won't do.'

'What more do you want?' Richard asked, and I could tell from his tone that his mood had not improved a jot since I last saw him.

'Oh, I don't know,' Giles said. 'How about a little country pile of my own? Nothing as grand as Crows-an-Wra Manor, of course, but something comfortable.'

There was silence. I looked around me again, conscious of my eavesdropping, to be sure that I was still alone. The last thing I wanted was for Mariah to come along and catch me with my ear pressed to the keyhole.

'And if I agree?' Richard said, pausing again as his voice trailed off as if in thought. 'That will be the end of the matter?'

'For now, yes,' Giles said. 'But we'll have to see, won't we? I mean, all the while you expect me to keep your little secret, surely I should expect you to pay for it.'

There was silence again as Richard considered his answer. It gave me time to ruminate over what I had just heard. What secret was Giles referring to? It was certainly nothing I was privy to, but it explained a lot. So this was the reason Giles had been invited to stay, and why Richard had sided with him over Lucy's dismissal. I could only conclude that whatever this secret was, it was of a most serious nature, given my husband's long-standing resentment of his brother. I heard a coarse clearing of the throat then, which was something I had noticed Richard did from time to time, when he was feeling particularly uncomfortable about something.

'Very well, I'll buy you your house,' Richard said, 'and I'll give you a generous sum of money to go with it if you'll leave here within the week and never return.'

'That's very generous of you, I'm sure,' Giles said, still with that same haughty smugness about him, 'but you know I'm no good with money. It has a way of slipping through my fingers all too quickly.'

I was startled then by what sounded like something being slammed down on the desk. It caused me to recoil from the door a little.

'Get out of my sight!' Richard yelled. 'You may have the run of this house for now, but you are not welcome here in my study.'

'Oh, I'm going, don't you worry,' Giles said. 'I'll let you know when I've found somewhere – shouldn't be too long, given that money is no object.'

I was about to run from the door, thinking that I would not now be welcome in Richard's study either, given the even more foul mood his brother had put him in, but just as I began to turn away, the door shot open and Giles saw me standing there.

'Hello, what's this?' he said, studying me curiously as he stepped out and pulled the door shut behind him. 'Been out here long, have you?'

I tried to conceal what must have appeared to be an awkward expression with a smile. 'No,' I said, in a very matter-of-fact way. 'I just arrived. My husband has asked to see me.'

'Has he indeed?' Giles said, stepping aside and gesturing to the door. 'Well, don't let me keep you. He seems to have had enough of my company for now. Perhaps you'll fare better.'

I wanted to tell him that I had had enough of his company, too, but I bit my tongue. I passed him without further discourse and entered my husband's study, closing the door behind me with a click.

'Ah, Grace,' Richard said. He sounded as weary as when I had last left him sitting there behind his desk. 'I can't begin to tell you how pleased I am to see you again.'

I was surprised to hear him say that after all I had just heard. 'Because of Giles?' I said, supposing that had to be the reason. I noticed then that he had been pulling at his sideburns, no doubt in frustration over the matter.

'Yes, because of him, and after this morning I had my doubts that you'd care to see me again today, or tomorrow for that matter. I take it you saw Giles on your way here?'

'Yes, I did,' I said, raising my eyebrows. 'Right outside your study door, as a matter of fact.' I was not about to pretend to Richard that I had not been outside all this time and had not heard a word of what was said. While a husband may not be expected to divulge every trial and tribulation to his wife, I felt that this was of a serious enough nature to press the matter a little. 'I heard something of your conversation,' I added. 'He's blackmailing you, isn't he?'

Richard stood up, and I noticed then that his features

suddenly took on a wary appearance. 'It is of no importance,' he said, shaking his head as if to dismiss it altogether. 'A trifling matter you need not worry yourself over.'

'If it is of no matter,' I said, 'then why do you not send him on his way?'

Richard sighed again and sat down. He did not look at me for several seconds, focusing instead on the papers that cluttered his desk. When he looked at me again, he said, 'Very well, I shall. By the end of the week, I promise. Will that suffice for now?'

'Yes,' I said. How could I say otherwise? Even though Richard had not actually divulged anything, it was enough to know that Giles Trevelyan would not be staying with us for much longer. 'And thank you,' I added, feeling obliged to do so. 'Crows-an-Wra Manor will be a far happier place without your brother beneath its roof.'

'Hear, hear!' Richard said. He smiled at me then, and it was quite unexpected. 'Now, don't you want to know why I asked to see you?'

In truth, I had forgotten all about it. 'Yes, of course.'

'Then come around here beside me and take a look at these plans for your Italian garden by the lake. I had intended to keep them as a surprise for your birthday, but I felt the need to make up for this business with Lucy.'

If there was any trace of the conversation I had overheard still lingering in my mind, it left me that instant. I leaned over the plans, stroking the back of Richard's head as I began to study them. 'You can be very sweet, Richard,' I said. 'To think that you've had all this drawn up for me when you have so many more important things to attend to.'

'I may seem aloof to you at times, my darling, but I

know where my priorities lie. Now tell me, is this the kind of garden you were hoping for?'

I didn't know where to begin answering the question. It was so much more than I'd hoped for. There were a number of marks on the plan, representing a plethora of statuary. My pergola was there, abutting the lake, and behind it was what appeared to be a sunken amphitheatre, which was something I had not considered. If that was not enough, it was located at the centre of a boxwood maze. At least, I imagined it would be created from the Buxus sempervirens.

'What are these circles on the lake?' I asked, indicating them on the drawing. 'Are they fountains?'

'Of course. What Italian garden would be complete without at least one?'

'But there are so many.'

'The more the merrier, I thought,' Richard said. 'To own the truth, I've always thought the lake needed a fountain or two. Do you remember the gardens at Tivoli?'

'How could I forget them?' I said, recalling the wonderful Neptune fountain and the water organ behind it.

'Well, I can't promise you anything quite as grand as that, but you shall have jets of water that reach just as high, assuming the architect of these plans can fulfil his promises.'

'Oh, Richard, I don't know what to say.'

'Then don't say anything,' Richard said. He turned and kissed me, his lips lingering on mine in such a way that I had not felt since we returned from Europe.

'But the east wing,' I said, when at last we separated. I quickly calculated the months that had passed since the fire happened. Last September, Richard had told me, and it was now August. 'It's been almost a year since the fire. As much as I'd love to see the work on my Italian garden commence now that the plans have been drawn, the restoration of the east wing must take priority. I cannot be selfish in the matter.'

'Nonsense,' Richard said. 'And it was barely seven months ago. You shall have your garden just as soon as it can be created.'

'Seven months?' I said, wondering how I could have been mistaken. I distinctly recalled Richard saying it had happened last September, two months before we met.

'That's right,' Richard said. 'Should I not know the month well enough?'

'Yes, of course,' I said, sure that he had to be right. How could any man so quickly forget the month of his wife's death, especially when it occurred in such a tragically memorable manner?

But what did it mean? Richard had clearly lied to me about it, but why? It dawned on me then that it meant we had met before the fire, not after, as I had always believed. Was his lie simply to conceal the fact that his first wife was still alive when our courtship began? It was a plausible explanation, but it left me wondering whether there was more to it.

CHAPTER TWENTY-SIX

Rosen

Richard came to me again last night.

He had not called upon me to satisfy his carnal needs in months, and not once since his new wife arrived at Crows-an-Wra Manor. Why had he done so again now? What had changed? I imagined he must have become displeased with her, and I took some comfort from the thought. Perhaps she would not let him do the things to her that I was powerless to prevent?

Or was there another reason?

I stirred from a fitful sleep with another familiar headache and pulled the bedcovers up around me. There was daylight at the little window above me, which was covered with condensation, the air in my room now thankfully so much cooler than it had been. Was it yet September? I imagined it was, if barely. I think a week must have passed since I heard Mariah talking to the maid, Lucy, and I had drawn attention to myself by screaming and banging on the shutters, but nothing had come of it. I had not heard her voice again, and I truly feared for her.

Since then, I had been the good girl I had promised Mariah I would be, made so by her threat to harm my Sophia if I was not. How could she say such a thing? I had told myself over and over that Mariah could not harm her own granddaughter, but how could I know? Before this cruel fate befell me, I would have thought her incapable of a great many things, but I no longer knew her, or the dark thoughts that occupied her mind.

I wiped the sleep from my eyes, and as I did so I heard a sound by the lower hatch. I quickly sat up. There was a bowl of food and a cup of water on the floor. Yes, I was being given food and water again for my good behaviour.

'Mariah?' I called, supposing the sound of the hatch opening had awoken me, as it sometimes did. 'Are you still there?'

I was sure the hatch had only just closed. I listened, but I could not hear anyone stepping away from the door.

'Jenken? Is that you?'

I got up and went to the door as quietly as I could. I thought I could hear breathing – heavy breathing. It was not Mariah.

'Jenken, I know you're there. Please talk to me.'

Several seconds passed. Then at last he spoke.

'I brought you a book,' he said, speaking in a whisper, presumably because he had been told never to speak to me, and he did not want Mariah to find out.

I looked down at my feet and saw it. Jenken knew how much I loved to read. He would often find me in the grounds somewhere, lost in a book. I stooped and picked it up. It was the first volume of Gulliver's Travels. I rose again, thinking there were few books better capable of transporting the mind to the far-away places I had come to crave. 'Thank you, Jenken. Is it our secret? Should I hide it from Mariah?'

'Our secret,' Jenken repeated, and I imagined him nodding his head emphatically on the other side of the door.

Clearly, he had taken a risk by bringing it to me, and I had to smile to myself at his endearing stupidity. However would I have known to keep the book a secret from Mariah had I not awoken in time to speak with him and ask him? But that was Jenken. He was not the type to think too far ahead, as Mariah had recently reminded me, or of the consequences of his actions. I silently blessed him for it, and at the same time I wondered whether I could use that to my advantage. If I was ever to escape and be with my Sophia again, I would need help, and who better was there? Still, I had to be careful. I did not want to arouse his suspicion and turn him from me now that he had shown me this kindness. I had to gain his trust again first.

'Jenken,' I said, my mouth close to the door. 'Will you open the upper hatch so I can see you?'

'Not supposed to,' Jenken said.

'But will you, for me?'

Silence.

'I mustn't, really,' Jenken said, but I could tell from the uncertainty in his tone that he had been thinking about it.

'Then will you at least stay a while and talk with me? I miss having a friend to talk to.' I thought perhaps letting him know I still considered him my friend might help my situation.

'Not supposed to do that, either,' he said. 'I'd best be going.'

'Please wait!' I said with some urgency, hoping he would hear the desperation in my voice. 'Something's troubling me. Perhaps you can help.'

'What is it?'

'It concerns my husband's new wife, Grace. You know Grace, don't you?'

'I do.'

I had been thinking about the other possible reasons why Richard had come to me in the night again, and one stood out. 'She's with child, isn't she?' I said, knowing that if she were, then Richard likely considered his work done, and would not wish to go near Grace again in that way for fear of hurting the child growing inside her. 'Has her condition been announced yet?'

There was silence again. This time I half expected to hear Jenken walking away, but he did not.

'Yes,' he said a moment later, and I let go of the breath I had been holding. My supposition was correct. Now, although I had no reason to wish Grace well, I hoped for this unwitting interloper's sake that her child would be born a boy, for if she did not give Richard the son and heir he so desperately yearned for, I feared she might soon find herself lodging alongside me, or worse.

'Will that be all?' Jenken said, cutting into my thoughts.

'No, there's something else,' I said. 'If you will indulge me a moment longer.'

'Go on, then.'

What I said next I knew Jenken would not wish to hear, but I had to tell him the truth. 'I would never harm my daughter,' I said. 'I did not start that fire. I did not try to kill Sophia.'

'That's what she said you'd say. That's why she told me I must never speak to you.'

I had expected as much. I silently cursed Mariah for it. 'But I didn't do it!' I pleaded. 'You must believe me.'

I heard him walking away.

'Come back, Jenken, please! You've been told a lie. If Sophia's in danger from anyone, it's Mariah, not me.'

But Jenken did not come back.

CHAPTER TWENTY-SEVEN

Another week or so passed, this time in utter frustration. I had to speak with Jenken again, but the only person I had seen or heard since he brought me the copy of Gulliver's Travels to read was Mariah. I had formulated another plan to escape, a well-thought-out plan this time, and even if he did not yet know it, Jenken was vital to its success. I was also as bored as ever. I had quickly devoured my book, having read it by nightfall that day, and I craved another more than I had previously craved food in my belly when it was denied me. I did not know whether Jenken had intended to bring me more books, or why he had not since returned, but I had had to content myself with Lemuel Gulliver's adventures over and over, and had even taken to acting out the various parts for variety, filling my room with imaginary scenery and the voices of the cast. I prayed that Jenken had not told Mariah about our brief conversation, although I expected she would have had something to say about it if he had and she had said nothing. In truth, I thought

Mariah unusually quiet of late, rarely opening the upper hatch for longer than was necessary to look in on me.

It was raining today. The weather had certainly turned because it was also far cooler. Although I could not see the signs, I knew that autumn was under way. Before long it would be winter, and come January I would be commiserating, rather than commemorating, the first anniversary of my heinously unjust incarceration. But come January I would not be here – I could not be here. My latest plan to escape had to work. There was far too much at stake if it did not. If it did not, I was sure Mariah's punishment would kill me this time, and what of her threats regarding my Sophia? No, this time I had to succeed.

I was sitting in my armchair by the shutters, feeling a little uncomfortable because I had adopted the habit of hiding Gulliver's Travels beneath the cushion so that Mariah would not see it. It was late in the afternoon by now, and I had not been reading today, or acting out the parts. Today, I had sat in meditative silence, going through my plan over and over again in case I had missed something vital that might upset it. Getting Jenken on my side was paramount, and the answer to that problem had not come easily to me, but come it had. I had found a way to make him believe me – to see the truth for himself, if only he would look. That was the first part of my plan. With that accomplished, I merely had to fool Mariah into thinking I had somehow fled my room when I had not. Then I would slip out quietly to meet Jenken while she – and the remainder of the household for all I knew, for I was sure they had all been told the same lies – were out looking for me.

But wherever was Jenken?

I imagined something must have been keeping him busy, and all manner of reasons sprang to mind. At summer's end, there was always so much work to do in the grounds, and with so few staff now in service at the manor – so few people who could be trusted not to talk about the mad woman who tried to kill her daughter – there was every chance he had been called upon to help out there, too. There were also the demands I knew Sophia could so often place on him whenever she was bored and in need of someone to amuse her. Perhaps the answer was simply a combination of all of these things. I just had to be patient and bide my time, which was something, of course, that I had plenty of.

I settled my head back and gazed up at the grey skylight, wondering if I would ever be free to walk in the rain again. The sound it made as it hit the glass and the roof tiles above me was comforting in its way, but how I yearned to feel it against my skin, and to smell the damp ground at my feet. They are the simplest of things, but oh, how we miss what we once took for granted when it is denied us. I closed my eyes and tried to recall the memory of it, but even that which I had experienced so many times was beginning to fade. Instead, I listened, and so comforting was the sound that I quickly began to drift into a pleasant half-sleep that was filled with daydreams. One minute I was walking through a field of long meadow grass, and the next along the wide sandy beach at Sennen Cove where I used to take Sophia. I was sure I was smiling to myself as I dreamed, for I was laughing gaily in the rain, walking freely beneath it without a care.

A moment later – or so it seemed, because judging from the fading light at the window above me an hour or more must have passed – I was brought back to my dire reality by the sound of the lower hatch opening. I drew a sharp breath and sat up with a jolt, suddenly wide awake again, my eyes focused on the small opening. I was just in time to see my empty cup and bowl being slid out. Was that Jenken's hand? My heart began to race with hope, but the light in my room had by now faded so much that I could not be sure. I sat forward and squinted through the half-light, blinking several times the better to see. I held my breath as my second meal of the day was slid through the hatch, and then I let out a long sigh. The hand was too small to be Jenken's. It had to be Mariah again. When the upper hatch opened, it was confirmed.

'Bit of a treat for you tonight,' she said. 'Beef and potatoes, and a whole steamed carrot.'

Treats, though rare, always made me wary. Did this particular treat mean that Richard intended to visit me again? I hoped it simply meant that it was time for my bedding to be changed, and my body to be scrubbed rather than abused, but I feared the latter as I had not seen Richard since he had first started coming to me again over a week ago. Still, as unpleasant as the ordeal was for me, I could endure it for the greater purpose that lay ahead. I was hungry, and I had to keep up my strength in order to give myself the best chance of escaping when the time came.

'Thank you,' I said, rising from my armchair.

I went to the door and looked down at my plate. It was equally rare for my meals to be served on a plate rather than in a bowl – dry food of any kind being unusual. It typically consisted of broths and stews, which could easily hide Mariah's sleeping draughts. It made me less wary, although it was easy to imagine that the substance had been ground into the seasoning, the taste disguised by too much salt and pepper. Perhaps that had always been the way of it.

Mariah began to close the hatch, but I could not let her go just yet. I was too keen to understand the reason for Jenken's absence, and more importantly to know if and when he was likely to return.

'How are things at the house?' I asked, thinking that I could hardly be direct about it.

Mariah fully opened the hatch again and studied me with suspicion. I swear it was as if she already knew that I had no real interest in the goings on at the house, but was in fact fishing for something else entirely. 'Busy,' she said, her tone quick, her eyes boring into mine as she tried to work out what I really wanted to know. She took a guess. 'You want to know about that maid, Lucy, don't you?'

I could see why Mariah might think that. I knew Lucy had heard me that day. She knew I was here, or at least that someone was. For a time, I had pinned a certain degree of hope on her talking about what she had heard, and that in time questions might have been asked about who was being kept at the cottage like a dog, living on scraps from the kitchen.

Confident that she was right, Mariah continued. 'She's gone,' she said, smiling to herself. 'So don't expect any salvation from her.'

'She's gone because of me?'

'Yes, of course. Whom else?' Mariah said with impatience. 'Because of you, I've wanted her gone from the day she arrived. I was fearful from one hour to the next that she might discover you, and then she did.'

'Is that why things are so busy at the house?' I said, bringing the conversation back to what I was really interested in. 'Because there's one less maid to help out?'

'That, yes, and because Richard's new wife has everyone involved in her preparations for the Italian garden she's been promised – even the cook!'

Mariah spoke with such vehemence that it was as if she no longer cared to speak Grace's name. 'And Jenken, too, no doubt,' I said, eager to hear her reply.

Mariah scoffed. 'She has Jenken running around all day with sticks, poking them into the ground by the lake, moving them here and there as she sets out the dimensions for this feature and that, so keen is she to have it all just so. When Jenken is not at her beck and call, he hardly has time left to attend to his own duties in the grounds, let alone help out elsewhere, but I intend to put a stop to it.' She took a short step away from the hatch and sighed to herself. 'There,' she added, sounding frustrated. 'Is that enough news of the household for you?'

It was. Mariah had told me exactly why Jenken had not returned to me, and above all that he would likely do so again very soon. I nodded, and without another word between us, the hatch closed.

CHAPTER
TWENTY-EIGHT

Grace

'Further!' I called to Cobb, the string held tightly between us. 'That's it. Now a little to your left.'

I was out by the lake, making the finishing touches to the layout for my Italian garden. I pulled down the wide brim of my hat to shield my eyes from the sun's glare so that I could better see her precise location, which was perhaps a hundred feet away.

'There!' I said, holding my arm up to signal her to stop.

I reached into the pocket of the apron I had borrowed from Mrs Pengelly's kitchen and pulled out another of the wooden stakes I had had Jenken make for me, this one painted blue to mark out the statuary walkway that would run alongside the lake towards the terrace at the rear of the house. I watched Cobb kneel down and hammer her stake into the ground where I had indicated, and then I did the same, pulling the string tight before tying it off. Although dry today, the ground was thankfully soft, if a little muddy in places from the recent rain. I doubted that even the sharpest of Jenken's stakes could have penetrated the summer-baked ground a month ago. Standing up again, my hands on my hips, I surveyed our work. It was all a bit of fun, and quite unnecessary, Richard had said, but I wanted to get involved, and I had so little else to do with my time.

The maze had already been marked out, and Jenken had been most useful there, although Mariah had told me just the day before that he could no longer be spared – that he was already behind with his duties on account of my Italian garden and had far more important things to attend to. In truth, I thought her manner a little brusque to the point of being rude about it, but I saw her point, which was why I had enlisted Cobb's help for the finishing touches. I had asked Sophia initially, convinced that it would help bring us closer together, but she told me she thought it a silly garden and wanted no part of it. Although she would not admit it, I suspect it was she who had begun to remove and reposition some of my stakes during the early part of my preparations. That is, until Mariah gave her a stiff talking-to, keen as she was to see the back of it so that I would no longer tie up the servants' time. I was fortunate that Cobb had been allowed to help me finish up.

I was beginning to warm to Ada Cobb. I think she liked working outside, rather than being cooped up in the house all day and night. I even caught her smiling at me once, when I pulled the string too tightly before she had managed to tie it off and it pinged from her hands. I waved to her to come back to me for the next length of string.

'Ada!' I called. Yes, I was even addressing her by her first name now, as I had with Lucy. I think she liked the familiarity, too, but unlike Lucy, Cobb remained too mindful of her station in life to let it show. 'We'll do the other side now,' I said to her as she approached.

'Very good, madam,' she said, as conservative with her words as ever. I was still having a difficult time getting her to talk more openly to me.

I snipped the ball of string with my scissors where I had tied it to the stake and handed the loose end to her. 'You're not married, are you?' I said. 'You have no children?' I had not considered it before, but now that I was myself with child, I had become more mindful of such things.

'No, madam. Not exactly.'

'How do you mean?'

A frown set into Cobb's brow. 'I mean there was someone, but we never married, and there was a child. Darling little boy, he was. Died of the cholera before his first birthday.'

'I'm so sorry to hear that.'

'Probably for the best. I could hardly feed myself at the time.'

She sounded so sad as she spoke that I wanted to put my arms around her, but instead I gave her the kindest, most sympathetic smile I could muster. It was heartfelt. I could only pray that my own child suffered no such fate.

'Here,' I said, handing her another stake to take our minds off the matter, but just then a cry went up from the terrace. It was Jenken.

'Ada!' he called. 'You're to come at once! We've got visitors.'

'Visitors?' I said, as much to myself as to Cobb, questioning the likelihood. 'I wonder who it could be.'

Whoever it was, I had not been informed of their visit, and judging from the urgency in both Jenken's step and his tone, I suspected that no one else at Crows-an-Wra Manor had, either.

I heard loud talking as soon as I went back into the house. The parlour doors were open and an indiscernible number of male voices were spilling out. Who were they? Why were they here? I wanted to run up to my room and quickly change out of my mud-streaked dress and boots, but I was too eager to find out. I untied the bow beneath my chin and removed my hat as I walked, slowing a little, mindful that I did not arrive in the parlour out of breath or, heaven forbid, having broken out with perspiration. I saw Richard first. He had his back to me and was in his shirtsleeves. Presumably he had not been allowed time to see to his attire either. Standing before him in their tailcoats were three other men of no acquaintance to me, their hats uniformly clutched beneath their arms.

'Richard,' I said, smiling as I approached them. 'You did not tell me we were expecting company.' I looked down at my clothes and laughed. 'I might have dressed more appropriately if you had.'

Richard turned to face me, but it was one of the other men who answered. He was an ox of a man with a balding pate and a day's stubble on his chin. He gave me a courteous bow. 'Forgive us, madam,' he said. 'The blame rests entirely at our feet. Our arrival at Crows-an-Wra Manor was not pre-arranged.'

One of the other men drew my attention then. He

was a younger man, clean-shaven and only marginally less heavily set. 'You must be Grace,' he said with a bow. 'We've been looking forward to meeting you ever since we received notice of your marriage to our niece's father.'

'Yes indeed,' said the third man with enthusiasm, and when he spoke I could not help but stare at him. He was the younger man's twin, down to every small detail.

'Do excuse me,' I said, realising that I had been staring at them both far longer than was polite. I smiled again to hide my embarrassment. 'Yes, I am Grace Trevelyan.' I put my arm through Richard's. 'Will you not introduce us more formally, Richard?'

Richard cleared his throat. 'Of course,' he said. 'Where are my manners? Grace, these three gentlemen are my late wife's brothers.' He held his hand out towards the eldest of the three. 'This is Jago Blake,' he said, 'and beside him, Harry and John.' Richard laughed awkwardly to himself. 'I swear for the life of me, I never know which is which!'

One of the twins stepped forward and bowed his head. The only way I could differentiate them was by the colour of their tailcoats. This fellow's was dark green, while the other's was blue.

'I'm John,' he said. Then he, too, gave a small laugh and, glancing back at his twin, added, 'It is a simple matter to tell us apart, for it is plain to see that I am by far the more handsome.'

Harry laughed with him and playfully slapped his brother's shoulder. 'If not the more modest!' he said. He bowed his head and added, 'I'm sure I speak for all three of us when I say that we're very pleased to make your acquaintance, Mrs Trevelyan.'

'And I yours,' I said, smiling in turn at each of them,

noting as I did so that Jago did not return my smile. He was studying me, and I could only suppose it was because he wished to get the measure of the woman who now stood in his late sister's place. My eyes did not linger on his. In truth I found his stare a little unsettling, so I turned back to the twins, whose demeanour seemed far more agreeable. 'And what is the nature of your visit?' I asked them, certain that it could not merely be to satisfy Jago's curiosity about the new mistress of Crows-an-Wra Manor.

'We have come to see our niece,' John said.

'Yes, it's been far too long and we miss her,' Harry added.

Jago stepped forward and placed a hand on Richard's shoulder. I could see at once how ill at ease it made him. 'I trust Sophia is well?' Jago said, narrowing his eyes. His questioning tone sounded almost threatening.

Richard laughed it off. He took a step back and Jago's arm fell to his side. 'Yes, of course she is. Why ever would she be otherwise?'

'I saw her tutor recently,' Jago said. 'He told me his services here had been discontinued, which is understandable given that Sophia was sent away for a time, but what of her formal education now that she's back?'

'Her formal education?' Richard repeated. 'What need does Sophia have of a formal education? She can already read and write remarkably well for her years, and she will marry well, too. In time she will resume her appreciation of music and dance, flower arranging and so forth, as befits a gentleman's wife.' He paused to catch his breath. 'I'll thank you not to tell me how to bring up my own daughter,' he added. 'I've sent Mother to find her. They should be along soon. Here, let me take your hats. You must be tired of holding them by now.'

I watched Richard collect their hats and set them down in a neat line on the table by the fireplace. Then he went to the drinks cabinet.

'Brandy, anyone?' he said as he poured himself one. 'Some sherry for you, darling? Madeira perhaps? It's a little early for tea.'

I saw that the three brothers looked keen and I didn't wish to be the odd one out. 'Madeira, thank you,' I said. 'Just a small one.'

Richard poured the drink and handed it to me. Then he passed a glass of brandy to each of our guests. 'To your good health,' he said, raising his glass. 'Now, where the devil is that maid? A man cannot be expected to pour too many drinks in his own home, and collect hats, for heaven's sake.'

'I heard Jenken say that Mrs Pengelly needed her in the kitchen,' I said. 'You gentlemen will join us for something to eat?'

'Thank you,' Jago said. 'We would be most delighted.'

At that moment, the parlour door burst open and Sophia came running in, pushing a toy perambulator ahead of her. She was full of smiles as soon as she saw who was there to see her.

'Uncle Jago!' she squealed.

She ran to him and leaped into his arms, and only then did I see Jago smile.

'Steady, Sophia!' he said. 'Look, now I've spilled my brandy.' He put her down again and she leaped at each of the twins in a similar fashion.

'Uncle Harry! Uncle John!' she cried, seeming to have no difficulty at all telling them apart.

They both began to laugh at her exuberance. 'I swear

you've grown two inches taller since I last saw you,' John said, and as soon as he put her down, she began to look about the room, her smile gradually turning to a frown.

'Where's Uncle Edward?' she said. 'Is he unwell?'

The laughter died down almost immediately. A moment later I caught the twins exchanging awkward glances, and noted that their features had darkened. Jago's expression was suddenly no less serious.

'In a manner of speaking, yes,' he said. 'Though what ails him he brought upon himself.'

'Has he been drinking too much wine again?' Sophia asked. 'Mother always said it would make him ill some day.'

Harry scoffed. 'It certainly makes him behave ill,' he said, addressing John, but everyone could hear him.

'Yes,' John agreed, 'but he'll think twice next time.'

'Harry, John,' Jago warned. 'Not now.'

Where was Edward indeed? I must confess to wanting the twins to continue right there and then, but clearly Jago did not feel it a suitable subject for Sophia's young ears.

'Sophia,' Jago continued, 'I thought your grandmother had gone to fetch you, but where is she? Did you run here so fast with your perambulator that her old legs fell behind?'

He was smiling heartily at Sophia as he finished speaking, and Sophia beamed back at him. She skipped over to him, quite the little darling. I wondered whether her uncles really knew her as I did. But how could they, or anyone else for that matter? No one else was trying to fill her dead mother's shoes as I was.

'She told me her head hurts,' Sophia said. 'She's gone to her cottage to lie down.'

'Her cottage?' Jago said, looking to Richard for explanation. 'Does she expect us to visit with her there before we leave?'

Richard coughed into his brandy and drained the glass. 'No,' he said, firmly shaking his head. 'My mother has taken to living in the gatekeeper's cottage because she prefers her privacy. We must respect her wishes.'

John gave a humourless laugh. 'A headache be damned! She means to avoid us. That's what it is.'

'John!' Jago snapped. 'I shall not tell you again.'

John drew a deep breath, as if frustrated by the obvious hierarchy that existed between the twins and their older brother. 'But you know she does not like us, Jago,' he persisted, unwilling to let the matter go.

'She has never liked any one of us,' Harry added in his twin's defence.

Richard spoke up then. 'I am quite sure my mother likes you all as well as anyone,' he said. 'Her head pains her, as you have heard. Mariah would not lie to her own granddaughter. Perhaps she will join us presently for our meal.'

As if oblivious to the tension building in the room, Sophia giggled to herself and skipped away from the gathering, drawing everyone's attention. 'Don't you want to see what I have in my perambulator?' she asked as soon as she reached it. It was half the size of a real perambulator, with a gleaming white undercarriage and a navy-blue half-canopy. She wheeled it closer, and I was naturally curious to see what was inside.

'Is it your favourite doll?' I guessed, thinking that was most likely.

Sophia shook her head.

'Potatoes for Mrs Pengelly?' Richard joked.

Sophia laughed so much at the idea that it bent her double. 'No, silly!'

'Then whatever can it be?' I asked, smiling along with everyone.

'It's your baby,' she said, inviting me to look more closely. 'Father said he couldn't wait for my little brother to be born, so I made one.'

'A baby!' Jago said with hearty enthusiasm.

'Congratulations!' all three of the brothers seemed to say at once.

I was now all the more keen to see the contents of Sophia's perambulator. I leaned in, and what I saw drained the smile from my face in an instant. I drew a sharp breath. 'It's hideous!' I gasped, stepping away again. 'Get it away from me!' I screamed, without a care for whose company I was in.

As if to contradict my reaction, Sophia began to laugh again. She pointed her finger at me and laughed so fully at her joke, as she must have seen it, that I wanted to slap her insufferable little face. Inside her perambulator was a doll of sorts, but it was no fitting toy for a child. It was a dead squirrel, dressed in dolls' clothing. Its head was squashed and deformed as though it had been captured in one of Jenken's traps, its skull later smashed with a rock, and it was crawling with maggots. I was horrified that Sophia had created this monstrosity as a substitute for my baby, of all things. And yet here she was, laughing at me. I could not stand to look at the wretched child a moment longer.

'Sophia!' Richard scolded, even before he had seen it. 'What have you done?'

Everyone gathered around the perambulator to take a look, while I retreated further into the parlour to distance myself from it. I sat down before I fell down. Then I heard at least one of Sophia's uncles laugh to himself. Not openly, but in that quiet way one does when one knows it is wrong to do so. I am sure he must have thought it all meant in good-natured humour, but I could not see a humorous side to the matter.

And still Sophia's laughter mocked me.

I saw Cobb enter the room then, her face a picture of bewilderment, as she no doubt wondered what all the fuss was about. 'Mrs Pengelly sent me to say that the meal will be ready in ten minutes,' she said, trying to get a peek at the contents of the perambulator herself.

Richard turned to her. 'Good,' he said as he wheeled the perambulator to the door, where she was standing. 'Take my daughter and this hideous thing away with you. It's stinking the place out. And see to it that Sophia is thoroughly washed.'

'No!' Sophia yelled. 'I want to stay with my uncles.'

'Very good, sir,' Cobb said, ignoring her. She looked inside the perambulator and pulled a sour face. 'What do you want me to do with it, sir?'

'Burn it, woman!' Richard said. 'Give it to Jenken. He'll know what to do.'

'Very good, sir.'

Cobb took Sophia by the wrist and led her out, almost dragging her as she awkwardly wheeled the perambulator away. Even now, Sophia would not let up.

'It's far prettier than your baby's going to be!' she called from the hallway.

Richard poured me another glass of Madeira and stood beside my chair. 'I'm so sorry,' he said, handing the drink to me. It was a full glass this time, and I needed it. 'I can only imagine her mother's death has taken a far greater toll on her young mind than any of us imagined. I'm sure it will pass in time.'

'I hope so, Richard,' I said. 'She's gone too far this time. I really don't know how much more I can take.'

Sophia's last remark had left everyone looking grim-faced.

'If she were a boy, I would have beaten him,' Jago said. 'Family or not.'

The remark caused Richard to grit his teeth, and I understood why. He had never, to my knowledge, condoned any form of violence where Sophia was concerned, and despite everything that had just happened, I suddenly found myself regretting my earlier desire to slap her face. She was just a child, after all. She had lost her mother. She needed love and kindness – if only she would allow me to show it to her. If only she would accept me.

Richard turned slowly to Jago and his brothers. 'I suppose that's what happened to Edward, is it?'

Jago's features darkened. He stepped closer to Richard until there was less than an arm's length between them. 'Any man who abuses his wife deserves a beating, sir!' Jago said. 'Do not presume to judge how I mete out my justice.'

Harry and John sidled up beside Jago.

'He had to be taught a lesson,' Harry said. 'His wounds will heal.'

John nodded. 'Yes, but he'll think twice before he raises his hand to his wife again.'

'If he does,' Jago said, his face reddening, 'I swear it will be the end of him. I don't care who he is. He's been warned.'

Richard said no more about the matter. Instead, he

went to the drinks table and poured himself another glass of brandy. I saw that his hands were shaking as he did so, and as he turned to me I noticed there was sweat on his brow, and wondered what had come over him.

Quite unexpectedly, Jago began to laugh. 'But what's all this talk of violence?' he said. 'If the dining table is prepared, shall we not eat and be merry? I'm positively famished.' He slapped Richard on the back. 'You know, Richard, Edward could learn a thing or two from you. Perhaps you'll have a word with him. Our sister never had a bad word to say about you. You were always so kind and considerate to her.'

As I took Richard's arm and we all made our way to the dining room, I shuddered to think what such men would have done to him had he not been.

CHAPTER TWENTY-NINE

Rosen

I had an embroidery needle and three colourful lengths of silk: one green, one yellow and one violet. I knew they were a bribe to keep me busy, and above all quiet, but I didn't mind. I was so happy to be able to embroider again, although my fingers were no longer as steady as they once had been. So many things about me had begun to deteriorate since my incarceration that I did not care to think of my condition a year from now. If indeed I was alive by then. I knew the silks were a bribe because Mariah had not left me once since she brought them to me, all red-faced and flustered, and because she had done so no more than a few minutes after I heard a carriage arriving. Few sounds escaped my ears these days, and the sound of carriage wheels echoing in the chimney was unmistakeable. There had been visitors at Crows-an-Wra Manor, of that I was in no doubt. Who they were was another matter entirely.

I did not ask Mariah who it was. What purpose was there in knowing? I was dead, after all, and they had not come to see me. I was, however, grateful they had come, because during their visit I had been able to embroider several pretty violas with yellow faces into the white fabric of my nightgown, all under the watchful eyes of my keeper. When I heard the carriage leave again, I drew no attention to the fact that I had heard it, for I was sure Mariah had not, but she was soon made aware. Jenken must have thought I could not hear him as he came to her and told her, but his footsteps on the stairs, and his whispers outside my door, were clear enough to my sensitive ears. Needless to say, when Mariah eventually left me, she made me give back the needle and silks.

Jenken...

It was dark now. Bathed in moonlight I sat by the door, staring at the lower hatch as I waited for my evening meal to arrive. Would he come today? If he did, would he stay long enough to talk to me and let me prove to him that I was innocent of the lies levelled against me? If he would listen, I would show him without a doubt that he had been lied to.

If he would listen.

I had grown accustomed to disappointment where Jenken was concerned. At times, since discovering his complicity, I had wondered whether Mariah would ever let him bring my meals to me again, but with so few servants and so much to do, how could she not? Of all the dreary days that had passed since I formed my plan to escape and be with my Sophia again, I was sure that today was the day; visitors, whoever they were, surely meant there would be things to do at the manor, and now they had gone and there was no longer the need for Mariah to keep such a close eye on me, she would no doubt relish the opportunity to be free of me for a while.

But where was Jenken?

Although I could not be sure, I felt that it was already past my usual mealtime. The nights were fast drawing in, making it difficult to tell from one week to the next what time of day it was, but there were other signs. When the wind was blowing in the right direction, I could sometimes sit at the fireplace and hear the chimes of the parish church. I had not heard them lately, but three days ago their faint ringing had told me it was eight o'clock and my meal arrived very shortly afterwards. Then, it had not long been dark. Now, it felt as if I had been sitting in the moonlight for at least an hour, so it was perhaps as late as nine.

Maybe I was to receive no meal tonight.

Whether through boredom or physical weakness, my eyelids suddenly began to feel heavy. I pinched my skin through my nightgown until it stung, but it offered only temporary reprieve from the drowsiness that arrived in waves, one after another, each more difficult to fight off than the last. I had to stay awake. I went to stand up, thinking to pace my room, but then I saw light in the cracks around the door frame – the amber glow of an oil lamp. I settled again and watched as the lamp's intensity grew. Then at last the lower hatch opened and my meal was slid through. My heart began to race. It was not Mariah's bony hand I saw.

It was Jenken.

'Jenken?' I said, speaking softly so as not to alarm him.

I watched his hand pause briefly as I spoke. Then he quickly withdrew it and closed the hatch.

'Jenken, please don't go!' I said. 'I must speak with you.' The light that filled the cracks around the door remained and I edged closer. 'Please open the upper hatch so I can see you.'

I waited. The hatch did not open, but neither did Jenken leave. That was a good start, but I had to mind my words this time. I had to keep him there long enough to convince him that he had been lied to.

'I promise I would never do anything to harm Sophia,' I said, and I immediately heard a shuffling sound on the other side of the door, as if Jenken were about to go. 'I've been locked away in this room for another reason,' I quickly added, 'and I can prove it.'

The air fell silent again. A moment later, Jenken said, 'How?'

'Open the upper hatch and I'll tell you,' I said, sure now that I had interested him enough to stay and hear what I had to say.

There followed a good deal of huffing and sighing on the other side of the door, as though Jenken were fighting with his conscience over whether or not he should disregard this most sacrosanct of Mariah's orders. Then his curiosity clearly got the better of him because the upper hatch slowly opened and his large, weather-worn face filled the frame. The deep lines on his skin were accentuated by the lamplight.

'Be quick!' he said in a whisper.

I smiled at him, just for the joy of seeing his face again at last, although he offered me nothing but a grim expression in return. 'I shall,' I said, 'but you must first ask yourself how it is that my husband was free to marry again. We are not, after all, divorced. Such a thing is rarely granted, as I'm sure you're aware. How is it, then, that my husband has a new wife while I still live?'

My question was met with a blank expression.

'I am not mad, Jenken,' I continued. 'Nor am I dangerous, especially not to my Sophia. There can be only one answer to my question. As far as the world beyond Crows-an-Wra Manor is concerned, I am dead. Mariah did not tell you that. Did she? But how could she, when she has in part charged you with my care?'

Jenken looked confused. That was good. Perhaps he was beginning to question what he had been told.

'Can you not now see for yourself that you've been lied to?' I asked. 'They have told you I am mad and dangerous – that I started the fire to kill my daughter so that you would help them to keep me locked away here, when it was my husband who started the fire so that he could make everyone believe I was dead. Even poor Sophia believes I died in that fire, yet you know I did not.' I felt my lower lip begin to tremble at the thought and I paused. 'Richard did all this because I could not give him a son. Now, perhaps, his new wife will. Don't you see it?'

Jenken drew a deep breath. His brow set into deep furrows as he continued to think over what he had heard. A moment later, he said, 'You told me you could prove it. How?'

'You can prove it for yourself,' I said. 'All you have to do is go to the churchyard at St Buryan and look for my grave. Another woman's body was buried there in my place. Once you see it you will know I'm telling you the truth, and that you've been spun a web of lies.'

I studied Jenken's face, trying to gauge his response, but he gave nothing away. 'Please!' I implored him. 'Go and see for yourself. Then perhaps you may find it in your heart to help me.'

All Jenken said in reply was, 'We'll see.'
Then he closed the hatch.

CHAPTER THIRTY

Two days passed before I saw Jenken again. It was mid-morning when he came to me with my water and my first meal of the day, and this time he opened the upper hatch without prompt or persuasion. It had turned bitterly cold, the wind howling off the Atlantic Ocean day and night without a moment's respite, so I had remained in my bed with the blankets pulled up around me for warmth. As soon as I knew it was Jenken, I ran to the door at once to speak with him.

'Did you see my headstone?' I asked him. 'It was there, wasn't it, just as I said it would be?'

Jenken nodded.

'And you believe me now, don't you? Will you help me?'

Jenken nodded again, and my entire body seemed to sigh with relief. I would have run to him and embraced him as my saviour were I able to, but it was enough for now to know that, because of him, the day would soon come when I could.

'Thank you, Jenken,' I said, thinking of my Sophia and daring to imagine that we would soon be reunited. How would she take to seeing me again, believing me dead all this time? I hoped it would not come as too much of a shock for her – for a shock it would surely be – but I imagined it would soon pass, and then she would smile and throw her arms around me. Of course, she would hate her father for it. I would spare her that if I could, but it was unavoidable, and Richard deserved no better for what he had done to us.

'What do you want me to do?' Jenken asked, cutting into my thoughts. 'If I unlock the door and go about my business, she'll know.'

I heard a degree of fear in Jenken's voice as he spoke, and I understood why. He knew Mariah would have him punished for it when she found out. For his sake I would avoid that, and fortunately I had had plenty of time to think on how to go about it.

'Don't worry, dear Jenken,' I said. 'I have a plan that, if successful, will absolve you of any guilt.' I caught myself. My plan had to be successful. There was too much riding on it. Thankfully, the most difficult obstacle – securing Jenken's help – had already been overcome. 'I need you to break my window,' I added. 'Then Mariah will believe that's how I escaped.'

Jenken peered at the window. 'But it's boarded up.'

I smiled to myself. 'You'll have to remove one or two of the boards first, of course – just enough for me to have squeezed through. Perhaps Mariah will imagine I used the edge of my spoon to gradually work the nails until I could prise the boards free. The slats are already loose in places, and the glass is old and would no doubt be easy enough to break with my hand if I cared to push hard enough.' I paused and took a breath, aware of the excitement rising in my voice. I reminded myself to slow down or Jenken would fail to fully comprehend my plan. 'Anyway, I doubt Mariah will consider the matter for too long. With the window broken, you simply need to let me out and lock the door again after I've gone.'

Jenken scratched at his chin. 'You want me to do this now?'

'Heavens, no!' I said, horrified at the thought of making even the slightest sound in broad daylight, and without first ascertaining where Mariah was. 'It must be done under cover of darkness, at a time when Mariah is otherwise preoccupied.'

Jenken began to nod to himself. 'I know when that will be.'

'You do? When? Please tell me it will be soon.'

'Soon, yes,' Jenken said. 'In three days it'll be the new mistress's birthday. She's had us all running around after her in preparation for it. You'd think the Duke and Duchess of Cornwall were coming to dinner.'

'Who is coming?' I asked, wondering whether my sudden and unexpected appearance in the dining room would be enough to save me. Surely I had only to be seen by those who had previously thought me dead. Questions would be asked, and how could Richard deny what he had done then?

'No one,' Jenken said, dashing my hopes for a simple and speedy solution. 'The master won't allow it.'

Of course he won't, I thought. As far as Richard was concerned, the fewer people there were on the estate the better, while I was still alive. It didn't matter. I knew what I had to do. I had to leave Crows-an-Wra Manor and its vast estate, and go to my brothers. They would know what to do.

'On the night of the birthday dinner, while everyone

is at the manor, you must bring Sophia to me,' I told Jenken. 'And you must bring a change of clothes for me – anything will do – and provisions to see us through a day or two.'

'But where will you wait for us?' Jenken asked.

I hadn't thought that far ahead until now. I considered the copse of trees where Sophia liked to play, but it was too close to the cottage. I wanted to get as far away from this place as I could. That also ruled out leaving via the main gates as they, too, were close by and were the most obvious means of escape should anyone notice me gone too soon and come after me. The strong walls that encompassed the estate were sturdy and too tall for me to climb. I could not simply escape with Sophia wherever I chose to, but thankfully, there were other ways.

'Do you remember the little secret we had, you and I, soon after Sophia was born?'

'Do you mean when you used to take Sophia to show her the sea without anyone knowing you was gone?'

'Yes, that's exactly what I mean. I used to walk barefoot in the stream that runs through the estate, out through the west culvert, following the water's course until the sea came into view and Crows-an-Wra Manor was far behind me.'

Jenken began to shake his head. 'You can't get out that way no more.'

'I can't? Why ever not? The lock on the gate rusted through years ago.'

'That it did,' Jenken said, 'but the master had me replace it not six months ago.'

I frowned, but the answer presented itself to me far more quickly than it had to Jenken. 'As groundskeeper, though, you hold the key, surely?'

It was as if a lamp had just illuminated above Jenken's head. As he realised what I meant, he rolled his eyes. 'Ah, I see,' he said. 'Yes, I have the keys. I can bring them with me to unlock the gate when I come to meet you.' He paused and scratched at his cheek. 'So that's where you'll wait then?'

'Yes, at the west culvert,' I said. 'We'll leave that way. In three days, I'll be ready.' I smiled at him. 'I shall never be able to repay you for your kindness,' I added, at the same time reaching up to touch his face through the hatch. I meant it only as a kindly gesture, but he backed sharply away.

'In three days then,' he said, and then he left me alone again with my thoughts.

CHAPTER THIRTY-ONE

During my isolation I had suffered many long and empty days, but none as long as the days that had passed since Jenken had left me with such hope in my heart I could scarcely believe it to be true. I was leaving this room. I was going to be with my Sophia again. For three days I had thought about nothing else.

But would he come?

I was sitting on the edge of my bed, repeatedly scrunching the folds of my nightgown so tightly in my hands that my fingers ached. The skylight above me had fallen dark some time ago now, and I had been watching the door for his lamplight ever since, listening intently for the slightest sound that might signal his approach.

He had to come.

The moonlight on the floorboards in my room was pale tonight. That was good. With no more than the slightest sliver of moon visible in the night sky, the countryside would be dark. It would be easier for me to flee from this place unseen. Nonetheless, I would have to be careful. I would have to keep to the trees as much as possible, although to get to the stream there would be times when I could not. But who would expect to see me out there? By the time I reached the stream, I imagined Richard and his new wife would be enjoying themselves too well to notice anything beyond their own reflections in one another's eyes. Or perhaps that was not the type of relationship they enjoyed. Perhaps, as I suspected, Richard cared only for his son and heir.

I began to wonder where the focus of Mariah's attentions would be during the birthday dinner, but I did not have long to ponder over the question. Cutting through the empty silence, I heard the distant squeal of what I imagined was a rusty door hinge – the back door, perhaps. Had Jenken come to the cottage at last? I strained my ears, leaning ever closer to the door. A moment later I knew for certain that someone was coming because I heard the familiar sound of a creaking floorboard. I caught my breath and waited. Amber light soon filled the cracks around the door again.

'Please let it be Jenken,' I whispered to myself. 'Please, please, let it be Jenken.'

I expected the lower hatch to open at any minute, but it did not. Instead I heard a key in the lock, and I began to smile. Of course, my meal would not be delivered through the lower hatch this time. This time, if Jenken had brought it, there would be no need. I stood up to greet him. The door began to open. And there he was, larger than life itself, or so he seemed to me, my glorious knight in shining armour.

'Jenken!' I said, suddenly feeling quite breathless. 'You came.'

'Of course,' was all Jenken said in reply.

He lumbered into the room and put his lamp down on the floor, lighting the small space with its glow. He had a little sack with him, which he handed to me.

'Pheasant, boiled eggs and potatoes for your journey,' he said. 'You should eat some now. You'll be needing your strength.'

'Thank you,' I said as I took the sack from him. I peered inside. There was more good food there than I had eaten all week. 'What about clothing – a pair of boots?'

'Too risky,' he said. 'I'm expected to bring you food of an evening, but I couldn't trust myself to give a proper answer should anyone see me coming to the cottage with a bundle of clothing beneath my arm. Don't you worry, though. I'll have one of the master's old greatcoats for you, and something for your feet, when I bring Sophia. There's a chill in the air, mind. You think you can manage until then?'

I was sure of it. The cold was something I had become quite hardened to, and what did I care for my feet in the short term? 'I'll be fine,' I said. 'Please ensure my Sophia is appropriately dressed, though, won't you?'

'I will,' Jenken said. He reached behind him, and from beneath his belt he withdrew an iron crowbar. 'No time to waste,' he added as he went to work on the boards at the window.

I sat on the edge of my bed again and wildly devoured a leg of pheasant as I watched him, biting into it with the tenacity of a starving dog. Every now and then I found my eyes straying to the open door, and I do not know how I found the will to resist running for my freedom right there and then. But I had to be patient. I had to follow my plan.

'Almost done,' Jenken said, as if he could read my

thoughts and knew how desperate I was to leave now that the time had come.

He dropped another board on to the floor beside the rest and was through the slats in seconds. Before long I could see the glass beyond. It was black against the night, causing it to reflect the room. I stood up and went to it, peering around Jenken, the better to see myself in its dark mirror. I did not know the woman staring back at me.

'Stand back,' Jenken said, aware that I was now close beside him. 'I'm going to break the glass.'

I only wished he would hurry up and do it so that I did not have to look upon my wretched self a moment longer. I stepped back towards my bed as he struck the windowpane once with his crowbar. The glass shattered and tinkled, and I prayed that no one beyond my room had heard it.

Jenken turned to me then. 'Go on with you now,' he said as he picked the broken glass from the edges of the window frame. 'I'll make good here so it looks like you climbed out. Then I'll lock the door as I leave, just as you said.'

I went to him and threw my arms around him. I felt so weak that I'm sure he barely felt my embrace, but I wanted him to know how grateful I was.

'No time to waste,' he said. 'Go on now.'

I was smiling at him as I withdrew. At the door, I paused with my little sack of provisions and turned back. 'I'll see you at the west culvert then,' I said, as much for my own reassurance as to be sure that he understood perfectly where we were to meet. 'And please tell Sophia not to worry,' I added. 'Everything is going to be all right.'

Jenken nodded. 'At the west culvert,' he repeated.

'We'll be there.'

My first breath as I stood beneath the waning moon out-side the cottage was like no other I could remember. The cool air stung my throat and made me feel light-headed. It had intoxicated me and stopped me in my tracks be-fore I had taken two steps. I had drawn cold breath on many a morning in my room, but it was never like this. This was the breath of freedom. I drew it in as I threw my head back and gazed up at the countless stars, the sky so black that I could see deep into its fabric. I could have remained there for hours, captivated by the power of my own senses, now rekindled and wide awake, but I quickly reminded myself that while I remained within the walls of Crows-an-Wra Manor, I was not free.

Ahead of me was the carriage drive. To my left I saw the main gates, and to my right, the manor house. I stared at it with hate in my heart for all the pain and suffering its master had forced upon me and those I love. I would have chosen to run away from it, behind the cottage and through the trees to the east, but I knew it would take twice as long to reach the west culvert that way.

I had to go closer.

The lamps were lit in the west wing, where I imagined my husband's new wife was laughing gaily, enjoying her birthday celebrations. I would have to pass that way, but I would choose my route carefully. Thankfully, I did not have to pass by the ruins of the east wing, for it was pain-ful enough simply to look upon its bleak silhouette. I would keep to the trees as much as possible, but the open spaces to the side of the house, and behind it in particular, were largely unavoidable because much of the estate boundary to the rear of the house was thick with prickly gorse and other dense shrubbery.

It was without conscious thought that I suddenly found myself running. It was only when I felt pain in my joints from having used my legs so little this past year that I gave any consideration to it. I was like an animal, acting on instinct, eager to seek cover so that I could not be seen. There were trees to either side of the carriage drive, running all along the southern perimeter, the cottage nestled between them. With my little sack of food in my hand, I crossed the drive and was soon crunching twigs and dry leaves beneath my feet, keeping the manor house to my right. It was not long before I wished I had made Jenken go and fetch me some appropriate footwear before I left, because I was soon forced to slow my pace by the pain in the soles of my feet. I knew they would be cut to shreds before long, but I kept going, hobbling from time to time as if I were walking on hot coals.

I quickly found myself longing for the soft grass I would soon have to cross, and so I was thankful to reach the gorse, for there I did not dare to tread barefoot. I stopped short of it and came out to the edge of the trees, where I peered out from my cover towards the house. I was aware that my heart was racing fast. I was not used to any form of exercise, of course, but that was not the only reason for it. I was afraid. As much as I preferred the grass to twigs and thorns beneath my feet, I dreaded the open spaces I now had to cross in order to reach the stream.

The land to the west of the house was a mixture of manicured lawns and parterre gardens, filled with rose bushes and other pretty flora. I had come far enough to avoid much of the area that had been laid to lawn for now, but there was still a good stretch to cover before I reached the stream. I found myself cursing Jenken for not yet bringing me the coat he had mentioned, too. It was sure to be of some dull colour, and despite the dark evening, I felt all the more vulnerable in my nightgown, although it was not now as white as it had once been.

But what choice did I have?

I took a deep breath to help calm myself, sank into as low a crouch as I could manage, and began to run again. I kept my head down, not looking at the house again until I felt I had gone far enough to pass the west wing entirely. To give my back some respite, I straightened up a little when I reached the parterre gardens and the now leggy stems of the roses and tall verbenas. Beyond that, I made for a small patch of wild grass in the north-west corner, where I sank down until my eyes were level with the seed heads. Gingerly, I peered through them at the house.

I could see the rear terrace now. There were fewer lamps lit at the back of the house, which gave me some small comfort, but I was far from safe yet. My eyes wandered away then to the north, in the direction I had to take, and I saw the lake, flat and calm, like an enormous black mirror, reflecting the pale crescent moon and the stars in the near darkness. Once I had passed beyond that, I would breathe easier. After that, every step I took would take me further and further away from Crows-an-Wra Manor and its wicked inhabitants.

Apart from the lake and the lawn that now stood between me and my freedom, the grounds behind the house were more or less unimproved. By daylight, one could see the estate spread away for miles. Here and there were little copses of windswept trees amidst the meadows that were largely left for winter feed, save for the large paddock area to the east. It was all open ground from there on. Then I would become lost to darkness amidst the vast landscape and would be safe.

Waiting only as long as it took to catch my breath, I continued to run, fully upright now, sprinting as fast as my feeble legs could manage. I did not look back, only ahead into the blackness, which seemed to intensify the further I went. Within no time I had all but passed the lake, but then I felt a tug at my ankles. A second later the hem of my nightgown caught on something. It felt as if someone had reached up from the earth and grabbed me, pulling me down. I fell with a thud, momentarily dazed and confused.

Once I had collected myself, I saw that the ground was covered in a maze of string and wooden stakes, which, in the darkness and my blind eagerness to flee, I had not seen. I remembered then that Mariah had told me Richard's new wife had had everyone helping her with the preparations for an Italian garden by the lake. It was this, then, that I had literally stumbled across. I stood up and looked back at the house momentarily. Nothing had changed. No lamps were moving as they might were someone coming for me. I did not linger, although I was forced now to make slow progress by the web of strings that lay before me.

Step by step I left Crows-an-Wra Manor behind me, and before long I reached the tall meadow grass, where I began to breathe more easily. The grass here reached to my waist and I no longer felt the need to crouch. Behind me, the entire manor was now no more than a dark silhouette of chimney stacks against the night sky. I could not see the lighted windows, and those within could not see me.

As I walked, I began to think of my reunion with Sophia. I prayed that she would not be scared – that she would not think me some unholy reincarnation and run from me, afraid to look upon me again. I supposed that Jenken would have to tell her where he was taking her and why, and in doing so would at least prepare her for the shock of seeing me again, alive, not dead as she had been told. By daybreak we would be close to my family home and my brothers, and I did not care to imagine their bitter retribution for all the suffering Richard had put us through.

The stream that ran across the estate between the east and west culverts, dividing the land in two, was thankfully impossible to miss as long as I kept heading north. There was a small bridge at its widest section, but I needed no bridge where I was going. I began to cut a diagonal to my left, pushing through the tall grass to the west, drawn to the roar of the sea, which was faint but already clearly audible to me. Ten minutes must have passed before I felt the ground change beneath my feet. I winced as I trod over the first sharp stones I came to, my already bleeding feet crying for respite. Then, as the grass began to thin out, I heard the delicate tinkle of the stream ahead.

There is nothing quite as satisfying, to my mind, as the feeling of having one's feet in water, especially feet that were as tired and sore as mine. I drew a sharp breath as I stepped into the stream. The water felt ice cold, but that was all for the better as far as I was concerned. It soothed me instantly. I stood there for several seconds, until the water numbed my soles and washed away my pain. I gazed up at the heavens and turned in slow circles until I felt dizzy, for I had no fear of losing my bearings now. I simply had to follow the water's course, and in time I would arrive at the west culvert, where I would wait for Jenken to bring Sophia to me, along with the key to my salvation.

CHAPTER
THIRTY-TWO

Grace

I can honestly say that the occasion of my twenty-second birthday was without exception the dullest day of my life. As I sat alone at the breakfast table the following morning, waiting for Richard to join me, I could not help but reflect on it. It began with good enough intent. Richard was to take me to Penzance for the day. He had wanted to buy me a gift to mark the occasion of my first birthday living at Crows-an-Wra Manor as his wife, but Mariah had other plans. Rather than going to the trouble of buying some new jewel for me to wear, she thought it more fitting that Richard should present me with something personal – something from the family – which of course meant that there was no need for us to go anywhere.

I was wearing the gift now, having put on the plainest of my white day dresses to best show it off. I absently reached up to my neckline and touched it, a cluster of emeralds in the shape of a pear that had once belonged to Richard's grandmother, and more recently to Mariah. I was not ungrateful to receive it, simply frustrated that it had kept me here, on my birthday of all days. Would I never leave this place? I kept telling myself that next year would be different – that as soon as the work on the east wing was under way, Richard would yearn to take himself off somewhere, and I with him – but I was beginning to have my doubts. More and more I felt that Crows-an-Wra Manor was a prison to us all.

Footsteps in the hallway distracted me from my thoughts. I knew from their hollow sound and cadence that it was Richard. He entered the breakfast room with no trace of his usual swagger, still half dressed in close-fitting casual trousers and shirtsleeves, the buttons at his neck unfastened to the middle of his chest. I cannot say that his appearance did not in some way appeal to my senses, but it was clear at once that my arousal was not his intention. He sat down in his usual place at the opposite end of the table without uttering a single word, pushed his tousled hair back off his forehead, and sighed so fully that I thought I felt his breath on my cheeks.

'Good morning, Richard,' I said, keen to maintain propriety. 'Is everything all right? You're wearing such a frown.'

Richard had not been looking so much at me as through me since he sat down, as if he were deep in thought about something. Only now did he seem to notice I was there. 'Am I?' he said, relaxing his expression. 'I'm sorry. Yes, good morning. I trust you slept well?'

'Thank you for asking, Richard, but frankly I did not sleep well. I did not sleep well at all.'

'Well, that makes two of us,' Richard said, his eyes now surveying the contents of the table. 'Where's Cobb?' he added. 'No, don't tell me. I suppose as it's after eleven she's cleaning some part of the house somewhere and I must serve myself again.'

'Would you like me to serve you?' I asked, not caring for his attitude.

'No, I would not!' he said. 'If Mother were here, I'd have her do it, for letting so many of the servants go.' He stood up and lifted one of the silver lids from the assortment of serving dishes Cobb had previously laid out. 'Devilled kidneys again. I really don't think I have the stomach for it this morning.'

'There are poached eggs,' I said. 'Although I expect they, too, will be cold by now. Perhaps something simple will suffice. There's bread and cheese, cold meats.'

Richard sat back and sighed again. 'I'm not really hungry,' he said. 'So why couldn't you sleep last night?'

I knew precisely why, but I did not dare to come straight out with it for fear of further upsetting Richard's already ill-tempered mood. 'I've been trying to fathom why I was not allowed to invite any guests to my birthday dinner.'

Richard gave an impatient harrumph. 'For heaven's sake, Grace. I've already told you – you do not yet know anyone worth inviting.'

'How can I, when I'm not allowed their company?' I asked, my own face now set in a frown. 'Having met three of Sophia's uncles recently, I would have liked to invite them and their wives, and I'm sure that Sophia—'

'I did not want them here!' Richard cut in. 'Can you not understand that every second I look upon them I am reminded of my first wife!' He stood up and slammed his fists on the table so hard that it shook the lids on the serving dishes, jarring my nerves. 'I have far more important things to think about!' he said, his face now quite red with anger.

I blamed the wine and the brandy for his outburst. He had consumed far too much of both the night before and was clearly now suffering the effects. I wondered what other, more important matters were on his mind, but I did not ask. Instead I stood up, aware that his outburst had caused my nerves to get the better of me. I could feel my hands shaking as I folded my napkin and neatly set it down. I was about to leave without saying another word, but just as I turned to the door, Sophia entered. She had already taken her breakfast in Mrs Pengelly's kitchen, along with Jenken and Cobb, so I knew she had not come for something to eat.

'I heard shouting,' she said. 'Are you quarrelling?'

'No, no,' Richard said, sitting down again. 'I'm just a bear with a sore head this morning. That's all it is. I'm sorry if my shouting upset you. Now, come here, and please tell me that you at least slept well last night.'

Sophia skipped across the room to her father and sat in his lap. 'For the most part, I did,' she said, and then her eyes drifted across the table to me. She stood up again and came towards me. 'Last night,' she told me, 'I saw a ghost.'

'Did you?' I asked, and I dreaded to think what she would say next. I suspected it was the opening line to some new torment, such as she had seen the ghost of my as yet unborn child because it was already dead inside my womb, but I was glad to be proved wrong.

'Yes,' she said, nodding so much that her ringlets began to bounce up and down like a clockmaker's springs. 'It was by the lake, all dressed in white.'

I smiled to myself. 'And I suppose it was this ghost who pulled out some of my stakes again,' I said, recalling how Sophia had practically ruined my first day's efforts to lay out the plans for my Italian garden. I had not yet been out to put them back, but had seen them from the rear terrace earlier when I stepped outside briefly to survey the design and take the morning air. There was no doubt in my mind that it was Sophia who had removed them, just as before.

'I suppose it must have been,' Sophia said, with the innocence only a child could own. 'I didn't do it. Perhaps it was you, Father,' she added, turning back to him. 'Did you do it?'

'I most certainly did not,' Richard said. 'And there are no such things as ghosts.'

Mariah joined us then, although I did not notice her come in.

'What's all this talk about ghosts?' she said, in such playful tones that she could only be addressing Sophia.

'I saw one,' Sophia said with enthusiasm. 'It was last night by the lake. No one believes me, though. Do you believe me?'

'Of course I do,' Mariah said, and I noticed that her eyes had now shifted to Richard. 'We shall have to do something about it, shan't we, Richard? We can't have a ghost roaming the estate. It could be very dangerous for all of us. Who knows what it might do, or who might see it next?'

Richard began to scratch irritably at his sideburns. His mother's words had clearly troubled him, although I could not fathom why. They were purely hypothetical, surely, for Sophia's sake.

'Yes, I suppose we shall,' he said, nodding heavily, his words sounding far more grave than the situation seemed to call for. Even Sophia had begun to frown, as if sensing that they carried more weight than she or I could as yet comprehend.

CHAPTER THIRTY-THREE

Rosen

It was all for nothing.

As I sat huddled by the fireplace in my hateful little room, listening to the birds caw-cawing and screeching in the near distance, I continued to wonder how I could have been so blind. My escape had failed, and now even the birds had come to mock me. I could only imagine they had, because there was no sign of a storm raging outside – no howling wind or lashing rain at my skylight. To the contrary, the sky was clear of the angry grey clouds that usually brought the gulls inland, and they were not all of them gulls. I could hear crows and other carrion eaters amidst the cacophony, all of them fighting over themselves to be heard. Why else would they come in such numbers, if not to mock me in my defeat?

I pulled my blanket more tightly around me and pressed my hands over my ears to shut them out. I closed my eyes and tried to recall a happy memory, but I could not. In my mind's eye, all I could see was my own self as I was the night before, splashing through the stream beneath the pale moonlight towards the western culvert. I recalled my joy as I saw it, the steel of the new lock, bright as a beacon against the rusting gate, drawing me closer and closer to my freedom. I must have waited there, crouching beneath the low stone arch, for close to an hour before Jenken came. I was shivering uncontrollably in my nightgown, my bare feet by then freezing cold and blue from the icy water.

'Jenken?' I called when I heard someone approaching. 'Is that you?'

I peered out from my cover to be sure, and I saw that it was Jenken. I remember smiling so much at the sight of him that my cold face quickly began to ache.

'Sophia?' I said as I came out from beneath the arch, squinting through the half-light to get a glimpse of her.

But it was not my Sophia I saw.

In that instant, it was as if the cold air had suddenly reached into my chest and stopped my heart dead. 'No!' I screamed, fear stifling my cry. 'Not you. It can't be you.'

'Yes,' Mariah said, a cruel smile on her lips. 'And what a silly girl you've been.'

I had been betrayed, and I feared now that it would be to my end.

Even now, as I sat awaiting my fate, I could not understand how Jenken could do such a thing. Clearly, he had not believed a word I told him, and I doubted now whether he had ever gone to the churchyard to look at my grave. I could only imagine that he had dismissed everything I said as nothing more than the rantings of a mad woman who was bent on killing her own child.

The upper hatch shot open suddenly, and with such force that it startled me. With my hands over my ears I had not heard Mariah's approach. I lowered them now and stared back at her, her sharp features more hateful to me now than ever.

'I suppose you thought yourself clever, didn't you?' she said, a satisfied smile twitching at the corner of her mouth. 'But it is I who have been clever.'

'Go away!' I yelled, thrusting my face towards her like a venomous snake.

Mariah's smile flourished so triumphantly then that she was soon laughing at me. 'Come now,' she said. 'Do not be so sour in your defeat. Did you really think you could best me – that Jenken would trust your word above mine and risk putting Sophia's life in danger?'

I drew a long breath and sat back against the fireplace again, saying nothing in reply. In truth, I no longer knew what to think.

'He came running to me as soon as you asked for his help,' Mariah continued. 'Just as I had instructed him to. He told me everything, and I told him what to say in return.' She laughed to herself. 'You may as well have been talking directly to me, you foolish girl.'

Yes, I had been foolish. I had previously believed that my plan to escape had been entirely my own, but it was clear to me now that it was not. Mariah had dictated its course from the moment she came to hear about it, but to what end?

When Mariah spoke again her voice had softened considerably, but in a manner that was laced with threat. 'Richard is quite concerned about you now,' she said, and I began to see why she had allowed, perhaps even encouraged, me to escape. 'He's going to have to do something about you, isn't he? What if you got out again? Where might it lead?'

'Stop it,' I said, knowing full well that she was teasing me, only this time I feared she truly meant it. Richard was going to do something about me. I could feel it now more than ever. He could not let me go on like this, living here in this room, continually worrying over the possibility – even the probability – that I would escape again.

'What if someone saw you?' Mariah said, voicing my own thoughts. 'The risk has become too great, hasn't it?'

'What will he do with me?' I asked, my voice sounding diminutive even to my own sensitive ears.

'What he should have done with you long before now. But can you not imagine?'

'I don't want to imagine,' I said. 'Imagining is all I do and I'm tired of it.'

Mariah scoffed. 'Well, it won't be long now. Then you won't have to imagine anything ever again.'

With that, Mariah turned and left, but the upper hatch remained open. I heard her going down the stairs and I sat up, trying to understand why she had not closed it. Then I heard her returning. At least, I initially thought it must be her, but I quickly realised that the footfalls were too heavy. Jenken? Had he come to gloat? Why else would he come? Surely Mariah would allow him no apology for his betrayal.

I eased closer to the door, my eyes fixed on the opening. Then suddenly it was filled, and I caught my breath when I saw Richard's face looking back at me. Neither of us spoke. He just stared at me as I stared back at him, lost for words. Although he did not voice it, I could see that there was a degree of sadness written in the lines on his face. Richard had never looked in on me like this before.

Now, as he slowly closed the hatch, I sensed with utter dread that he had come to say his final goodbye.

CHAPTER THIRTY-FOUR

Grace

After breakfast, I parted company with Richard and his foul mood and went up to my room to collect a shawl. I was keen to reset the stakes that had been pulled up by Sophia or her 'ghost' but, while it was fine out, I thought the autumn air cool enough to warrant another layer. Entering my room, I made straight for the lower drawers in the wardrobe where I kept them, thinking that sage green rather suited the season. I had to pause, however, as I passed the floor-standing mirror that was just inside my door. My bump was definitely showing today. There was no question about it. I had been studying myself, clothed and unclothed, every day since I learned that I was carrying Richard's child, looking for the signs, but today was the first day that the child growing inside me had really made his, or her, presence known to me.

It filled my heart with such joy.

I stroked my belly and smiled down at the reflection in the mirror, imagining that I was looking directly at my baby, and that it was looking back at me. The notion instantly lifted my mood, but I was quickly distracted. One of my windows was open, and perched on the frame was a small grey-headed crow – a jackdaw.

'Shoo!' I called, waving at it to go away.

The bird began to flap its wings. A moment later it gave a shrill cry and swooped away. I went to the window to close it and saw that the jackdaw was not alone. There were other birds, lots of them, and it was only now that I became fully aware of the din they were making. The gulls I had heard many times before, but never to such an extent, and why were there so many crows among them?

I fetched my shawl from the drawer, thinking little more about it for now. I had not, after all, lived long at Crows-an-Wra Manor, and I supposed the house, and the tiny hamlet that shared its name, had been aptly described. I recalled then that Richard had once said the name had something to do with a witches' crossing or a white cross in the old Cornish language, so perhaps it had nothing to do with crows at all. I had to confess to knowing very little of the area, which was something I planned to address if I was ever allowed the freedom to do so. Richard had also once told me that the grounds were surrounded by farmland, so, as I left my room to go outside, I imagined that was the reason. Perhaps the local farmers were spreading something on their fields, in which the birds had now taken an interest.

Once outside, however, I began to have my doubts.

As I left the terrace at the back of the house, heading for the lake and the layout for my Italian garden, I could not help but crane my neck this way and that as I took in the spectacle above me. The crows, of one type and another, were continually swooping at the gulls as if to attack them, and the gulls were skewing this way and that to avoid them. They all combined to make such an unpleasant racket that I doubted I could remain outside for long. It was not until I reached the first of my uprooted stakes and turned back to the house, however, that I saw the full extent of the matter. My jaw literally dropped as I took in the sight. There were hundreds of birds circling immediately above the manor, and many more still, perched on the chimney pots and along the gables and roof parapets. They were not interested in the farmland that surrounded the estate. It was the estate itself, or the very house, in which they were interested.

Although I could barely take my eyes off them for wondering what they were fighting over, I looked away – down to my feet, at one of the lines of string I had come to repair. It was then that I noticed something else that struck me as odd. I stopped to pick up the stake. The string was still attached to it, but there was something else: a small piece of off-white fabric, spattered with mud. It had somehow become caught on my stake. I pulled it free and brushed away the dirt, and I saw that the fabric was not plain. It had a small section of embroidery sewn into it. I creased my brow, perplexed as to how it came to be there. Then I realised. Was this another of Sophia's little jokes? I imagined it was. It all fitted together very well with her story of the 'ghost' she said she had seen roaming the grounds in the night. Now, here was the piece of white gown to prove it.

I laughed to myself, wondering what kind of ghost she thought might roam these grounds dressed in an embroidered gown. Then I stopped laughing as the answer struck me. I pictured Sophia's comforter with all those embroidered animals. I had tried to take it from her when we first met, and she became upset because her late mother had embroidered it. This piece of cloth, then, had likely belonged to Rosen Trevelyan. If this was another of Sophia's little games, set to torment me, the poor girl was in greater need of help than I could give her.

But what other answer was there?

I looked up at the house again, and at the gulls and the crows. Then down at the piece of cloth once more, knowing I had to tell Richard about them both. I imagined he would be in his study as usual, so I made my way around to the front of the house, and as I turned the corner I saw Jenken heading along the carriage drive towards the gate-keeper's cottage. He had a stack of what appeared to be old floorboards balanced on his shoulder. He was almost tripping over himself as he, too, kept looking back towards the manor house, at the birds circling and cawing in the sky above it. At least I was not the only one there who seemed to think their behaviour unusual.

Entering the house again, I made straight for Richard's study. I knocked, hoping his ill mood had eased, but there was no answer. I knocked again.

'Richard?' I called softly as I teased the door open, but I quickly discovered that he was not there.

I frowned, although I did not think long on what to do next. I was too intrigued by now to leave the curious behaviour of the birds alone, so I decided to go up to the roof and see for myself what it was that they were so interested in.

CHAPTER THIRTY-FIVE

Although I had not yet ventured into the attic rooms at Crows-an-Wra Manor, having previously only so much as considered going up on to the roof during the heat of summer for the promise of a cool breeze, I found they were easily accessed. With so few servants to run the house I was also able to reach them unseen, which I somehow felt was important. Now that I had started out on my little expedition, I was keen to see it through, and I imagined that if anyone saw me, Richard or Mariah would soon come to hear about it. As I made my way along one of the narrow corridors, wishing I had thought to bring a lamp with me because the light was so poor, I felt glad that Richard had not been in his study. I had not had this much excitement in the middle of the day since my arrival earlier in the year, and he was sure to put a stop to it if he knew.

Now that I was higher up, the sounds of the gulls and the crows cawing and screeching outside was so loud and so unpleasant that it set my face into a constant wince. I opened one of the attic-room doors to throw more light into the corridor, and the din intensified to the point where I wanted to close the door again at once, but I did not. Through the cloud of dust I had disturbed merely by opening the door, I saw an interior that was as shabby as everything else I had seen on this level of the house. I could not see out of the window, so small and filthy was the glass, but it let in enough light to see by. The room was full of discarded and seemingly long-forgotten things, all covered in a layer of dust and grime so thick I could easily have written my name in it.

The same curiosity that had brought me up here now took me inside. There were books here and there, the covers and spines all grey and wordless to my eyes beneath their veils of dust. I saw a pile of swords and other old weaponry in one corner, their shapes unmistakeable even though their shine had long diminished, and there was a table against one of the walls. I felt myself being drawn towards it, wondering at all the indistinct objects randomly placed upon it. I should have liked to rub my thumbs across everything there, just to know what it was, and perhaps to learn something about the family I had married into from the subtle clues each item might impart, but I stopped myself. If I had not, I fear I would have become lost in this room or the next, until I had quite forgotten my purpose.

I turned away and stepped back out into the corridor. There had to be a door on this level somewhere that led out on to the roof, and I had to find it. I opened the doors to several more rooms as I went along the corridor, lighting my way without so much as a glance inside so as to remove the temptation to linger. I came to a junction and turned to my left, passing old paintings stacked against the walls and furniture that no longer had a place in the main part of the house. Given that I had come up from the west wing and had walked towards the heart of the manor, I supposed I was now heading towards the back of the building, which faced north. Ahead of me, I soon made out the shape of a small staircase of no more than half a dozen steps. There was a door at the top, and I imagined it to be the door I was looking for.

Would it be locked?

My pace quickened. I was eager to find out. At the same time I supposed that if it were, then surely there had to be other doors that led out on to the roof. I had all day. I would try every one of them if I had to. Just as I grabbed the handrail beside the stairs to ascend them, however, a loud clatter from one of the rooms stopped me cold. Were I an old woman, I thought my health might have suffered as a result of the shock it gave me. I spun around and listened. A moment later the noise sounded again, and although I was expecting it this time, it set my nerves jangling nonetheless.

'Hello?' I called, expecting no answer.

To my knowledge, there was no one up here but me, but if that were so, then what had caused the sound? I took a step closer, my eyes fixed on one of the doors to my right. It was ajar, and I could not stop myself from thinking again about Sophia and her little ghost story. Could it be true? I shook my head. It was more likely to be Sophia herself. Had she followed me up here just to frighten me?

'Sophia? Is that you?'

As I arrived outside the door, listening intently, I stole a peek through the gap, but I could see very little. I nudged it open, just a few inches more, and in that moment I could not decide whether my coming up here in the first place was brave or merely foolish. Either way, I cursed my curiosity and pushed at the door again, harder this time. It swung open, and the clatter I had previously heard sounded again from further inside the room. My heart was by now pounding in my chest. I wanted to turn and run back the way I had come, but I could not go without knowing who or what was there. I really do not know how I found the courage, but I stepped fully into the room then, and I immediately saw the cause of the commotion. It was not Sophia. Nor was it the ghost she had spoken of. It was a gull, perched atop an old chest of drawers, its piercing eyes fixed on mine.

I let go of the breath I had been holding, but my fear remained. To say that it was a large example of the species would be to understate its presence in so small a room. I saw at once where it had got in. There was a broken skylight above me, the pieces of glass still scattered on the floor beneath it. It would not have surprised me to learn that the bird's weight alone had been enough to shatter the glass, although I suspect it must have already been cracked and badly in need of repair. Not wishing to alarm the creature any more than I already had, I was mindful not to make any sudden movements, yet at the same time I wanted to free the poor thing, so I pulled the door to behind me so as to contain it.

I caught my breath as the bird began to flap its wings, further disturbing the contents of the room and kicking up such a cloud of dust that it made me cough. The sound seemed to excite the bird further. It let out an almighty screech as it flew at me, wildly flapping its wings. It was all I could do to turn my back to it and duck to avoid it striking me. When I looked again it was standing on the floor on the opposite side of the room, its eyes once again fixed on mine.

'Go on!' I said, pointing up to the broken skylight. 'Go back and join your friends.'

The gull screeched at me again and I covered my ears. I would have liked to help it out of that room, but I quickly realised this feat was far beyond my capabilities. Without taking my eyes off the bird, I slowly opened the door again, just enough for me to squeeze through.

'You can find your own way out then,' I said. 'The same way you got in.'

I closed the door on the matter and made sure the catch clicked into place. Perhaps it would follow my advice and fly out again. If not, Jenken would have to deal with it. As I went back to the steps and the door that led out onto the roof, I thought there was indeed a bird problem at Crows-an-Wra Manor, and I was now all the more determined to understand why.

CHAPTER
THIRTY-SIX

As soon as I stepped out on to the roof, I found myself being mobbed by crows, their inky black wings flapping and thrashing so frantically in front of me that I was forced to cower momentarily.

But I would not be deterred.

'Shoo!' I shouted, waving my arms at them. 'Away with you!'

I realised then that it was not me they were interested in. My arrival at the very moment they passed me was nothing more than a coincidence. One of them had something in its beak. The rest were simply chasing it to rob it of its find. Nevertheless, I was glad to see them go. There were by now so many birds above Crows-an-Wra Manor that the sight of them, now that I was among them, and in particular the noise they combined to make, made me ill at ease. As a result, I proceeded slowly, determined not to draw their attention if I could help it.

As I suspected, I had emerged towards the back of the manor, amidst tall chimney stacks and the ceilings of the attic rooms, which jutted out from this seldom seen landscape like small grey pyramids of lead and stone. My eyes quickly found the broken skylight I had seen in the room I had just left, and I wondered whether the unfortunate gull had found its way out again. I suspected it had not, but I had no intention of traipsing over all the guttering to find out.

Instead, I took the narrow walkway that now presented itself to me, and I quickly found myself standing beside the manor's north-facing parapet, looking out over the lake towards a vast landscape of fields. When I had stood in the grounds below earlier, I had only been aware of the slightest breeze. Now, however, it tugged at my dress and threatened to blow my day bonnet clean off my head.

I tightened the bow beneath my chin as I moved on, continuing along the walkway to my left, alongside the parapet. Ahead of me, I could see that I was closing in on the cause of all the excitement. The birds here were squabbling so aggressively among themselves that I had to pause for a moment to take a breath. Whatever could it be? I supposed there had to be something here to interest them, but what?

I passed several attic-room windows before I saw anything to further arouse my own interest. It was just as I was approaching the manor's north-west corner. I was no more than a dozen or so yards from it, and I could see the edge of what looked like a brown tarpaulin. It was poking out from between one of the chimney stacks and the roof of one of the attic rooms. Easing myself forward to find out what it was, clutching the parapet as I went, I was soon able to see that it was indeed a tarpaulin. There were several birds sitting on top of it and around it, picking and poking at it, and at one another from time to time.

A gull landed on the parapet ahead of me, distracting me momentarily. I waved my arms at it and it flew at the tarpaulin, disturbing the crows. There were birds all around me now, screaming in my ears, but I no longer cared. I was far too interested, as they were, in what was beneath that tarpaulin. I went closer. Two more gulls joined the first, pecking and tearing at the tarpaulin with their long, hooked beaks while the crows stood watch, waiting for their turn to come again.

I was no more than six feet away now, and it was only then that the stench that had presumably drawn the birds hit me. It stopped me cold. It was so strong that I wondered how I could not have smelled it as soon as I stepped out on to the roof, but I supposed it was because of the strong breeze coming off the parapet, carrying the smell away from me until I was too close to miss it. I knew the foetid odour well enough. It was not unlike that of the dead squirrel Sophia had brought into the parlour the day her uncles came to visit, only this was no squirrel, and the smell was far more pungent.

I leaned in. A gull began to squawk at me, warning me off. Another bird flew at my bonnet, catching me off guard. My heart was racing, but I had to see what was there. A length of rope had been fastened around the tarpaulin, but I could see that it had come loose, or more likely had been torn loose by the birds. It must have left the contents partially exposed on the side furthest from me, because it was there that the birds were jabbing their beaks and pulling at whatever was inside.

Moving slowly in and around to the other side of the tarpaulin to see what it was, my eyes were met with a sight I could never forget. There was a hand protruding from the tarpaulin, a human hand that had been all but stripped to the bone. The gull that had squawked at me was tearing at what little flesh remained, and it was all I could do to quell the scream that began to rise in my throat at the hideous sight of it. I put a hand to my mouth. I had to look away momentarily.

Whose body was this? Why was it there?

I tried to think of a practical answer, something to tame the sudden sense of evil that had washed over me, but there could be no satisfactory explanation for this. Dead people were not laid to rest on rooftops. With my hand still covering my mouth, more now as a feeble barrier against the stench than from shock, I ventured closer still to see if I could identify the poor soul. My close presence had further disturbed some of the gulls. Now several crows had moved back in at the opposite end of the tarpaulin and were feasting heartily on this most horrific carrion.

I could not stomach it. I wished I had something to throw at them, but I did not, so I stepped boldly towards them, flapping my arms. The gull closest to me took flight instantly, letting out a throaty 'ha-ha-ha-ha' in alarm as it went. The crows were more tenacious. They lingered until I was almost upon them.

'Yar!' I yelled at them. 'Shoo, all of you!'

'Caw-caw-caw!' they replied as they flapped away like death's own shadows.

When they left, I screamed. How could I not? I put both my hands to my mouth this time to stifle the sound. I was staring into the empty eye sockets of Richard's brother, Giles Trevelyan. What was left of his face was barely recognisable, but bearing such a close resemblance to my husband, how could I not know it? The birds scattered, my own cry joining the cacophony. What madness was this? I reached in to further peel back the tarpaulin, having gauged from the size of the bundle that there had to be something else there, but just as I did so I heard a sound that chilled me to my core. I looked up, listening.

Someone was coming.

I had heard a door opening in the near distance, perhaps the same door by which I had emerged on to the roof. I heard voices, still faint for now, but there was no doubt in my mind that they were coming this way.

I had to hide.

Frantically, I looked around for somewhere to conceal myself. The voices were growing louder by the second. I had little time. I knew I could not run out on to the main walkway again, or I would likely be seen at once. There was just the chimney stack to one side of me, and the sloping roof of one of the attic rooms to my right. The latter offered limited cover, so without another thought I stepped quickly and quietly past the tarpaulin to the corner of the chimney stack, and hid myself away on the other side, just as the voices became loud enough for me to pick up their conversation clearly. I heard Mariah first, and to my horror it was soon clear to whom she was talking.

'Didn't I say it was a bad idea?' she said, her tone as grave as the situation I now found myself in. 'They should have been buried deep in the woods long before now.'

They? I thought, momentarily perplexed, although it addressed my suspicion that there was more beneath the tarpaulin than Giles Trevelyan. There was another body, but whose?

'There wasn't time,' I heard Richard say in reply. 'And what about Jenken? We can only expect to fool him so far. Had I buried them in the grounds, I would not have slept a night since for worrying when he might uncover them.'

'Well, we must do something with them,' Mariah said. 'They cannot be left out here. The birds draw too much attention.'

'I'll drag them into one of the attic rooms for now. The birds won't get at them there.'

'Be sure to lock it behind you.'

'Of course. Not that anyone has reason to come up here these days. I'll take them deep into the woods when I can be sure no one will see me.'

'We could send the servants into Penzance for the day,' Mariah said. 'Tomorrow perhaps, or the day after. A reward for their hard work.'

'Yes, that should do it. Grace can go with them. She bleats on enough about her need for a change of scene.'

I could not help but frown at Richard's remark. To hear him talk about me in such a way made me wonder whether I really knew the man. Clearly, I did not, any more than I knew what he was capable of, although even now I prayed to hear something that might absolve him of this most heinous of sins. I feared, however, that I would not. I did not know this man at all. Had he really murdered his own brother? Why? I had said I wanted Giles gone, but not like this.

My thoughts returned to the second body beneath the tarpaulin, but I was distracted by Richard's heavy breathing as I imagined him first uncovering the bodies, and then lifting them or dragging them apart, ready to be taken to the attic room he had previously spoken of.

What I heard next answered my thoughts, although with all my heart I wished it had not.

'Do you suppose anyone will miss her?' Richard said.

'Why should they?' Mariah replied, sounding a little breathless herself. 'As far as anyone else is concerned, you took her to Penzance. Cobb will vouch to that should it come to it, but why should it? What happened to Lucy after she left us is no business of ours. No blame for her disappearance will be laid at our door.'

At hearing that, my jaw fell open and my eyes welled with tears as I pictured poor Lucy's innocent face lying cold and ashen not ten feet from me. I wanted to cry out the pain that suddenly felt so tight in my chest. I wanted to step out from my cover and confront them both, to understand why they had done this. Lucy had not been dismissed as I was led to believe. She, too, had been murdered.

CHAPTER THIRTY-SEVEN

I could not return to my room quickly enough, although a good hour passed before I was safely able to do so. My hands were trembling uncontrollably on the doorknob as I turned it and entered, and pressed the door quietly shut behind me. I put my hand to my face and felt my fingers quiver against my lips, unable to dispel the images, both real and imagined, of Giles and poor Lucy lying dead beneath that tarpaulin. How could Richard do such a thing? And how could his mother, for that matter? Clearly, I did not know either of them, and I hated them both for what they had done.

Why had they done this?

I went to the window, shaking my head in disbelief as I continued to wonder. I recalled how odd I found it that Giles had been invited to stay, and so soon after I had witnessed for myself the bitter feelings Richard harboured for him. I had later overheard them talking in Richard's study, and their conversation had left me in no doubt that Giles was blackmailing Richard. Surely, that was it.

Richard had killed his brother to put an end to his blackmail, to protect the secret Giles had spoken of. But what about Lucy? Had she also come to know what Giles had known? If she had, then Richard's secret had to be something close to home – close enough for a maid to have discovered it, for I very much doubt Giles would have told her.

I began to pace my room, going over every peculiar thing that had happened since my arrival at Crows-an-Wra Manor. The first was that all but a few of the servants had been dismissed. Ada Cobb had been appointed to replace a good many of them – a woman who could be trusted to work hard and ask no questions, in light of the situation with her mother. It made it necessary for her to earn her wage, regardless of what she may see or hear. That, coupled with the fact that the only visitors we had received had arrived uninvited, now gave me cause to suspect that it was a case of the fewer people at the manor the better, as far as Richard and Mariah were concerned. Were they afraid that someone might see something they should not?

I wondered then whether that was why Richard had not taken me anywhere off the estate, and why I was not allowed outside its walls on my own – in case I had seen or heard something and might tell of it. In light of what I now knew, I also thought it odd that Richard should have left the east wing in ruins for so long. I had believed it was because he was not yet ready to face the repairs, but surely the best way to move on after the death of his first wife was to make good that which continually reminded him of it. And yet how could he, when by doing so he would bring so many people to Crows-an-Wra Manor? What of his secret, then? The thought made me wonder whether his consent to my Italian garden was merely to keep me amused – to preoccupy my mind so that I would remain blind to whatever else was going on at Crows-an-Wra Manor.

I stopped pacing my room and sat on the edge of my bed, where I stared at the bright window, focusing on nothing but the dark conundrum that lay before me. What of Mariah? What was her part in all this? Protective mother, perhaps? Was she helping to keep her son's secret, or was it the other way around? Then again, I supposed they could just as well be equally complicit. I considered the first thing about Mariah that had struck me as unusual. Why had she moved out of the manor house by the time Richard and I returned from Europe? She had said it was to give us our privacy, and that by moving into the gatekeeper's cottage she would also have hers, but I had always thought that a little peculiar, given the size of the manor. It was so large that I hardly saw Richard unless I went looking for him. Privacy was surely of no great concern.

So why had Mariah insisted on moving out?

She had been equally insistent that I should never bother her at the cottage, which suggested to me at the time that her own privacy was something she took very seriously, but this now also seemed odd to me. Was it not, after all, quite normal and welcome in most circumstances for a wife to visit her mother-in-law from time to time?

In most circumstances, I reminded myself, which these clearly were not.

I flopped back on to my bed with a sigh, unable to see the bigger picture, and yet I was sure it was there. If only I could put the pieces of the puzzle together. I considered what else had happened, and Richard's lie sprang to mind. Before I came here as his wife, he had told me that the fire occurred two months before we met, and yet in his study recently he had unwittingly let slip that it had happened after we met. I recalled that he had been most insistent about it. It had puzzled me at the time, but I could make little of it then. I had supposed he merely wished to conceal the fact that his wife was still alive when our courtship began, lest I refused his advances, and rightly so. Thinking about it again now, I realised it meant that we were not only courting prior to the fire, but we had also become engaged to be married. The thought horrified me. I had previously wondered whether there was more to the lie. Now, in light of everything that had transpired, I was sure of it. Why else would he not simply state the truth of the matter? What difference would it have made now, given that Rosen was dead and we were married? The lie, then, was to help conceal a truth.

A secret...

A moment after the thought struck me, a wave of excitement coursed through my body and I sat up. Richard's secret had something to do with Rosen. Of that I was now certain.

But Rosen was dead.

I felt the blood drain from my cheeks then. I was suddenly light-headed. In my mind I saw the torn piece of embroidered cloth I had found by the lake that morning, and a chill ran through me. Sophia had said she saw a ghost in that very area. I had thought it another of her ghastly games, set to torment me, but what if it were not? What if Sophia really had seen someone by the lake? What if she had seen her own mother?

I stood up as random thoughts rushed through my

mind. I saw everything over again, but now in a new light. Of course there was only a skeleton staff at Crows-an-Wra Manor. Of course visitors were unwelcome and I was not allowed to leave. Of course... I paused my next thought, recalling how I had seen Jenken that very morning, carrying what appeared to be a stack of old floorboards towards the cottage. Of course Mariah did not want me to go there.

I began to question what business Jenken had with those floorboards, and it was easy now for me to imagine that he was not going to the cottage to repair the floor. If Rosen was at the cottage, being held there against her will, then she had escaped, and Sophia had seen her. Perhaps Rosen had broken a window and that was the business Jenken had been about when I saw him.

If Rosen was at the cottage.

If she was alive at all, for that matter, I reminded myself. I knew I was merely constructing what I felt to be a logical explanation for everything that had happened since my arrival, but it all fitted together so well that I could see it no other way. I did not concern myself with why Richard should wish to lock his wife away at this time. For now, it only mattered whether or not I was right. It would be a simple matter to find out. I need only go close enough to the cottage to see if any of the windows had been boarded up.

And what if they had?

I was all too aware of the mortal danger I was now in should it be known that I had found two dead bodies on the roof, let alone if I were right about Rosen. A part of me wanted to leave Crows-an-Wra Manor without a moment's delay, to go to the authorities and bring them here, but how could I? No excuse I could conjure would be agreeable to Richard or Mariah, given what they had done, and to insist would only serve to raise their suspicions. No, I had to go to the cottage. I had to see for myself whether Rosen was there, but I would have to be careful.

I left my room with a book under my arm, in case anyone should see me and wonder what I was about. To my knowledge, no one had done so since breakfast, and to all intents and purposes I had been in my room ever since. Now I was going outside for some air, to continue reading my book in the grounds. Although the air was a little cool, it was a pleasant enough afternoon, especially now that the squabbling birds had all but gone. I glanced down at the spine of my book as I made my way along the corridor towards the main staircase, to familiarise myself with the title. It was an old copy of The Vicar of Wakefield by Oliver Goldsmith.

I heard laughter as soon as I reached the top of the stairs. It was Sophia, but she was not laughing at me, not this time. It had come from one of the open rooms further along the corridor on the opposite side of the staircase, towards Richard's room. Perhaps they were together, although he had spent so little time with Sophia since she had returned to Crows-an-Wra Manor that I had cause to doubt it. It was Cobb then, I imagined, cleaning the rooms while Sophia, out of boredom, was making a nuisance of herself. As I made my way quietly down the stairs, I thought it some small consolation to know that her mischief was not aimed solely at me.

I could now account for two people who would not see me going to the cottage, but where was Richard? And where was Mariah, for that matter? Above all, I had to be sure of her whereabouts. I had to know that she was not already there, waiting for me. I listened at the door to Richard's study for any sign that he may be inside, but I heard nothing. I went to the dining room, although I did not expect either of them to have an appetite after the unspeakable things they had been doing. They were not there.

It was not until I arrived outside the parlour that I heard their voices coming from within. I could not make out what was being said between them, but I did hear glass clink against glass. It was not in the delicate manner of a toast, but more akin to the sound of a decanter being rested none too lightly on the rim of a brandy balloon. It did not surprise me to learn that Richard and Mariah were in need of restorative fortification.

I thought that as another drink was being poured – for I did not suppose it to be their first – they would be there for some time yet. Time enough for me to prove, or disprove, my theory. My only other concern was Jenken. At this time of year, however, he would have plenty to occupy himself with in the grounds, so he did not trouble me too much, any more than Mrs Pengelly, who was rarely far from her kitchen. I turned away from the door, keen now to go about my task with all haste, but no sooner had I taken two steps than I heard Richard's voice behind me. It chilled me to the bone.

'Grace?' he said. 'Whatever are you doing here?'

'I live here, Richard,' I said, my words as cold as my affections for this man I could now barely bring myself to look at. 'Or had you forgotten?' Under the circumstances, it was perhaps bold of me – any form of confrontation with the murderer standing before me was the last thing I wanted – but I could not help myself. I noticed he still had the smell of death and decay about him. It was faint, but there nonetheless, trapped in his hair and the fabric of his clothes.

Richard gave a small laugh. 'Still mad at me for my ill temper at breakfast, are you?'

I wanted to laugh back at him. He could not begin to understand how I now felt towards him. I wanted to slap his face and tell him I knew what he and his mother had done. Were I a man, I have no doubt that I would have done far worse. As it was, I could not speak. I felt suddenly paralysed by fear.

'What have you got there?' he asked when my silence had dragged on too long.

I showed him my book, my hand wavering a little as I did so. 'I've been reading in my room since breakfast,' I said, studying the jacket, refusing to make eye contact with him. 'I wanted some air, so I thought I'd continue reading in the grounds for a while.'

Richard took the book from me and looked it over. 'My first wife liked to read,' he said with a distant tone. 'I suppose she would have turned these pages at some time or another, as you now are.'

'Do you mind me reading it?' I asked. I no longer particularly cared what he minded, but I sensed his melancholy, and in light of my suspicion that Rosen was still alive I wanted to understand why. Was it really out of sadness for his loss, or was it regret? I suspected the latter, whether for the things he had done, or was yet to do if I could not somehow prevent it.

'No, I don't mind,' he said, snapping out of his thoughts. 'You go along and enjoy it. Books are for reading, are they not?'

'Yes, they are,' I said. 'Well, if you'll excuse me.'

I turned away, but Richard's next words stopped me cold.

'It should be much quieter out there now for you.'

'How do you mean?'

'The birds,' he said. 'Surely you've heard them?'

I studied him, trying to understand why he had brought the matter up. I would have thought it the last thing he wanted to talk about. Was he trying to ascertain whether or not I knew why the birds were there? Did he suspect that I did? I wondered then whether he or Mariah had seen me, and the thought must have drained the colour from my cheeks because Richard suddenly began to frown at me.

'Is everything all right?' he asked, eyeing me with a puzzled expression.

'Yes, of course,' I said, rushing out my reply. 'The birds, yes, I've heard them.' To deny it would be utter folly. There was nowhere at Crows-an-Wra Manor where one could not have heard them. 'Should we expect stormy weather? Isn't that usually the case when the gulls come inland?'

Richard smiled, as if satisfied with what he'd heard. 'Usually, yes,' he said, 'but the weather is quite fine, as you know.'

The statement gave me the impression that Richard was leading me to ask him what else might have caused the birds to come inland, and to the manor in particular. Was he trying to catch me out? I had no choice but to go along with him.

'Then why else are the birds here?' I asked, knowing I had to choose my words very carefully.

'Rats,' Richard said. 'The attic rooms have become infested with them. Jenken has been setting traps and putting poison down. That's what's drawn the birds.'

'Dead rats?' I said, suspecting that Richard knew I must have thought the bird activity peculiar, and so felt the need to go out of his way to tell me an appeasing lie.

'Yes, and rats will die from poison just about anywhere. The roof was littered with them.'

'Was?'

Richard nodded. 'I've taken care of the matter. The birds will not bother us further, but you must not go up there. Apart from the smell, it would be quite unhealthy for you.'

I was sure by now that Richard did not know I had already been up to the attic rooms and out on to the roof, but just the same, I could not help but take his words as a threat. I should have agreed with him and left it there, but I now saw a way to find out where Jenken was.

'You took care of the matter yourself?' I said. 'Would such unpleasant work not have been more suited to Jenken?'

'Jenken is out threshing the fields for winter fodder,' Richard said. 'A task that is already some weeks overdue. With so few servants, I must be expected to do my part.'

'Of course,' I said. 'Well, that explains the matter.'

'Yes, it does, Richard said with some insistence. 'And do not concern yourself with the unseemly tasks I am currently drawn upon to perform. It will not be long now before the servants are so many they shall be getting under our feet.'

'You're hiring more servants?'

'Yes, and about time, too. You shall have your own maid again – of your choosing, of course – a wet nurse, a nanny, and as many tutors for our son as I can bring here.

Things will soon be very different around here. That, I promise you.'

Richard was smiling so fully at me by the time he finished speaking that I could not help but smile weakly back at him. There was no warmth to it. It was too late for his promises. Things had been done that, as much as I would wish it otherwise, could not now be undone.

More servants at Crows-an-Wra Manor...

That could only mean one thing to my mind. If I was right about Rosen, Richard was no longer concerned that someone might see her. I sensed that if she was still alive then her time was quickly running out.

Or was I already too late?

CHAPTER THIRTY-EIGHT

I did not go directly to the cottage. The parlour windows faced the front of the house, and I was sure Richard and Mariah would be watching for me. They would have a clear view of the carriage drive and, although distant, sight of the cottage itself. Instead of taking that route, I made my way around the front of the house and past the charred ruins of the east wing, where I was forced to slow my pace, although I was encumbered only by my thoughts. What significance did the fire hold? It had supposedly taken Rosen's life, but if I was right it was all an elaborate ruse.

I pushed on, crossing the lawn from the south-east corner of the manor, almost running as I headed for the copse of trees where Sophia had played one of her cruel games on me. As I went, I was mindful of the worm casts and the fallen leaves, thinking it would not do to leave any sign that someone had been to the cottage while Mariah was away. Every now and then I found myself glancing back over my shoulder at the house in case anyone had come outside, but I saw no one. I reached the trees and paused to catch my breath, then I made my way among them towards the cottage.

I had only been outside for a few minutes, but it already felt like an eternity. My mouth began to feel dry as I approached the cottage, which now obscured my view of the manor house entirely. What would I find? If nothing, then I would be unable to make sense of anything that had happened since my arrival. If, on the other hand, I found Rosen, then... My thoughts trailed off. What if I did find her? What would I do about it? More alarmingly, I began to question again whether I was already too late. What if she were dead? I did not think I could bear to find another dead body today.

As I moved around the cottage, I looked up at the windows to see whether any had been boarded up, hinting at the escape I had earlier imagined. I was looking at the back of the house now and nothing appeared out of the ordinary. There were windows on two levels, all intact, and a black-painted door set between them. There were fewer windows to the side, where I saw nothing to further raise my hopes. It was not until I came to the front of the house, which faced the carriage drive and the main gates to the estate, that I had cause to draw a sharp intake of breath. I felt my heart pounding harder now. There was a main entrance door and windows on three levels here, and at the top was a single dormer. I saw no glass at this window, only wooden boards to seal it up – presumably the same boards I had seen Jenken carrying earlier that day.

Conscious that sharp eyes might now be able to see me from the manor house, even at this distance, I quickly retraced my steps back the way I had come, until I found myself staring at the back door. I did not wish to enter. Surely the boarded-up window was enough to satisfy myself that I was right? But I could not leave. I had to be absolutely sure that Rosen was there, alive or dead. How else could I testify to having seen her when the time came for this evil to be undone?

There was no lock on the door, only bolts on the inside, suggesting that Mariah had left this way, perhaps in haste, when she went to help Richard with their business on the roof. I entered the cottage unhindered and found myself standing in the scullery. I made straight for the door at the far end, listening intently for the slightest sound as I went – any sign that there might be someone else there. I came to a staircase beyond and I took it without delay. There was only one room I was interested in, and I was ever conscious that time was not on my side.

I climbed the steps with some urgency until I reached the top floor, and there I came to a single, blue-painted door. I put my hand to my mouth as soon as I saw it. It was like no other door I had seen, only heard of – the kind one might expect to see in a prison, with an inspection hatch at eye level, and another abutting the floor.

'The poor woman,' I said under my breath as I went to it.

I was about to unbolt the upper hatch and open it, nervous of what I might see, when a woman's voice from within stopped me. It sounded so frail, so lost and ethereal.

'Yea, though I walk through the valley of the shadow of death, I will fear no evil, for thou art with me.'

Very slowly, very carefully and quietly, I slipped the bolt and opened the hatch. I saw a fireplace opposite the door, a single armchair to the left, and a bed to the right.

There was someone lying on the bed, her pale, drawn face staring at the ceiling, her body shrouded in blankets.

'Yea, though I walk through the valley of the shadow of death, I will fear no evil, for thou art with me.'

Although the woman looked nothing like the portrait I had seen of her, it was surely Rosen. She was chanting those familiar lines from Psalm 23 over and over again, as if she now knew her fate and had accepted it.

'Yea, though I walk—'

'Do not be afraid,' I cut in, and the chanting stopped.

When Rosen sat up, I do not know which of us appeared the more shocked. I was looking at the apparition Sophia had said she saw, but it seemed as if it were Rosen, not I, who had seen a ghost. Her bony jaw hung open at the sight of me, and her pinkish eyes bulged from their hollow sockets, though more from malnutrition, I supposed, than from the surprise of seeing me. I had no idea whether she knew who I was or not. I was about to introduce myself as Richard's wife, but I stopped. How could I, when Richard's wife was there in front of me? My marriage to the man was nothing more than an unlawful lie.

'I'm Grace,' I said. 'Please believe me when I say that I had no idea you were here until today.'

Rosen did not say anything as she pushed back her bedcovers and swung her near-skeletal legs out of bed. She did not speak until she came close to the hatch, staring at me in wonder all the way, as if to convince herself that she was not hallucinating. There were tears in her eyes; tears that I sensed were born not of sadness, but of overwhelming joy, in a place that had seen none in a long time.

'I thought you were Richard,' she said, her thin voice wavering, 'come to kill me at last.'

I could have cried myself at the thought. What a monster he truly was, to have done this to his own wife. Even now, I could not fathom why, but Rosen surely knew.

'Why?' I asked her. 'Why has he done this to you?'

'You already have the answer to that question,' Rosen said. 'How can you not see it?'

'I do?'

Rosen nodded. 'You carry it inside you.'

I reached down to my belly and ran my hand over the bump. 'My child?'

Now Rosen shook her head. 'Richard's child,' she corrected. 'You carry Richard's precious son and heir. At least, I pray so for your sake. I could not provide one for him, so he faked my death, allowing him to start over again with you.'

The thought that I had, albeit unwittingly, been a party to this woman's misery made me hate Richard all the more. It made me sick to my stomach. And what if I did not carry Richard's son and heir? What if, like Rosen, I could not bear him a son at all? Would I then share her fate?

'I had no idea,' I said. 'Please forgive me.'

'Of course you didn't,' Rosen said, her voice so frail. 'There is nothing to forgive. My husband has fooled everyone – he and his mother. But how did you know to look for me? Was it the maid, Lucy? She knew I was here.'

Poor Lucy. So she had discovered Rosen, and it had brought about her terrible end. 'No,' I said, saying no more about her for now. It was all too fresh – too painful. 'I'll explain everything as soon as I can. I don't know how much time I have.'

'What will you do?'

'To own the truth, when I first saw you I had no idea.'

'But now you have?' Rosen said, hope rising in her voice.

'Yes,' I said, and I was about to elaborate when I became dumbstruck with fear. Somewhere below, a door had slammed shut.

'Mariah!' Rosen hissed.

CHAPTER THIRTY-NINE

Rosen

I wished I had asked Grace to tell me about my Sophia before she left, but there was no time. At hearing Mariah's name, knowing she had returned to the cottage, I saw Grace's eyes grow wide with fear, just moments before she closed the hatch. She had to get out unseen. My life, and now hers, depended on it. I pressed my ear to the door and listened as she fled down the stairs. I willed her to go more quietly, but even so, where would she go? I was in no doubt that Mariah would come straight up to look in on me. Their paths had to cross. I heard distant footsteps on the stairs, but they did not belong to Grace. I knew them well enough by now to know that Mariah was coming.

I stepped back from the door and crossed my chest, praying that Grace would make it safely out, that the next sound I heard would be that of the hatch opening and for Mariah's face to appear in the frame, oblivious. Several torturous seconds passed, and then my prayer was answered.

'What are you up to?' Mariah asked, screwing her face up in displeasure at the sight of me. 'I thought I heard stomping.'

'Like this?' I said, and I began to stamp my feet on the floorboards, trying my best to mimic the sound Grace had made on the stairs as she went. I wanted Mariah to think it was me she had heard, and at the same time I thought that any noise I could make now would serve to help Grace further.

Mariah snorted. 'The madness has found you at last then, I see. Well, stomp all you like, while you still can. It won't be long now before things are back to normal around here. We shall have more servants than ever before, and plentiful fancy balls the likes of which you have never seen, nor are now likely to.'

As if I had not heard a word Mariah said, I smiled. It was a sight she had not seen before, not here in this room. She must have thought I was smiling at her, from somewhere deep within my insanity, but I was smiling because she had not seen Grace, and I could not help myself. I began to dance, shuffling my feet as energetically as my weak legs could manage, prolonging the illusion. I had to keep Mariah there long enough to allow Grace time to make it back to the relative safety of the manor.

Mariah began to laugh with a pitying cackle. 'Richard will be doing you a favour when he puts a sack over your head,' she said, and then to my alarm she began to close the hatch.

'Wait!' I called, rushing to the door.

'What is it?' Mariah snapped, opening the hatch again.

She looked as impatient as she sounded.

I had no idea what I was going to say to her, only that I had to keep her there a while longer, so I said nothing. I spat in her face instead, and it was about time.

'Wretched creature!' Mariah cursed, wiping her cheek with the back of her hand.

I began to laugh then, and I danced again and stomped my feet with happiness in my heart while Mariah looked on in disbelief. Madness had indeed overcome me, but it was the madness of joy! I went to the shutters and played them like drums. Bang! Bang! Bang! I beat them as loudly as I could. I did not have to speak to Mariah now to keep her there. She could not leave me all the while I was making such a din. She would not dare. She would go and fetch Richard or Jenken before long, perhaps, to hold me while she administered the ether that would calm the devil inside me, but it would not matter. They could starve me and beat my bones if they wished. What did I care now, as long as my distraction afforded Grace the time she needed?

All my hopes now depended on her success.

CHAPTER FORTY

Grace

Thank goodness I did not bump into Richard on my return from the gatekeeper's cottage, as I had on my way there. If I had, he would have known at once that something was wrong. He would have seen how shaken I was and would have demanded to know why. What would I have told him? Lying was not something I had ever felt comfortable with. As a result, I was not at all good at it. He would have seen through my deceit in an instant, and what then for Rosen?

What then for me?

Fear of discovery had been with me since I came down from the roof earlier. Even now that I had made it safely back to my room, my hands were trembling as I sat down at my little bureau beside the window and took up my writing pen. With two dead bodies in the attic, I was not naive enough to think that Richard would allow me the freedom of sending a letter at what was surely the height of his devilry, and I wondered now whether any of my letters home to Northumberland had been sent. It did not matter. I knew how to get word out, and in a manner Richard could not refuse.

As I squared up the piece of paper in front of me, I tried to relax. I had to compose myself before my letter, or my shaking hands would render the words utterly intelligible. But I could not still the fear. It was lodged inside me like a fish bone in my throat, making it difficult for me to breathe. It were as if I had not left the cottage but was back there, with Mariah coming up the stairs as I made my way down. I had hidden in one of the rooms on the floor below Rosen's without a second to spare, pulling the door to just as she appeared. Thankfully, she seemed too concerned with Rosen to linger in the hallway, or she might have seen that the door I was hiding behind was not quite as closed as she had left it. As it was, I had managed to leave the cottage without being discovered, not least because of the noise Rosen soon began to make, but still... I could not help but keep imagining the consequences if I had not.

I tried to think of better times, before I had ever met Richard Trevelyan. Several minutes passed, and gradually I began to breathe more easily again. When I felt my hand was steady enough, I dipped my pen into the inkpot and began to write. There was no need for lengthy correspondence. My message was simple, and the smaller my note, the better.

Rosen Trevelyan's death is a lie.

We are both in danger.

Please bring help!

I blotted the ink, and then I took a small pair of scissors from one of the drawers and cut around the words, making the paper as small as possible so that it could fit unseen in the palm of my hand. I read it to myself again and, satisfied that it said all it needed to say, I went to my bed and slipped the note beneath my pillow. Then I tugged on the bell pull for Cobb to come, hoping she would not be long; the afternoon was fading, and I did not wish to spend another night under the same roof as my husband.

As much as I wanted Ada Cobb to arrive at once, it was a good fifteen minutes before I heard a knock at my door.

'Come in, and be quick!' I called, my voice sounding purposely distressed.

The door opened and Cobb came rushing to my bedside, alerted by the anxiety in my voice. 'Whatever's the matter, madam?' she asked, her face a picture of puzzlement. 'Are you ill?'

'My stomach,' I said, clutching my belly. I winced as if in pain. 'It's the baby,' I added. 'Something's terribly wrong with the baby.'

'What do you want me to do?'

'Fetch my husband, quickly! I need a doctor at once!'

The poor girl looked more afraid than I at the prospect of there being something wrong with my baby. I judged that Richard, with his desire to have a son and heir by any means imaginable, would be no different. I watched Cobb run from the room again, obvious panic evident in every stride she took in her haste to go and find him. When she returned with Richard, just a few minutes later, he seemed less afraid for the well-being of our child than angry at me, for some reason. As if it were my fault that there was something wrong with his precious son. As soon as I saw him, I silently prayed for a girl, for I do not know whether I could bear to look upon his likeness and love any son of his as a mother should.

'What have you done?' Richard demanded, his eyes

fixed on my swollen belly as I continued to cradle it in my hands.

I smoothed out the fabric of my dress over the bump, thinking that if I needed any further confirmation of his accusations, there it was.

'What have I done?' I said, my own tone now sounding angrier to my ears than I had intended. I could not help myself. I had to give voice to my indignation, even though there was nothing whatsoever wrong with me. Richard, after all, did not know that. 'I have done nothing!' I added. 'My stomach is cramping. I need a doctor!'

Richard leaned in and placed a hand on my belly, as if by doing so he could diagnose what was wrong with me. 'Has this happened before?'

'No,' I said. 'It started soon after I came back to my room. I'm afraid for the baby, Richard. Fetch the doctor, won't you?'

'You're being hysterical,' Richard said. 'You've been overdoing things, that's all it is. I expect you've overexerted yourself in the grounds this afternoon, looking for somewhere to read that damned book.'

I began to fear that I had been wrong – that nothing, not even the threat of losing his son, would induce Richard to allow anyone through the gates of Crows-an-Wra Manor. I sat up sharply, gritting my teeth as I gave a low grunt of pain.

'Please, Richard! Bring the doctor!' I insisted. I began to pant. 'It hurts terribly. Please!'

I saw a look of consternation wash over Richard's face, as if he were re-evaluating the situation. I helped him along with a little scream.

'He's dying!' I shouted. 'Your son is dying! For heaven's sake, won't you do something? Won't you call for the doctor before it's too late?'

'All right!' Richard said, putting his hands up to stop my wailing. 'I'll send Jenken to fetch him at once. Cobb?'

'Yes, sir,' Cobb said, jumping to attention at his side.

'Bring towels and warm water. Sit with my wife and soothe her as best you can until the doctor arrives.'

I had to keep up my pretence for almost two hours before Jenken returned with the doctor. During that time, Richard only came into check on me once, and Mariah did not come at all. But then, how could she? I imagined both she and Richard had been busy ensuring that Rosen could not make a sound while the doctor was here. I pictured them putting a gag in her mouth and tying her to her bed, or worse. Poor Rosen. Although I did not really know her, I prayed with all my heart for her suffering to be over, and that she would not end her days like this.

Ada Cobb, on the other hand, had proved to be the most diligent of nurses. As soon as Richard left us, she had helped me into my nightgown, fussing over me as though I were of her own flesh and blood. She only left my side to replenish her bowl of hot water, which had quickly reddened my brow to the extent that by the time Richard brought the doctor in to see me it must have seemed that I had quite a fever.

'Cobb,' Richard said as soon as he came in. 'How has Mrs Trevelyan been?'

'She's calmed down a good deal, sir,' Cobb said, 'but still moaning and groaning much of the time. I've kept her comfortable like you said.'

'Good. You can leave us now.'

'Very good, sir.'

Richard came to my bedside with the doctor beside him. He was a rangy, middle-aged man, with grey hair, a clean-shaven face, and a pronounced nose, upon which sat a pair of round-framed glasses.

'This is Doctor Tremethyk,' Richard said. 'His family have taken good care of my family for many generations. I assure you, you're in the very best of hands.'

I sat up a little as the doctor put his bag down beside the bed. I smiled weakly at him and offered out my hand, which he took in his briefly before resting it at my side.

'Please, madam,' Tremethyk said, speaking slowly, with a nasal tone to his voice. 'Try not to exert yourself until we can be certain of what ails you.'

I relaxed again and saw that Sophia was standing in the doorway, staring at me, her face quite without expression. Curiosity had no doubt drawn her out of her room, come to see what all the fuss was about, and when she saw that I had noticed her, she smiled at me. It was not in the sympathetic manner one might expect under such circumstances. It was more a smile of satisfaction than concern, as if she were pleased to find me in need of a doctor, or that there might be some chance I could lose my child. It was a horrible thought, and perhaps I had read more into it than was there, but after the way she had treated me since her return to Crows-an-Wra Manor, I found it impossible to imagine her capable of any good thought where I was concerned.

I groaned and clutched my belly again. 'Leave us, Richard,' I said. 'Let the doctor do his work.'

I thought Richard might have insisted on staying while Doctor Tremethyk examined me, but thankfully, he gave no protest.

'Of course,' he said. 'Do excuse me, doctor. I shall wait in the parlour for your report.'

With that, he turned and left, taking Sophia with him.

As soon as my bedroom door had closed, Doctor Tremethyk placed the back of his hand on my forehead, and then on my wrist. From his waistcoat he took out his pocket watch and began to count the beats of my pulse.

'You're a little feverish, perhaps,' he said, as I had expected he would, 'but nothing too serious.'

He pulled back my bedcovers, and as he went to lift up my nightgown to examine me, I reached down and caught his wrist to stop him.

'There is nothing wrong with me, doctor,' I said in a low voice, yet with such gravity that I immediately stole his attention. 'I have brought you here under other pretences.'

'Nothing wrong with you?' he repeated, his brow furrowing. 'Pretences? What pretences?'

'I cannot say,' I whispered. 'Someone may be listening at the door.'

Had the doctor's cool fingers still been on my wrist, he would have felt the sudden rise in my pulse as I reached beneath my pillow and retrieved the note I had placed there. I pressed it into his palm.

'Let no one here see it,' I told him, my voice barely audible. 'Lives depend on it, though it is already too late for some.'

'Too late?' the doctor queried.

'Yes,' I whispered, 'and I beseech you not to talk openly about the matter.'

He turned his palm over, and he began to look more puzzled than ever as he read my note. I watched him intently as he did so, and I quickly saw the alarm in his eyes. He folded the piece of paper and slipped it inside his jacket pocket.

'My word, this is most serious,' he mused. Then, maintaining my pretence, he asked, 'When did these symptoms first manifest themselves?'

'Today,' I said, understanding his question to mean, when did I first discover that Rosen was still alive?

'Good,' he said, and almost to himself added, 'Such matters are best dealt with while they are in their infancy.'

He leaned in, and one at a time he lifted my eyelids and studied my pupils, perhaps to see if the shock of my recent discovery had affected me in ways I had not yet come to realise.

'I believe I have seen enough.' he said. 'Rest, and try not to worry yourself. I will do all I can for you.'

'Thank you, doctor,' I said, sighing as I spoke, relieved to know that help was at hand.

CHAPTER FORTY-ONE

Half an hour passed before I heard the carriage leave. I watched it go from my window, taking Doctor Tremethyk and all my hopes with it. I wondered how long it would be before he would return with the parish constable and his men, and I prayed it would be soon. I began to pace my room, back and forth, nervously wringing my hands. Then I heard someone coming and I quickly jumped back into bed. I barely had time to pull the covers up around me before the door opened and Richard walked in, the sleeves of his shirt rolled up to his elbows.

'I've brought you something to help you rest,' he said. 'Doctor's orders.'

He came to my bedside, stirring a honey-coloured liquid, the spoon tinkling against the glass as he approached.

'What is it?' I asked, taking it from him.

'A simple nerve tonic I had Mrs Pengelly put together, along with something from the doctor's medicine bag for your pain.'

'Thank you,' I said. I took a sip. 'It's rather pleasant.'

'Yes, well, don't expect me to tell you what's in it. Herbs and whatnot, I expect, like that Campari fellow's aperitivo you enjoy so much.'

I drank some more. Then, from over the top of the glass, I asked, 'What did the doctor say?'

'Finish your tonic first,' Richard said, pointing to it. 'Then I'll tell you.'

Eager to know what Doctor Tremethyk had said, I drank the rest of my tonic in one go.

'That's it,' Richard said once I had finished. He took the glass from me and set it down on the bedside cabinet. 'Now, as to what the doctor said, I'm afraid your condition is far worse than either of us could have imagined.'

Knowing there was nothing whatsoever wrong with me, I was more than a little taken aback at hearing this. 'Worse?' I said, my brow set with confusion. 'How do you mean?'

'I mean, my dear Grace, that he believes a madness has taken you.'

I felt the colour drain from my cheeks.

'He said that you are suffering from delusions, perhaps brought about by your fear of not being able to live up to the standards set by my first wife.'

I began to shake my head, but he continued.

'I told him you're having a difficult time trying to be an effective mother to Sophia, which he felt further qualified the matter. As a result, you feel inferior to Rosen.'

'No,' I said, gasping for breath again.

Richard reached into his trouser pocket as he continued. 'To the extent that you have conjured her from the dead and believe her to live here still, thus absolving you of any responsibility for the child.' He laughed to himself. 'A preposterous notion, of course.'

When I saw Richard's hand again, slowly rising in front of me, he had my note between his fingertips. I felt light-headed. I tried to get up, but my limbs felt so heavy. I was drowsy. The tonic...

'It's no use trying to struggle,' Richard said, his hand firmly squeezing the top of my arm to restrain me. 'That draught I gave you will soon send you into a deep sleep.' He shook his head at me. 'Did you really imagine the doctor would believe you?'

I saw someone else come into the room then. My eyelids began to close. My vision was blurry, but I knew it was Mariah. She had something coiled in her hands.

'Rope?' I said, my voice sounding slow and hollow. 'What are you going to do with me?'

'With any luck you'll never know, my darling.'

CHAPTER
FORTY-TWO

If death is absolute, then I have surely glimpsed behind its dark veil, for I have never before known such empty sleep, devoid of dreams and all awareness. When I awoke, it felt as if I had been wrenched violently from the clutches of the Grim Reaper himself and thrust so suddenly back into life that I found myself gasping for air. And yet, this was surely not my life. Gone was the comfort of my bedroom – my last waking memory – replaced by damp earth beneath me and darkness all around. The Reaper's cold touch lingered in my bones. I began to shiver. I blinked, and gradually my eyes began to see. What I saw startled me at first. It was a face, as pale as the dead.

It was Rosen.

Was she dead? I thought she was. The air was cold enough to see the traces of my own breath, but I could not see hers. She was lying on her side, as I was, and there was such a calmness about her, her blue lips so relaxed over the gag at her mouth, her skin so ashen, that I did not doubt she had passed.

Was I dreaming after all?

I tried to reach up and pinch my cheek, to wake myself if I was, but I could not move my arms. My wrists were bound together at my knees. I felt the rope cut into the back of my legs as I pulled at it. The rope... Yes, I remembered seeing Mariah with it just before I fell unconscious. I clawed at the ground and felt nothing but earth and twigs and fallen leaves beneath my fingers. I heard sounds behind me then: a thump and a scrape. It repeated over and over. I was not dreaming. It was the sound of someone digging. I had emerged from my empty sleep into a waking hell.

'Rosen?'

I tried to whisper her name, but all that came out from my own gagged mouth was a puff of breath, swirling between us in the chill night air. I began to envy her. If she was already dead, then she was at peace and would not suffer as I imagined I now would. In the near darkness, I had already made out the trees around me. I was in the woods, presumably somewhere on the estate, and I could guess my fate well enough by now. Was I to be buried here with Rosen for having discovered Richard's secret? Would he kill me first, or simply roll my body into the open grave he was digging and bury me alive? I feared the latter. As cold a man as I now knew Richard to be, I did not credit him with the courage to murder me first.

'Deeper!'

The voice startled me. It was Mariah's unmistakable croak. She was close by, somewhere behind me, presumably standing over Richard with his spade, overseeing his work, as I was convinced she had overseen all of his dark deeds.

'I have already dug down a good number of feet,' Richard said. 'Surely, it is enough.'

'I'll tell you when it's enough,' Mariah said. 'No one must find them. Not ever.'

I heard a huff from Richard and he began to work his spade faster. So I was right. I was to die here in my own grave, buried deep in the ground and left to suffocate – to die, along with my unborn child. I wanted to scream, but what use would that serve me now? Death was inevitable. I was powerless to prevent it.

Mariah interrupted my self-pity. 'If you had listened to me in the first place, Richard,' she said, 'you would not be down there at all. Did I not warn you of the risk you ran in keeping Rosen alive? Did I not tell you to let her burn along with the east wing?'

'I was not then ready to let her go,' Richard said, and the digging stopped.

Mariah scoffed. 'And you see now where that has got you. Now, if you're to have a son and heir, you will have to start over again. You must court another would-be bride, and this time she must never learn the truth as Grace has. So dig! Bury your secrets deep or they will be your undoing.'

'Surely, I am already undone,' Richard said as he resumed his digging. 'What will I say to those who ask after Grace – her family, for instance? What excuse will I give them?'

'I have given the matter some considerable thought,' Mariah said. 'You must make it known that Grace has run off with your brother. You must say that the child she carries is his, and that for all you know he has taken her far away, to a place where no one knows them, so they can marry.'

'Italy,' Richard said. 'That's what I'll tell them. She was always on about the blasted place, so as far as anyone else is concerned, that's where she is. It will also serve to quash any gossip concerning Giles's whereabouts.' He gave a harrumph. 'And what court would not sooner or later grant me divorce under those circumstances?'

'I told you I had given the matter considerable thought,' Mariah said. 'I always look after you, don't I? I always know what's for the best.'

I did not hear Richard's answer, if indeed he gave one. My attention was suddenly drawn from their conversation. I had been staring at Rosen all this time, and now I thought I heard her groan. It was such a low, barely audible sound that I quickly began to doubt my senses. I studied her deathly pale face again, looking for any signs of life. I saw a spider crawl slowly across her cheek. She did not twitch. I followed its path over her eyelids and on to her forehead. Then Rosen's eyes shot wide open and I recoiled, startled. She began to gasp as I had, her sudden need for air hindered by the gag at her mouth. She was not dead. The poor woman was still alive.

It gave me no greater comfort, however, to know that I would not now die alone; I would not wish for anyone to share my fate. I tried to smile at her, to comfort her in our last moments, but I doubt she saw it through my gag. She began to struggle and groan. She kicked her legs, which were bound together at her ankles, just as mine were. She thrashed and wriggled like a pale worm in the undergrowth, so much so that she quickly drew Mariah's attention.

'They're awake.'

'That's too bad,' Richard said. 'I would have spared them this.'

'Then you should have been quicker with that spade!'

I rolled myself over to face them. A dimly lit oil lamp drew my eye. I saw Richard then, up to his shoulders in the grave he was digging, his features silhouetted by the lamp. Twigs began to snap underfoot and I saw Mariah approaching. She was standing over me suddenly. Then I, too, began to thrash and wriggle.

'Calm down, the pair of you!' Mariah ordered. 'It won't be long now. Then all this will be over.'

She turned away and peered down into the grave. 'I think that will have to do,' she said to Richard. 'No sense prolonging this any longer.'

Richard threw his spade out, back towards the lamp. He climbed out after it. 'Hold the lamp up while I drag them to the edge.'

Mariah left us then. She went back around to the other side of the grave and picked up the lamp as Richard now came towards us. She stood on the far side with it held high, fully illuminating the grave and the area around it so that Richard could better see what he was doing. He knelt before me and grabbed the ropes that bound me. I shook my head, but he did not see. He would not look at me as he dragged me to the edge of the grave. I could see fully down into it now, and could think only of my family, and of the wicked lies they would be told about me. Behind me, I heard Richard begin to drag Rosen and I knew I would not be tormented by such thoughts for much longer.

Then I heard something else.

I looked across at Mariah, standing with the lamp on the other side of the grave. She had not moved, and yet I had heard movement – fast movement. The woodland undergrowth was being disturbed, as though a deer were running towards us. I saw a small shadow come out of the darkness then. It paused and stooped as if to pick something up. Mariah must have heard it too, because she turned towards it, but just as she did so the shadow came into the light and I saw that it was Sophia. She had picked up Richard's spade and now, as Mariah turned to face her, she struck her with it, catching the side of her head. Mariah fell, the lamp with her. I heard the glass break, and the oil must have spilled because there were suddenly flames around them. They lit the scene like stage lamps on a macabre play as, to my horror, I watched Sophia continue to swing the spade, bashing Mariah's head with it.

'Sophia! No!'

It was Richard, but I could already see that he was too late. Mariah was surely dead, and yet Sophia still did not stop. Richard dashed after her. As she swung the spade again, he grabbed it and took it from her, and just then I saw the light of another lamp, coming quickly through the trees towards us. Several paces ahead of it I saw Jenken.

'You leave her be!' he shouted.

He sprang at Richard, just as Richard swung the spade at him, but Jenken was already too close. He grabbed it by the shaft and wrenched it from Richard's hands. Then he hurled it into the darkness.

'You lied to me,' Jenken said, and Richard backed away. 'You lied to us all.'

Richard put out his hands. 'Calm down, Jenken,' he said. 'I'll make it up to you, I swear.'

Jenken wasn't listening. 'You were going to kill them.'

Richard threw a punch at Jenken. It caught him square on the nose, knocking his head back, but he appeared to be unfazed by the blow. He shoved Richard so hard in the chest that he fell back into the flames from the broken oil lamp. I saw Richard roll away from them, and now he was scrabbling on the ground for something. I thought it must have been a broken branch to hit Jenken with, but when Richard stood up again I saw something glinting in his hand. It was a long shard of glass from the lamp. He waved it in front of Jenken as Jenken came at him again.

I noticed Ada Cobb for the first time then. She had arrived after Jenken with the other lamp I had seen. She was coming around behind Rosen and me, perhaps to untie us. So, too, was Sophia. I paid them little attention. My eyes were fixed on the struggle playing out before me. I saw Richard lunge at Jenken, catching his side with the glass. I saw him slash at Jenken across his chest and now there was blood on his shirt. Then I watched Jenken grab Richard around his shoulders, restraining him. He lifted him off the ground and squeezed as if to crush the life out of him.

'Mama!'

It was Sophia behind me. A moment later I felt hands at my bonds and saw Cobb working to free me. Ahead, the fight had all but gone from Richard. He went limp and dropped the bloodied shard of glass. Jenken kicked it away and I sat up. I turned and saw Rosen and Sophia holding one another. Then, as we both stood up, we too embraced. There were tears in our eyes and quivering smiles on our lips. We were saved.

But what now for Richard?

Cobb's thinking was ahead of mine. She had the lengths of rope that had been used to bind us coiled in her hands, and was taking them to Jenken. We followed slowly after her, Sophia and I helping her mother, who was too weak to walk unaided. I watched Jenken force

Richard to his knees and restrain him while Cobb tied his hands behind his back. Another length of rope was used to bind his elbows to his torso.

'What are you going to do with me?' Richard asked, his voice now little more than a whimper.

Rosen stepped towards him, and I cannot describe the fear that washed over Richard's face as she said, 'My brothers will know what to do with you. Take him to the cottage.'

CHAPTER FORTY-THREE

As we brought Richard to the cottage, I learned of the lies Jenken and Cobb had been told about the mad woman who was being kept there – how Sophia's mother had supposedly started the fire in the east wing in an attempt to kill her, and how, for Sophia's sake, she was never to know that her mother was still alive. That lie had been exposed as soon as Sophia went to Jenken and told him about the conversation she had overheard between her father and Doctor Tremethyk. Sophia told me how, through the crack in her bedroom door, opposite mine, she had then seen Richard carry me out of my room unconscious, and how she had followed him and seen her mother for herself before we were laid out in the woods for burial. She had found Jenken and Cobb, and had told them both everything she had seen and heard, and they had run into the woods after her – our little saviour.

Before we left the woods that night, at Rosen's instruction Jenken rolled Mariah's dead body into the grave Richard had dug, and we each took turns to bury her.

Cobb was unsure at first.

'I don't want any more part in this,' she said, shaking her head quite emphatically, but I knew how to change her mind.

'Help us, and say nothing about what has happened here,' I told her, 'and your mother will be a free woman before the next sunset.'

It was Cobb who found the spade Jenken had thrown into the darkness, and it seemed she could not now find it quickly enough. It was Cobb who handed it to Rosen to throw the first scatterings of earth on to Mariah's body.

There was no need to tie a gag around Richard's mouth as we brought him to the room where Rosen had been forced to spend the best part of the past year. He did not speak as Jenken led him there and Rosen locked him inside. He just stared blankly out at us from the upper hatch, resigned to his fate as I had been resigned to mine. I had no doubt he would have more to say when Rosen's brothers arrived, and no man would wish to be in his shoes when they did, but for now, we had other things to think about.

Jenken was dying.

As soon as we left the cottage again, he staggered and fell. The stab wound Richard had given him with the shard of glass from the oil lamp had cut deeper than Jenken had let on. Blood soaked his shirt, and as I looked down at him, I imagined he must also have been bleeding a good deal on the inside. There was no colour left in his usually ruddy cheeks.

'Jenken?' Rosen said as she knelt beside him.

Jenken coughed, and now I could see dark blood bubbling from the corners of his mouth. 'Forgive me, madam,' he said. 'Jenken didn't understand, see.'

'I do forgive you,' Rosen said.

Then Jenken sighed his last breath and was gone.

I expected Sophia to fall over his body and cry for him, but she did not. She simply stood over him as I did. What a strange child she was. Although she and Jenken had been good friends, and had shared many happy times together, she seemed quite calm and accepting of his death.

'Leave him with me,' Cobb said, helping Rosen up again. 'I'll take good care of him. You get along to the big house and warm yourselves up before you all perish.'

And so we left Cobb and Jenken there outside the gate-keeper's cottage, and we walked the carriage drive back to Crows-an-Wra Manor with Sophia between us. She was holding her mother's hand, but it was not long before I felt her other hand reach up to hold mine. I had found her mother. I had brought Rosen back from the dead, and in doing so it seemed that Sophia had accepted me at last.

ACKNOWLEDGEMENTS

My thanks to Jenni Davis and Sandra Mangan for editing this book, to Kath Middleton for proofreading it, and to my wife, Karen, for her untiring support and contribution to all my books.

A special thank you to you for reading this book. I hope you enjoyed it. If you did, please tell someone. If you can find the time, please consider rating or reviewing it. If you would like to contact me, you can visit my website at www.steve-robinson.me, or you can send an email to mailspr@yahoo.co.uk. I'd love to hear from you.

ABOUT THE AUTHOR

Photo © Karen Robinson

Steve Robinson is a London-based crime writer. He was sixteen when his first magazine article was published and he's been writing ever since. A love for genealogy inspired his first bestselling series, the Jefferson Tayte Genealogical Mysteries, and he is now expanding his writing to historical crime, another area he is passionate about. He can be contacted via his website, www.steverobinson.me, or his Facebook page, www.facebook.com/SteveRobinsonAuthor, where you can also keep up to date with his latest news.

Printed in Great Britain
by Amazon

63272173R00180